DANGEROUS PITY

First published in 2010 by
Liberties Press
Guinness Enterprise Centre | Taylor's Lane | Dublin 8 | Ireland
www.libertiespress .com
info@libertiespress.com
+353 (1) 415 1224

Trade enquiries to CMD BookSource
55A Spruce Avenue | Stillorgan Industrial Park | Blackrock | County Dublin
Tel: +353 (1) 294 2560
Fax: +353 (1) 294 2564

Distributed in the United States by
DuFour Editions | PO Box 7 | Chester Springs | Pennsylvania | 19425
and in Australia by
InBooks | 3 Narabang Way | Belrose NSW 2085

ISBN: 978–1–905483–98–3

2 4 6 8 10 9 7 5 3 1

A CIP record for this title is available from the British Library.

The publishers gratefully acknowledge financial support from the Arts Council.

Cover design by Sin É Design
Internal design by Liberties Press
Set in Garamond
Printed and bound in the UK by CPI Mackays, Chatham ME5 8TD

DANGEROUS PITY

ELIZABETH WASSELL

for Manuel Linares

'Pour l'hôtel le Cecil est bien. Un Niçois d'ici me dit d'aller au PLM Palace avenue de la Gare . . . '

Apollinaire, *Lettres à Lou*

'Pity is cruel. Pity destroys. Love isn't safe when pity's prowling around . . . pity can be the expression of an almost monstrous pride.'

Graham Greene, *Ways of Escape*

I

That morning, I walked down the plunging streets of *vieux Nice*, beside the coral-coloured houses, the cafés and *socca* bars, the displays of mountain ham and olives. And I bought loads of food and a bottle of *vin du Var* for lunch, almost as though I were expecting a visitor.

But I was merely feeling better than I had in the four months since my mother's death, partly because I had just learnt that a British director wished to buy the film rights to my seventh novel. And it was a limpid October day, which recalled me to why Nice had captivated me in the first place – the salt shimmer of its skies; the walls of its old town; its Mediterranean balance of bustle and languor. I was falling in love with the world again.

Six years before, I had come to live in a small hotel close to the station. The entranceway was always dim after that vivid sky, and since I was carrying bags today, I had not removed my dark glasses. So I could just make out a slight figure standing by the lift. As I approached, it turned immediately, and said in the voice of a girl, though without shyness, 'Let me help you.' I looked anxiously towards the desk, but no one seemed to be there. The girl extended a hand for one of my parcels, which I let her take, too puzzled to protest. She followed me into the lift, where I took off my spectacles.

She regarded me from beautiful eyes, quite dark and lustrous, with heavy lashes. Yet they were her one and only beauty; she was a sharp-featured thing, painfully thin, with badly cut black hair, and a bold smile. She spoke English or, more precisely, Dublinese. 'Jesus, Sebastian. You *must* remember me, after I've come all this way just to visit you? I was your student, only last year.'

I stared at her. The year before, Trinity College had invited me to conduct a writing workshop for undergraduates. I had been reluctant at first; the prospect of callow youths looking earnestly at me in some dank Dublin lecture hall and expecting me to teach them *how to write* had not brought joy to my heart. But the money, to put it bluntly, had been necessary. And now, finally, I could recall the girl confronting me in the lift of my own hotel. Her name was Ursula Dowling. She had followed me from the lecture hall to my rooms after each session, chattering on about Hemingway or Joyce, inviting me out for coffee, asking my advice about this or that. Despite her pushiness, I had rather liked her. She was bright, and her gawky figure and guttersnipe grin had amused me more than if she'd been some conventionally pretty coquette.

Oh, I had liked her, all right, when she'd followed me along the cobbled avenues of Trinity College, full of her particular kind of exasperating yet endearing chatter. Only I had never envisaged her dogging me to my French home, as if she were entitled to a place in my private life. I surveyed her cautiously as the lift climbed, but when we arrived at my floor, I merely opened the grille, which made its customary loud clang, and beckoned her into the suite.

She dropped her rucksack on the sofa and immediately announced that she had no place to crash, as she put it, while those lovely brown eyes looked about, doubtless taking in the fact of my kitchenette, and the small second bedroom.

'You can stay here,' I heard myself say. 'For a night, at least. Until you find somewhere else. Nice is full of clean, cheap hotels, especially near the station. Would you like a coffee and some bread? You must be hungry after the journey.' I was astonished by myself. I should have given this cheeky creature her marching orders immediately. Instead here I was cosseting her, letting her into my rooms without a murmur of protest, then offering her not only a bed for the night, but food and drink as well. As though she were a distinguished guest whom I had formally invited, instead of an unwelcome ragamuffin whom I barely knew.

Yet I found myself pitying her: she had come, she said, all the way from Ireland, with practically no money, for the sole purpose of seeing me, because 'there was a light inside you that I was warmed by, last year when you were my teacher. And I need to keep on feeling it, Sebastian. I need it to become the writer that I *know* I am. And I believe your books speak to me in a special way, as if you wrote them *to* me. I really *understand* them.' Those long-lashed eyes gazed at me, and I surprised myself once more by pouring two kirs, and emptying the olives I had bought into a bowl.

So we talked about novel-writing, and I grew fond of her again. That had been it from the start, I realised; that was why I'd liked her in Dublin. She was in love with the novel form, with its elegance and sprawl; she loved characters and narrative and moments of rhapsodic reverie. Despite her plainness, she was radiant with this love. And it made my middle-aged heart melt in wistfulness: she reminded me of myself, when the world was young. Also, she was poor – as most students are, as I myself had been. While she munched handfuls of olives, I began to wonder when she had last eaten.

'You are very skinny,' I observed.

She made a gesture of disdain. 'I don't care about food. I practically lived on chocolate and apples when I was coming down here. I save all my money to buy books, which are the only important things.'

'You'll have lunch with me,' I said firmly, so that she would not demur, but of course she followed me quite happily into the kitchen, where I unwrapped my parcels and laid out plates, and opened the bottle of wine.

'Wine in the afternoon is *really* nice,' she cried, practically clapping her hands. I had already noticed, the year before at Trinity, that she could be childishly enthusiastic one moment – eyes shining above that lopsided grin – and morose the next. Now she suddenly scowled. 'I had to get away, Sebastian. Dublin is really soiled these days, you know? I could only respond to you. And I realised the feeling was mutual. All those talks we had, those rainy afternoons in the pub. We really *connected.*'

I could remember no rainy afternoon in any of the student pubs surrounding Trinity, but gave her a sympathetic smile anyway. She had eaten nearly all the goat's cheese and *jambon cru* and olives and radishes which I had bought that morning, and her thin lips glistened with olive oil. Yet she did not seem a glutton. She ate distractedly, tearing at the bread, slurping from her wineglass, all the time gabbling on and on about her favourite books and her own inchoate projects. She said she was working on short stories, and putting them together into a collection, since she wasn't yet ready to attempt a novel. 'Though I will be,' she declared, staring at me over the plates. 'I will be pretty soon, I'm sure of it. I mean, with you to inspire me, Sebastian.'

After lunch, and all her talk, we were both tired. She had done the washing up, which pleased me; at least she would be some help about the place. (I no longer considered billeting her in another hotel.) I brought her to the guestroom, and retired to my own, for my ritual siesta.

I had closed the shutters but the strong light blurred at their corners. Presently I dropped into a deep sleep, and dreamt that my mother stood at the side of my bed. Everything in the room was as it had been before: the light clouding round the shutters; a distant throb of traffic; everything normal and familiar. All except my mother, standing over me in the false dusk, and wearing the face of a demon. I stared in horror at *her* transformed into a gargoyle, with bulging eyes and a grimacing maw. Then I saw that she was naked; with a shriek of laughter, she whirled round and made an obscene gesture, crouching to display feral buttocks, which she opened out with both hands before bolting from the room.

My eyes opened. A siren was weaving a skein of noise in the road below, its donkey bray sounding like a taunt. Was that animal din the source of my terrible dream? Or from what unclean source in myself had it sprung, in the midst of my grief for her?

A smell of cooking, of garlic, green herbs and olive oil, floated up from the restaurant next door. I concentrated on this smell, and on my own breathing, until I was calmer. Then I got up, splashed water on my face, and stared into the bathroom mirror. I looked young for fifty-five; the grey eyes I had inherited from my father were still clear and wide, the hair – my father's light brown hair – only just beginning to glint silver at the temples. 'Your father always looked youthful,' my mother had assured me. (I had only ever known him in pictures.) She herself had always looked relatively young, even childlike, with the big blue eyes of a doll. Quite unlike the demon of my dream.

*

Even when Claudia and I decided to live abroad, my mother followed, first to Paris, where we had bought an eagle's eyrie of a flat in the *cinquième*; then onwards to Spain, where we had sojourned briefly in a raffish harbour town, simply because we loved such places. Each time, she'd declared guilelessly that she was merely going on a holiday, that she missed Paris and had found a charming little hotel in the *cinquième*, or that, coincidentally, she also liked the louche glamour of Spanish harbour towns. When she was not following me across the world, she rang me up every day.

She died suddenly, of a heart attack. I was perfunctory about the funeral, coolly buying a return ticket to Dublin; wearing a discreet dark suit to the ceremony; listening respectfully to the murmurs of relations and friends as they pressed my hand in her drawing room. *She was so proud of you, a famous writer* . . .

It was only when I arrived back in Nice that grief afflicted me, literally like a blow in the stomach. She had loved and oppressed me, and I had loved and hated her, had wrapped the tendrils of my imagination around her. Yet now, where she had once stood, there was only empty air.

*

I went into the kitchen, to find Ursula reading a grubby copy of Forster's *Aspects of the Novel* while eating some bread and jam. I made coffee but, still shaken from the dream, could barely speak. At one point, while we were silently drinking, she reached across the table and seized my hand. 'It's OK , Sebastian. You needn't chat. I can see you're worried about something. Really, *I understand you.*'

Hadn't she told me already today that she 'understood' me? Or was it my novels she understood, and which she felt had been written exclusively for her? While her admiration appealed to my vanity, I was disturbed by something complacent, proprietary, in these assertions by a near-stranger. It was as if she considered herself the custodian of my very dreams, just because I had been her teacher and she had read my books. I mumbled that I would be going out for a while, and suggested that she take advantage of the balmy evening. A stroll along the promenade, with a pause on one of the benches overlooking the sea, would be very pleasant, I promised her.

She accepted my advice, sauntering out with rucksack and book, calling, 'See you later.' Relieved to be alone, I had a shower, changed, and walked down to the desk.

'Monsieur Clare,' said old Hervé, in his gloomily formal way. He had a lugubrious face, with pouches beneath the eyes, and a drooping moustache.

'You must have seen a girl,' I told him. 'I mean, a girl leaving, just now. She is staying with me.' I had not thought that I would sound so flustered. Especially since Hervé was patently indifferent to the personal life of his guests, our visitors provoking nothing more than a sardonic smile, or a Gallic lift of his profuse eyebrow. And he never charged anything extra. Dear old Hervé, neither curious nor venal. 'A girl?' he muttered now. 'Fine. Congratulations, Monsieur Clare. Unless she stays *forever.*' And he laughed bleakly, as if at some private joke.

I decided to go to a nearby bar that had, over the years, become my local, since it was an ordinary French café where one could drink a thimbleful of coffee or a glass of wine, and read or work for hours without being disturbed. While I walked there, I wondered if Ursula, gazing at me with those fine eyes (their vastness and too-sincere expression reminding me uncomfortably of my mother), knew much about my personal life. I thought not, despite how well she *understood* me. On the other hand, I was by no means an autobiographical writer; had, indeed, grown all too adept at approaching the subject of myself obliquely. This desire for privacy was one of the reasons I enjoyed the expatriate life. Just then, for instance, I liked walking along avenue Georges Clemenceau in the ash-blue dusk, while perpetually bronzed young girls, retired gentlemen clutching sticks, shawled Arab ladies, and cross-border tourists speaking rapid-fire Italian all eddied past, everything around me at once familiar and bright with strangeness.

I also very much liked my *quartier*, which lay between the old *gare* and the rather burly cathedral. It was a district of cheap hotels, cheap clothing and souvenir shops, cheap homely restaurants, betting cafés and late-night sandwich vendors, with the occasional respectable *boulangerie* or *tabac* looking faintly censorious amidst such honky-tonk glamour. Also, it was an Arab quarter: there was an open market selling halal meat and furled pastries gleaming with honey alongside bottles of saffron and cinnamon, and boxes of henna for the women to redden their hair. The Arab men stood about on the streets, for all the world like the corner boys of an Irish town, huddled together, talking in soft voices, giving passers-by sidelong, perhaps hostile glances, though in our brief exchanges I had only ever known these men to be courteous. They had come from Morocco, Algeria, Tunisia; life here could not be easy for them. One often saw them queuing forlornly before the little shops that advertised cheap phone calls to foreign countries. Obviously most of them had left family behind; perhaps my exile's heart went out to them? I often wondered what they discussed, in their little clusters beneath those ragged palm trees at the back of the cathedral. Probably football or politics, about which groups of men standing on leafy squares throughout Europe are all experts.

Basically, I liked my district because it was not bourgeois, nor was it the opulent Nice of casinos and grand hotels. Despite the few dilapidated sex shops near the station (just like those near any train station, in any city), it was mainly simply itself, an honest sort of *quartier*. Nice did not feel like a resort here, but like an ordinary market town, though sweetened by a pure sea light, encircled by splendid mountains, and with, sometimes, a fugitive smell of lavender in the air, beneath the more ordinary French smells of coffee, cigarettes and car exhaust. And of course I had found my little hotel, its walls painted russet and gold like a Matisse, and with a small garden at the back. In a curious way, the hotel had rescued me, after Claudia.

I entered the café and looked about. The tables were fairly full, but I was alone at the *comptoir* except for two men I had noticed before, but to whom I'd never spoken. Something intimate about their exchanges – how they laughed softly and touched each other on the arm or shoulder – suggested that they were a gay couple. The smaller man had an animal look, with his narrow face like the tapering snout of a – what? – a vole or squirrel? But it was not an uninteresting face, its lines neat, almost Egyptian.

His companion was more conventionally handsome, though running a bit to fat. He was tall, with lots of coarse, greying hair. I had supposed that, with their hazelnut complexions and dark eyes, they were French. But all of a sudden the smaller man addressed me in a courteous English accent. 'André tells us you are Sebastian Clare, the writer?'

I glared at André, the barman, who ostentatiously turned his back on us in order to busy himself, meaninglessly, with some bottles of pastis beside the till. Then, sighing inwardly, I answered 'Yes, I suppose so.'

The larger man said, 'We have noticed you here before, though I am afraid we did not know that you were the famous

Mr Sebastian Clare! Léon and I have been living in Nice for three months now, you see, and today we finally decided the time had come to salute a fellow expatriate.'

'Only of course I am from Ireland,' I said resignedly. 'And you two are English, I believe?'

This gave them the opportunity to introduce themselves, an opportunity they had clearly been eager for and that I was too courteous, or perhaps too weak-minded, to discourage. They were Léon and Max, both psychoanalysts from London. They'd lived together for over twenty years; were 'actually married, in a way', offered the slight one called Léon, with a nervous smile. But when I didn't blanch, they relaxed, and went on to explain that they had decided to retire early and come to Nice, where they had bought a flat just round the corner.

Max, the larger man, explained, 'Our friends say we should have bought something in a more elegant part of town, but we *like* our quarter, don't we, Léon?'

The smaller man smiled, as did I – because of course I agreed. I volunteered: 'I enjoy living here too. I am intrigued by our Arab neighbours, though I think it would be impossible to fathom them, their cultures, their reasons for coming here, the distinctions amongst them. How would a Tunisian feel about a Moroccan, for instance, and vice versa? One can only observe. And we are lucky to have so many family restaurants in this area. They work very hard, you know, in those family places, with the husband cooking and the wife serving twice a day, that sort of thing.'

Once more they smiled. It occurred to me that I rather liked them, even though we had exchanged very few words so far. I liked them because they seemed, well, pleasant. I had received the impression that they enjoyed the sweetness of constancy, living comfortably together as in any successful marriage, and that they were generally thoughtful. Which was probably why they preferred our ordinary district, with its Monoprix and shoe shops and newspaper kiosks, to the florid life along the Bay of Angels.

Now I bought my new acquaintances another drink, and we talked a bit more, until little Léon suddenly said, 'Listen, why don't you take dinner with us, in one of the family restaurants that you like? We've already booked, but they'd be pleased to have one more. Do say you'll come.' And he placed a persuasive hand on my arm.

So we walked to the restaurant they had chosen, one of the few in the district to which I had never been. Very small it was, and decorated in a kind of gleefully kitsch style with pictures of French and Italian film stars adorning the stucco walls beside photographs of the family, the silver-haired chef, and his exuberant wife, who seemed to regard her establishment as a vivid little theatre in which she was the star. She and her daughter served us a *pichet* of red wine and a plate of olives, followed by a lovely meal – all for a pittance. I remember a terrine of rabbit within a ribbon of aspic that glowed like amber; then *loup de mer*, done plainly on the grill with a little olive oil; and finally cheese with a salad of *mesclun de Nice*. Throughout this charming dinner, Madame bustled about, stopping at each table to chortle coquettishly and admonish us all to eat up, every morsel, or she would be angry. 'She is like everybody's ideal mother,' observed Max over coffee. I suddenly remembered Ursula.

'Oh dear. I've got a girl from Dublin staying with me, a former student, and I am afraid I forgot all about her.'

Léon narrowed his intense little eyes. 'Surely you gave her a second key? Then why worry? I mean, is she a close friend who'd expect to take meals with you, or is she just an ex-student you're helping out?'

'The latter,' I answered hastily, as if compelled to reassure them – or perhaps myself. 'The latter, absolutely. She was my writing student last year in Trinity College, and she turned up suddenly this morning, out of the blue.'

'Good God,' exclaimed Max, frowning. 'Sounds a bit of a stalker. Was it wise to invite her to stay?'

Perhaps the wine we'd drunk had loosened my tongue, or perhaps I was reasoning that since these two were psychiatrists, they would receive my confidences more tactfully than most other virtual strangers. Or maybe I was simply puzzled by my own docility, by the unquestioning way I had received Ursula into my rooms, almost as if I'd been under some spell. Anyway, I found myself saying, 'I don't know. Of course it was importunate of her, but I think . . . ' I paused, then plunged on. 'I think I'm feeling guilty about my mother, who died recently.' And I told them how her blue eyes, wide with love and worry, had recently begun to haunt my dreams. (I did not tell them about the dream in which she had appeared to me as a gargoyle.)

Léon said gently, 'You know, all sons feel guilty. All of us feel we should have rescued our mother from death. You are experiencing what one might call a sort of primeval tumult.'

Max raised an admonitory finger. 'And you may be displacing some of that tumult onto this girl, who, as you say, appeared suddenly at your door without a by-your-leave, expecting hospitality. The fact that you have tolerated such an encroachment disturbs me, if you don't mind me saying so. You are quite vulnerable, Sebastian.' He scowled again. 'I presume this girl has a crush on you?'

'She says she feels as if I wrote my novels for her alone. But others have said that to me before; young people often do, when a book ignites them. They begin to believe they know you intimately through it. Also, students do sometimes convince themselves that your life revolves around them.' I pictured Ursula's determined face beneath the ragamuffin hair. 'Still, there is something odd about this girl: the vehement way she insists that she *understands* me, that we are *connected.*' I sighed. 'Is it a crush? She has, after all, followed me here to Nice like a dauntless lover. So I suppose she must have feelings for me, though I never encouraged her at Trinity last year. And it wasn't only because she was my student; it was also that she herself had seemed asexual somehow. She's a childish creature.' I hesitated before offering feebly, 'We mainly talk about books.'

We ordered more coffee, and Léon suggested a *digestif*. Max said, 'I worry about this girl insisting she understands you. That is precisely what these intrusive people always say, you know. If I were a writer like yourself, I wouldn't mind if, after a reading, an admirer declared, "I loved that story. When I heard it, I felt that you really understood me." That's genuine praise, in my book. But if the admirer said, "I loved that story. When I heard it, I knew that *I* understood *you* . . . " Well, in that case I'd be alarmed.'

'I think I see what you mean,' I answered slowly. 'It's possessive of her, to say that. She's trying to suggest that I belong to her somehow, isn't she?'

'I fear so,' said Léon in a sombre voice. 'You can't be too careful these days.'

Max gave yet another frown. 'In our profession, we are used to this kind of thing. We call it "the transference", and in a way it is the crux of any analysis. How the patient grapples with it and overcomes it is the heart of the drama, so to speak.' He inclined his large body towards me. 'But you say that you are used to it as well – to invasive readers or students who fall in love with you through your books or because you are their teacher. Surely, in the past, you have dealt successfully with these "groupies", as I believe one calls them now?'

'Of course,' I answered, feeling strangely embarrassed. 'But usually it was when I was teaching in America. I knew how to handle them there, for some reason, whereas Ursula is Irish, and now she has come to me here in Nice, so I suppose I'm a bit flummoxed.'

When I took leave of them, we felt comfortable enough with one another, after that pleasant dinner and the glow of brandy, to kiss on both cheeks in the French way. I accompanied them to the front door of their house, then realised I felt like walking. So I strolled past the bus station and returned to the old city, where a rose-gold glow flushed the dark air, and the clatter of pots and pans and the shouts and laughter from within the houses, and the roar of scooters along the roads, seemed tempered, at this hour, by a centuries-old stillness. When I got back to the hotel, Ursula was waiting on the sofa.

'Hey,' she said sulkily. 'Where were you? I was hungry.'

'I thought you didn't care about food.'

She pouted. 'Well, I was hungry. I walked through the old town and had a kind of pizza thing, with onions, but it wasn't enough.'

I sighed. 'Ursula, I believe that you are the type of thin person who is perpetually hungry.' I looked more closely at her, and saw that she had changed into a rather unbecoming skirt, pleated like a school skirt, which it perhaps was. So she had dressed up to have dinner with me. I softened. 'The restaurant next door stays open very late. Come on, I'll buy you a meal and have a *tisane* myself.'

We were the only customers, and the proprietor seemed drowsy as he served us. I drank a verbena tea while Ursula gobbled *salade niçoise*, a steak, and apple tart.

'There's no cream,' she complained, narrowing her eyes at the tart.

'The French don't glop cream over everything, as the Irish do,' I reproved her, but when she continued to gaze at me sullenly, I resignedly called for some *chantilly*.

She stared grumpily at her *café noir*, as well. No doubt she had envisaged an immense cup of weak, milky coffee. (*Jus de chausettes*, the French call it, or 'the juice wrung from socks'.) But this time I refused to acknowledge her displeasure; I would not indulge her in everything.

Suddenly she asked, 'Sebastian, have you ever been in love?'

Uncannily, at that moment, a beautiful young woman walked in. She was with one other woman and two men; clearly they'd been out on the town and, noticing that this little place was still open, had decided to take a late meal. The plump proprietor, who had a way of moving slowly from kitchen to window, where he would gaze inscrutably out at the road for a while like a pampered cat, now tore himself from his reverie and gestured them to a table. He described the *plat du jour* in his sleepy voice, and the four proceeded to ponder the menu, and to consult each other in the serious way of all French people when they talk about food.

'Once,' I murmured, trying not to stare at the young woman. Her eyes were dark – though not as dark as Ursula's – and slightly round, with long lashes. Beneath them, the lips curved in a smile that made the breath catch in my throat. Generally she was a faun type, with that delicate face, but it was not merely her loveliness that moved me. She was so like my Claudia, I very nearly could not bear it. At the time I had tried to be stoical, to accept that I would not see her, or hear her voice, or touch her, ever again. Yet this face in a restaurant brought it all back, the living woman, and for a moment I was overcome.

Ursula said, 'I *thought* I was in love, once. Only now I'm not sure.'

I made myself focus on her again. She sighed, then gave her abrupt scowl and demanded, 'So, what did you think of my work? My short stories? You were pretty encouraging last year. Were you codding me, or did you mean it?'

I supposed it would not do to confess that I couldn't remember a single syllable of her writing. Neutrally I answered, 'Yes, I meant it. But you must let me see what you are working on now.'

She brightened, in that way of hers. 'Super. I'll leave something beside your bed, for us to discuss at breakfast.'

'Ursula, you really are extraordinarily cheeky.' I regarded her – that cracked grin which could instantly darken to a frown. 'You know, I haven't asked you anything yet about your own means, your background. You coming here like this could seem desperate, or at least extreme.' I fiddled with my teacup. 'To be blunt, why in heaven's name did you do this? I mean, the way you did go about doing it. You could have written, you know, or rung me.'

She answered, for once without her customary blend of naivety and guile, but with what seemed a simple candour. 'I didn't have much money. Just enough to bring me here, really. But there's no one for me back in Dublin. My father left us ages ago, and my mum just died. I had no one left. So I came away, here.'

The coincidence shocked me, as the glimpse of that doe-eyed girl who resembled Claudia had done, but I said nothing. Revealing the fact of my own mother's death could, I thought, encourage her to presume even further. I had met this kind of thing before, mainly in America: people who expected an instant intimacy to spring up between us, just because they had spoken about personal things at some campus drinks party or after a reading. If I had said to Ursula now 'How extraordinary. My mother is also recently dead', what would she have concluded? That destiny had brought her to Nice, to succour me in our similar grief? On the other hand, I could not help wondering if there was, in fact, something mysterious, some kind of synchronicity, behind her coming.

When we left the restaurant (I did not glance at the table where the four young people were eating), I suddenly felt restive, in need of yet another walk, even though it had got very late. But my little companion was game, as I supposed she would be for most things – which at once unsettled and charmed me.

So we walked again through Old Nice, which was especially beautiful now that nearly everything was closed and still. The houses with their crooked shutters and black lamps seemed newly exotic to me, as if after midnight the district settled back into its ancient Italian self. Then we went down to the sea, which tonight was deep and still and the profoundest of blues, except where it furled whitely upon the shingles of the strand. The Mediterranean, *mare nostrum*, for me the heart of Europe. There were very few people about. A young couple stood on the middle of the quay lost in a kiss, while an old man wearing a greatcoat too heavy for the season trudged past. A police car was idling nearby, no doubt scouring the area for miscreants, but the usual prostitutes, pimps, dealers and grifters were not to be found tonight. After a while we curved north, and walked beneath the arcades of the Place Massena and along avenue Jean Médecin, back to my own *quartier*.

I was telling Ursula that this was an Arab area, when simultaneously I remembered two incidents. The first had taken place about two years before. I'd been up at the station, buying the English papers, and was walking along the little road that lay between the halal market and the cathedral. It was a late-December evening, perhaps eight o'clock, the sky full of an ashen darkness. Sprawling from the footpath into the gutter stood a number of Arab men, perhaps fifty or more, all facing eastwards, towards avenue Jean Médecin – towards Mecca! – their heads bowed in prayer. I hurried past, feeling obscurely clumsy, a raw-boned Irishman with bags full of newspapers who had stumbled on something he was too ignorant to understand.

The second image that flared through my mind was older. Fifteen or so years ago, Claudia and I had lived in New York, in a pleasant East Village flat, while I taught at New York University for a term. One evening we went to a downtown nightclub, which so entertained us with its offbeat atmosphere and diverse clientele we lingered there until dawn. When we emerged groggily into the street, it was a sailor's morning, the sky mother-of-pearl, the streets muffled in a mist so heavy, it seemed to lie like a counterpane over the traffic lights. All of downtown New York, wreathed in this fog, seemed spellbound and lovely, lovely enough to break the heart. Suddenly Claudia murmured 'Listen'. I stopped, inclining my head in the silence, until I detected a rasping sound. Presently three figures materialised through the mist, which broke before them like fabric tearing. They walked slowly, three very thin young men emerging from out of the fog, each clutching a white stick that rasped against the footpath. The middle one was wearing dark glasses, and the hand that held his stick was splotched with sores.

They walked past without acknowledging us. Then the fog curled and closed upon itself again.

Ursula said petulantly, 'We're nearly home, aren't we, Sebastian? It must be three in the morning.'

I realised that my legs were aching. 'Indeed we are. Do you think you can make it back on foot, or should we splurge and take a taxi?'

I was joking, since the hotel was in the very next street, but she seemed genuinely shocked at the idea of taking a taxi – which quite pleased me. Capricious she might be, and vain, but clearly she was not profligate with money. So we walked back home, where she disappeared abruptly into her bedroom. I hovered on the threshold of my own, wondering what she would think up next.

She reappeared, still wearing her street clothes, and clutching five or so pages of handwritten text. 'Here you are, then,' she announced solemnly. 'I hope you enjoy it.' And she vanished once more into the guest bedroom.

*

As I readied myself for bed, I reflected that we – Claudia and I – had chosen Nice partly in order to evade the literary life. We had discovered a café where the walls were burnished by years of tobacco smoke and where serious-looking Arab men drank coffee, smoked and played cards at baize tables all day long. At night the card tables were cleared away for jazz, and the proprietor served good cheap wine well into the early hours. We had fallen in love with the place almost immediately, and not only because it was an authentic bohemian bar. It was also that we were anonymous there – which we both found restful. I, because I did not have to be 'Sebastian Clare the famous writer', and Claudia, because she was regarded as her own self and not 'the companion of Sebastian Clare the famous writer'. We would drop in for an aperitif once or twice a week, and sometimes return after dinner to listen to the jazz. We got to know the regulars and were happy; the café seemed emblematic of Nice, or of *our* Nice, I suppose.

So we settled. And despite an occasional invitation to read from Nice University or the Princess Grace Irish Library in

Monte Carlo, and aside from a modest coterie of literary friends, we remained more or less on our own, in our flat in Old Nice. I could not live there now, though I continued to love it, despite the tourists.

It occurred to me as I cleaned my teeth that perhaps my longed-for anonymity was no longer so satisfactory. Perhaps I was a bit lonely, missed the greetings of fellow writers, journalists, editors or admirers on the street or in the pub. Perhaps part of me yearned to read a review of my latest book, or the book of a friend, in Grogan's or the long bar of the Shelbourne Hotel, instead of being sent clippings by my agent. Perhaps this was why I was so susceptible to Ursula now. She was from Dublin, and she was interested in writing. Perhaps it was as simple as that.

II

Neither Claudia nor I knew how to drive. This didn't trouble Claudia, especially after we had found a flat in the Old Town where, because of its warren of crooked streets, cars were not permitted anyway. As for myself, I had once tried half-heartedly to learn, but all my life I'd lived in cities with public transport to hand, and I loved to walk, so my ineptitude never seemed like a hardship. (Though at times I felt that as a man I *should* be fascinated by the internal combustion engine, like the fathers and sons of my Dublin youth who had almost seemed to live with their heads under the bonnet of some broken-down Ford, Austin or Vauxhall.)

We had been living in *vieux Nice* for about two years when I was invited to read at a translation seminar in Monte Carlo. The organisers, who knew I couldn't drive, offered to send down a chauffeur so that we wouldn't have to bother with train tickets and timetables. I discussed this with Claudia over breakfast on our small terrace. 'I don't like Monte Carlo,' she said, wrinkling her nose. 'It's all false and glittering, like being inside a Fabergé egg.' She extended her arm towards the sun-blistered house opposite, the market below. '*This* is real. Monte Carlo is not real.'

'Of course it's not real. It's full of moguls evading tax. But the foundation people are offering a hefty fee and dinner for us both. Plus a driver. I say we go. It's just one evening, after all.'

He seemed friendly, the driver – a gangly Englishman of fifty or so, who had meandered down to the Côte d'Azur for some reason. Perhaps a remittance man, or a casualty of the English class system, or even a criminal? Though as we drove past the lights of Villefranche towards Monaco, he surprised us by saying, 'I didn't make the connection when that director fellow told me to collect a "Monsieur Clare", but I recognised you the moment I saw you. I've read all your books, Mr Clare. I'm a real admirer. In fact, I myself would like to write a novel, perhaps a thriller or a detective story.'

Wonderful, I said to myself. *Another aspiring writer.* There were so many of them these days, and most, it seemed to me, merely wanted instant celebrity. Few were prepared to take on the real burdens of a writing life, the painstaking revisions, the fallow periods, the thwarted hopes, the nasty reviews. Few seemed to grasp the basic truth that writing is simply work: real, arduous work. That it takes years to get it right, if you ever do, and that you must do it for love and not for fame, or else you desecrate your gift, if you even have one. Yet how many taxi drivers or dentists or barmen or acquaintances at parties had told me that they intended to write a novel, as if it were something anyone could casually decide?

Although now, looking at the back of the driver's greying head, and the top of his leather jacket, where it hung off his shoulders, I was intrigued. He had been blandly deferential to Claudia and myself when we had descended from our flat to find him slouched against his car. I had not bothered to think much about him, only now he'd suddenly come into focus. Who was this tall Englishman who seemed to read literary novels?

On the drive back to Nice, I asked him about himself, his history, and he told us a sad story involving a wastrel father, a mother who had committed suicide and a brother who'd gone bad, and had become a gangster or something. 'Why not write about that?' I suggested. 'Don't bother with thrillers; tell your own story, which sounds fascinating.'

Next morning, I was making coffee when we heard a sharp knock at the door. Claudia opened it. There stood our driver of the evening before, wearing the same rumpled shirt, leather jacket and jeans. It occurred to me that he had slept in his car. Claudia looked startled but, always gracious, she murmured 'Please come in' and offered him coffee and a *tartine* of baguette and butter.

'I came back because I have a proposal,' he announced, touching a finger to his moustache. 'I would like to offer my services as your driver, your very own personal chauffeur.'

Claudia and I exchanged an alarmed look. He pressed on, 'I'll ferry you here and there, wherever you like. And I'll charge very little, just enough to keep me fed and watered and to buy petrol.' He placed his large hand palm-down on the table and stared at it, before looking up again with a smile. 'All I'm really asking for in return is advice. Literary guidance. From you, Mr Clare, as a novelist, and from you, Miss, because I know you're an editor.' (*How does he know Claudia is an editor?* I wondered. *He must have been listening pretty closely to our chat in the back of his taxi last night – more closely than either of us realised.*) Claudia said, 'I don't edit very much any more. And only children's books.'

'Still,' he said, fastening his flat light eyes not on her, but on myself. 'I'd like it if both of you would read the manuscript I'm working on, and suggest improvements. That's all I ask.'

'Where do you live?' said Claudia.

He continued to gaze levelly at me, without even a glance at her. 'I've an apartment,' he said vaguely, 'and a mobile phone. I can be at your beck and call.'

Why did we say yes? Probably because jewel-like towns and villages surround Nice, some beside the sea, others in that equally lovely world of the mountains, stone hamlets and fields of lavender and herbs. And here we had found a man – or he had found us – who would drive us to all those places whenever we summoned him, and collect us and drive us home. All in exchange for some cursory advice about his writing – the kind of instruction I was well used to giving from years of workshop teaching, and Claudia from her time in publishing.

What could have been easier? So we said yes, although we didn't even know his name.

*

His name was Clive, he announced the next evening. He was driving us to a seafood restaurant in Eze, which had been praised by friends, but to which we had never been because, typically, we had not wished to be at the mercy of the evening trains. So what better way to try out our new arrangement than this, relaxing in the back of his plump little Citroën as he swept us along beside the sea, in the radiant dusk?

But when he drew up in front of the restaurant, I felt uncomfortable at the thought of Claudia and myself sauntering into that pleasant-looking place and eating a good meal while he waited in the car. 'D'you like fish, Clive?' I asked suddenly. 'Why don't you come in with us and have a plate of prawns or something? It would be nicer than waiting out here.'

It was an awkward evening. He had little to contribute, though he swaggered in a hollow way. I asked if he'd driven other writers to and from Monte Carlo, and he mentioned two English poets, both men, and one female short-story writer, whom we knew since she lived in Nice. An accomplished and deeply thoughtful woman, she seemed to burn with an inward light that was, actually, fever, since she suffered from some wasting sickness. But Clive described her as 'that skinny bird' and 'a pain in the arse. She protested every time I struck a bump in the road. Hard to believe she's a famous writer.'

I forgave him because I thought he probably felt out of place in the restaurant. I registered that he was no good at extracting a mussel from its shell, and he complained that the sauces were too rich. And when he took a swallow from his half-glass of Vouvray (he had assured us that he drank little or nothing when driving), he made a face and announced that he preferred beer. No doubt he was used to gobbling a sandwich or a hamburger in his car between drives, and the fuss and ceremony of even this easygoing bistro had nonplussed him.

Back at our flat, Claudia looked at me through narrowed eyes. 'Sebastian, *why* did you invite Clive to have dinner with us without consulting me? I felt horribly uncomfortable.' She had seemed tense in the restaurant, but now, as she irritably threw her scarf on the sofa, I saw that she was more upset than I'd thought. Once more she faced me. 'Our first drive, and you immediately broke down the master-servant relationship. Surely it was unwise. Anyway,' she repeated, 'I felt horribly uncomfortable.'

'Oh, darling,' I answered, '*I* feel uncomfortable thinking in terms of masters and servants. You know that in Ireland we've been through centuries of that kind of oppression. It makes me squeamish, to consider imposing it on someone.'

She gave an exasperated sigh. 'I'm not suggesting that we should *oppress* him. I'm merely saying that if there are no borders, then where are we? That man is not our friend! He *is* performing a service for us. If we sweep away all the boundaries, all protocol, he could – he may – do anything. Don't you see?'

I remembered that before leaving the flat yesterday morning, Clive had offered to buy himself a uniform, complete with chauffeur's cap. I had said no, laughing, thinking that to trick him out in livery would be ridiculous. Yet now I wondered if it wasn't a good idea after all. On the other hand, I didn't see how we could put our arrangement in reverse, so to speak, and ask him to buy a uniform at this point. As if she'd read my mind, Claudia went on: 'Once you trample on the proper relationship, upset the balance, I think there's no going back. He'll just continue to take liberties.' She moved an impatient hand through her hair. 'I don't know, Sebastian. All of this is making me uneasy. We don't *know* the man, and his family life seems to be full of misery and criminals. What are we doing?'

'I don't know either, darling, but you must admit that we've stumbled on a marvellous piece of luck.' Recently, some friends had invited us to supper at their house in Villefranche, where the ancient streets unfurled from the harbour upwards into the mountains like the whorls of a seashell. Only of course we had been reluctant to go because of the bother with trains. I reminded her of this, and also of how we had been hoping to spend more time in St Paul and Carros. 'And now we can. He represents a new freedom for us, doesn't he?' When she still looked hesitant, I said, 'He'll take us to the airport, or drive us into Italy, or even as far as Cassis or Marseilles. Wouldn't it be a pity to reject this godsend? I'll try to observe the proper etiquette from now on. As long as we manage him in the right way, he's sure to be a boon to us, isn't he?'

Yet the next morning, when he arrived to take us to an art gallery on the other side of Nice, I instinctively opened the front door on the passenger side and slid in beside him, as one would in a Dublin taxi. But Claudia gave me such a look from the back that I scrambled out again and hastily took the place next to her.

But I suppose the damage had been done, for as we drove off I saw those colourless eyes surveying us in his mirror – a look I could not quite read but which troubled me slightly.

I never seemed to get it right. A few evenings later, he drove us to a party at the house of a photographer acquaintance in Antibes, and something I said on the way back – something too casual or familiar – encouraged him to criticise the other guests, whom he had glimpsed coming out of the house. This one was too fat, that one looked a bore, and so on. Stupidly, I was amused by such arrogance. It seemed so absurd that I just laughed.

About a week into this odd arrangement, he stopped open-ing the doors for us with the flourish he had shown at first, when he had seemed to be wearing that phantom driver's cap; now he let us climb into the car ourselves, and no longer offered help with bags or parcels. Clearly he had stopped regarding himself as our 'very own personal chauffeur'. So how *had* he come to see himself, in relation to Claudia and me? What was he expecting?

After that initial story of family woe and the admission that he'd like to write a novel, he did not press us for the literary advice he'd said he wanted when he first offered to be our driv-er, nor did he volunteer much more about his own circum-stances. We didn't know why he had come to the south of France or how long he had been there. He had only a few phras-es of French and seemed more or less indifferent to the place. Clearly he had had other driving gigs, since, after all, the Foundation in Monte Carlo had engaged him for us: perhaps he had advertised himself as 'the Only English Taxi on the Côte d'Azur'. But now it appeared that he had given up all his other clients to be at our disposal, since whenever we rang he was available. (Was this in itself not alarming?) I still suspected that his 'apartment' was a fiction, and that he slept in his car or per-haps under canvas in some mountain field like a superannuated

Boy Scout. I don't know why I thought this, except that he had no home phone and often looked a bit grizzled, and once I saw something like a sleeping bag in the boot of the Citroën. It was now early autumn, so I supposed that he could sleep in the open air without too much discomfort, but how would he manage when winter came? Yet, true to his word, he asked only for petrol money, and a bit extra for food and to help pay his mobile phone bill.

After another week, the situation began to trouble Claudia's dreams. She would cry out, and I would find her twisted up in the sheets. 'I dreamt of a dark place and a knife, gleaming,' she mumbled one night, while I smoothed back her hair and kissed her hot face. 'It's all right, darling,' I assured her, but the next night there was another cry after another dark dream.

Yet she did not insist that we dismiss Clive. After all, she too benefited from his services, even though he was becoming increasingly familiar, greeting us with nothing more than a grunt, rebuking us for our too-vague directions, continuing to make casual disparaging remarks about our friends. After driving us to a café one evening, he did not wait for us in the car but loped inside and settled at our table, explaining, 'I feel like a coffee.' We swallowed our own drinks guardedly while he talked about how much he disliked the French, with their 'incomprehensible' language, extravagant gestures and garlic breath. And after he'd gulped down his coffee, he didn't offer to pay. Generally he seemed to be presuming more and more that he was a pal and fellow *literato* of mine, or even a son; after all, I had encouraged him by inviting him to eat with us that night in Eze. His attitude to Claudia was different, though, and puzzled me.

Claudia. Often I was struck by what I can only call her otherness. Observing her chestnut eyes, the way a frond of hair fell across her cheek when she inclined her head to read or write, her narrow blue-white wrists, I would think: *She is herself.* Sometimes when we made love, I felt her warm skin, and the heart beating inside it, within me. And when the dark and shining skeins of ourselves wove together like that, self and other, other and self, I felt . . . I cannot say, except to seize on that vague and perhaps mawkish word *mystery*.

But I suppose my point is that while my feeling for her probably coloured my judgement, she was beautiful by any standard. When she glided along some narrow road towards the *terrasse* of a café where I was waiting, I would always be aware of others admiring her. Yet Clive seemed utterly unmoved by her loveliness, as if some ordinary sexual curiosity were dead in him. Of course he could have been homosexual, except that he seemed to give off no erotic charge at all, in any direction. His nondescript eyes stared impassively at us in the rear-view mirror, though he deferred to me more, and looked at me more, as he had on that first morning in our flat when he'd made his appeal mainly to myself, as if Claudia counted for little. She wondered if he was starting to think of her as a rival, but I laughed at the idea.

'No, really,' she protested. 'I sense he wants you all to himself. You're an only child, Sebastian, but I have a sister, so I know. What do you think he intends with all this driving us about? He wants to become so indispensable to you that you begin to prefer him to me. Oh, do stop laughing. After all, you're a successful novelist, which is what he would like to be, while I'm just a silly editor of children's books.' She walked over to the window and stared out. 'I don't know if I can tolerate this much longer.' She turned to me again. 'You know, I think you enjoy telling people you have a driver. It's a kind of fantasy for you, like being inside one of your own novels. But he's beginning to make me feel *very* peculiar.'

'All right, I take your point. I can't imagine him hovering around forever. What would we *do* with him?' I paused, considering. 'Would you agree to keep him on for a bit longer, give him some advice about his writing, and then dismiss him?'

A day or so later, he asked if we would read his manuscript – although, as usual, he made this appeal mainly to me, which further convinced Claudia that he was trying to move in on me, perhaps even wished to *become* me. I arranged to meet him in the café round the corner – an unusually homely place for that touristic part of town, frequented by garrulous old men, wearing braces and berets, who spoke *niçois*. They would drink pastis all evening while playing some elaborate card game and berating the *patron* in a friendly way. But at two o'clock, the time of my appointment with Clive, the place was empty except for the owner, and his white cat drowsing on the *zinc*. Claudia had said that she would prefer not to come along, so I waited by myself at a small table until he arrived, dressed in the same clothes as always, with a hand-rolled cigarette drooping from the corner of his mouth and some pages of foolscap in his hands. He was ten minutes late. 'Hi, Sebastian,' he said, giving an offhand wave. Then: 'You know, I'm so fucking *angry* with these fucking French drivers. First the bastards get me all tangled up in traffic, and then they call me these fucking names I can't understand. What's a *fis de pute*?'

I didn't feel inclined to translate, though I was chuckling inwardly. He muttered, 'Well, he's lucky I didn't know. Because if it means what I think it does, the next time I'm going to get out and seize him by the fucking throat.'

I looked over at the *patron*, who was eating a lump of cheese and reading *Nice-Matin*, a minute glass of red wine at his elbow. He and his clients were always exchanging insults that were a rough form of compliment, and the oaths that flew between drivers were a kind of verbal ballet, baroque and ritualised. Never had I seen anybody actually leave his or her car and physically attack another driver. And it occurred to me that Clive's language, his *fucking* this and *fucking* that, was more profane, and obviously far less imaginative, than the ceremonial insults one heard as a matter of course along European roads. As I called for the drinks – a small beer for him and a red wine for myself – I further thought that he had not spoken like this when he had first come into our life. In fact, his whole aspect had changed. The creature I was looking at now, legs sprawled beneath the table, cigarette ash crumbling onto that less-than-clean shirt, a sullen curl to the lip, bore almost no resemblance to the diffident man who had driven us to Monaco only a couple of weeks before.

While he drank his beer, I tried to apply myself to his manuscript, which was, to put it bluntly, pathetic – just two pages of almost illegible and clumsily written prose. It seemed to be an attempt at a story about a young man thumbing a lift along some rural English road. *He was neatly dressed*, it opened, *in collar and tie, but there was a haunting look in his eye.* Had he intended the rhyme? And surely he meant 'haunted'? The first paragraph continued to describe the man's clothes in a tedious, laboured way. And the meagre material that followed was equally pointless, with an appalling number of grammatical mistakes. An editorial nightmare.

Handing the two sheets back, I ventured, 'I must say, Clive, this story doesn't appear to have much of an anchor. What I mean is, I think your work would have more vigour if you tried to take on an aspect of yourself, even if you don't understand it. I've often said to students, "Write about something in your own life that you don't understand." Because the effort to fathom a part of yourself or your background that is a mystery to you can produce strong, tense writing. Whereas this story seems so vague. And it's so short! Do you try to write every day?'

Those eyes of his, which were at once opaque and clear as glass, stared at me, then slid away to look over my shoulder at the street. I suddenly realised that he had not wanted instruction from me, despite what he'd proposed that first day in our flat. All he had ever wanted, and had expected, was praise – which in this case I could not give. It also struck me that of course he was unable to write about a self he probably did not have. I guessed that he had always lived through others in a nearly vampiric way, which was why his chill eyes unnerved me so: perhaps they looked so lifeless because he had, in fact, no life of his own. He was, I was beginning to suspect, a parasite.

I continued to make suggestions but he had clearly lost interest. He crushed out his cigarette, moved about in his chair and sighed, then stared over my head or down at his hands, until I could no longer endure his rudeness. 'Well, Clive, that's about all I can say for the moment. If you decide to take me up on my advice, I'll have another look at your work. I must go now, but perhaps Claudia will ring you tomorrow. I think she'd like to do some shopping at that *marché* behind the station.'

'Oh, *Claudia*,' he grunted, and took a swallow of beer.

'What do you mean?' I asked stiffly.

He dragged the back of his hand across the foam that clung to his moustache. 'I bet you helped her along, didn't you? I mean, her editing jobs and all that. You arranged those posts for her, those good positions in the writing business. Your support would be very valuable to someone trying to break into that world, wouldn't it?'

I said levelly, 'Claudia is a prominent editor in her own right. She has a reputation in London as well as Dublin, and never needed my sponsorship. In fact, I am grateful to her for her sense of language. She is the first person to look at my novels and stories.'

I thought about those sessions with Claudia, generally at the hour of the aperitif. They were times of intense intimacy, with evening bringing a peculiar hush to the *quartier* and a lilac glow to the sky; the two of us slowly drinking at our dining table while Claudia read through whatever I was working on. For me, sounds and smells would become suddenly sharp: laughter from the café below, a busker singing in the distance, the savour of garlic from neighbouring kitchens. Then she would look up, I would say 'Well?' and, in her own honest way, she would tell me what she thought. Now, as Clive continued to stare at me with those pallid eyes, once more I asked myself, *Who is he? What does he want?*

Abruptly he announced, 'I can cook.'

'What?'

'I'm a good cook, mate. I could cook for you. And Claudia. I could even wear a chef's hat.'

'You want to be our cook as well as our driver?'

'I'm a good cook,' he repeated stubbornly. 'Do you have a guest bedroom? I could, you know, live in. It would be convenient for you. And for Claudia.'

Once again I felt my limbs stiffen. 'I thought you wanted to be a writer. When would you have time to write, if you were our full-time servant? As it is, you aren't producing very much material.' I regretted the pomposity in my voice, but couldn't help it.

He looked at me composedly, and I felt obscurely wrong-footed, as if it was me who had been ill-mannered. Then he said, 'I mightn't be the best writer in the world, Sebastian, but I have lots of really fantastic stories. I mean, *fantastic*, considering my brother and all, and the places I've been: drugs, sex, rock and roll, you name it.' He continued to appraise me coolly. 'We could collaborate, you and me. After all, you've got to admit, you and Claudia are a bit . . . hoity-toity. But I could pour some red blood into your work, introduce you to the dark side, if you know what I mean. With your talent and my stories, we could write a real best-seller.'

At that moment, a woman walked in, murmuring the ritual greeting 'Messieurs, dames, bonjour,' although there were no other ladies present. She was in her fifties or early sixties, and plump, with short curly hair and a pretty, smiling face. She and the owner had some exchange, then he laughed and pushed a packet of *Gitanes filtres* across the counter. She promptly paid for them, then cried 'Au revoir, messieurs, dames; bonne journée' in her lilting voice, and bustled out again.

Gazing after her, Clive said, 'She was nice, that one. I could fancy that one.'

For some reason, I was shocked. Perhaps because Clive had never shown even an idle erotic interest in anyone since I'd known him, or perhaps because while the woman had looked pleasant, she had also seemed matronly. I'd have said she wasn't the type who wished to be alluring, to excite carnal thoughts in a stranger. Also, there was something insolent in his gaze, and in his mumble, *I could fancy that one.*

When I did not speak, he grinned. 'Ah, you know, mate. Women of a certain age are quite nice. Grateful. One can get quite a lot out of them, even if the flesh is a bit tough.'

I still did not reply. He started to roll another cigarette. I noticed that his hands were badly cared for, grubby and with ragged cuticles. He said, 'Suit yourself. Only just to let you know I'm a fairly good cook. Could save you a lot of trouble, me doing the cooking. Think about it. Anyway, thanks for the advice about my writing.' He tossed some coins on the table – not enough, I noticed, to cover his beer – and stood up, extending his hand. I shook it, but remained silent, I did not quite know why.

*

When I returned home, Claudia was in the kitchen making a ratatouille. She had pinned back her hair, and was wearing a funny white apron with an immense radish painted on it. She was serious as a scholar about cooking; the watery light flowing in through the window struck her intent face, and glowed on the peppers and aubergines on the counter so that they flared green and red and violet. It was one of those moments that look like a painting – a Bonnard, perhaps – an ordinary moment, but vivid with sunlight and a kind of charged stillness. I looked at her for a while, and pictured Clive shambling about beside her, smiling superciliously, handling the food with his grimy hands, ash from his cigarette dropping into the pans.

She glanced up, smiling. 'Hello, darling. I'm glad you're home. You can give those tomatoes a rinse and chop some garlic. How did it go?'

'His stuff is crap,' I said tersely, moving towards the basin.

She gave me a startled look. I forced myself to smile, then kissed her cheek; she smelled pleasantly of herbs. 'If you don't mind, I'd prefer not to talk about it just now. Perhaps at breakfast tomorrow?'

'Of course I don't mind.' She smiled teasingly. 'Your mum rang. I told her you were out. At the *pub*. She was concerned about the early hour, so I said you were probably just having tea.'

'Well, I wasn't having tea. I had a drink. Not that it's any of her business.'

'Don't worry, Sebastian.' Again she looked up from the

vegetables, still with that mischievous smile. 'She's in Dublin and you're in France. She couldn't *possibly* engulf you from that distance.'

*

Next morning, Claudia stood, arms crossed, elbows cradled in her palms, staring out of the window, her habitual pose when troubled or thoughtful. I had just told her about my meeting with Clive the day before. After a few moments, she said, 'You know, Sebastian, the main trouble with him is that he's *boring*. He's not our friend; he's a mean-minded, slovenly, ignorant, boring stranger. Yet we've let him into our lives.'

I came up behind her and buried my face in her hair. And suddenly I was full of desire for her. Her hair against my closed eyes, the silk of her dressing gown beneath my hands, were making me, literally, tremble. She must have felt it too, the same thing, for she turned and gave me a fierce kiss. Perhaps it was what she had just said, about how we had done something foolish, perhaps even profaned something, by letting Clive encroach on us. Perhaps we wanted to make love at that moment not only to comfort ourselves, but also in order to perform some ceremony, some intimate ritual, that would protect our private life from him. '*Sebastian*,' she whispered, and I kissed the side of her neck. Then the phone rang. I wondered if we should answer, but Claudia sighed, 'Oh, go on. It's probably your mum. No one else would call so early.'

'I'll ring off as fast as I can.'

And indeed, 'Sebastian?' queried my mother from her house in Rathmines.

'Hello, Mum. Listen, it's a bit awkward for me at the moment. I'll ring back in a while.'

There was a pause. Then, tremulously, 'Your mother rings. Long-distance. You'd think a son would devote a particular attention to a *long-distance* call, from his *mother.*'

'Mum, you ring me nearly every day.'

'I didn't speak to you yesterday! You were *out*! At the *pub*!'

'Mum, there aren't really very many pubs in Nice. That was Claudia's joke. I was at a café, an ordinary French café, meeting someone. Am I obliged to give you an account of all my movements? Now please listen. I must attend to something and I'll ring you back shortly. All right? Goodbye.'

I turned to Claudia, who was still standing before the window, arms crossed once more over her kimono. She gave a dry laugh. 'Ring her back. You won't be peaceful until you do.'

'I don't know. I don't see why I should jump every time she makes one of her excessive demands.'

'Neither do I,' she said, with a curious, cryptic smile.

III

Before falling asleep, I read the first page of Ursula's story:

There was something wrong in the house. When did I first know? I feared outside things. The news was full of menace, even then. A man ensconced himself at the top of an American university tower, from which he could survey the peaceful quadrangles below. He slaughtered nine? ten? nursing students, with a rifle, before they caught him. Another sniper, a pallid skinny man, killed the American president; then he himself was killed. There was a picture, his mouth forming an 'O' of surprise, body buckling as the bullet blasted into it. Spy stories were popular, and I saw, on television, 'baddies' emptying phials of poison into the drinks of 'goodies'.

Those were my fears: standing with my back to an open window, where a sniper could get me; being poisoned. I went through a period of fearing dogs because I thought they could give me rabies; I would die horribly, frothing at the mouth. I remember when I was very small, shuddering with fear at the notion that the world might not be real, that the land of dreams might be the real world, while everything that seemed solid, the whole of my daylight life, was perhaps just smoke, an illusion. I feared that my heart would, all of a sudden, stop. I feared that I was not housed securely in my body, that some cruel god might transform me into a leaf or a cloud, as the Greek gods had done, changing girls into trees and boys into purple flowers. I think that I was always afraid . . .

*

She had prepared a charming breakfast, the table laid with a jonquil-yellow cloth (a present from my mother that I'd bundled into a cupboard and never used) and the pale blue coffee bowls bought by Claudia ages ago. I had not seen those bowls in a long time, but found myself glad, now, that they were being put to good use. There was a pot of Provençal honey; a plate of grapes, pears and apples; and a basket of croissants so fresh, the air smelled warmly of butter. She was making coffee.

'Hey,' she said, 'I had a really brilliant dream, where I had these gorgeous wings, and I was flying over the Mediterranean in this *blazing* light.' She emptied the coffee into one blue jug, and hot milk into another, and poured us each a frothing bowl of *café au lait*. 'I knew this French guy at college who taught me how to make proper French coffee,' she announced proudly, settling at her place and tearing a croissant apart in that voracious yet distracted way she had of eating.

She was wearing a black jumper and tight black trousers, with little black shoes like ballet slippers. With her short hair and those large eyes, she looked vividly bohemian, a *petite française* of the nineteen-fifties: Juliette Greco or a brunette Jean Seberg. I'd never seen her show any style before; this morning she was nearly pretty. 'I'll have you know,' she offered teasingly, 'that I used up the last of my money to buy this brilliant breakfast. The jam alone was a fortune, like.'

I wondered was it my reading of her story that had so animated her? The dark changeling, with its flashes of affability amidst an almost perpetual sulkiness, had, it seemed, turned overnight into a vivacious gamine. I said impulsively, 'Ursula, you look very well this morning, but your hair is a disgrace. No doubt you chopped at it yourself before you left Dublin, probably with blunt scissors. I will take you to a nice place today and have it cut properly.'

Her eyes danced at me over her coffee bowl; then she gave a low laugh and murmured 'Oh, Sebastian!'

I opened my mouth but no sound emerged: it rather shocked me that this, her first show of flirtatiousness, should so nonplus me. She went on, 'Well, what did you think of my story?'

'The writing is strong,' I said honestly, recovering my balance. 'The feeling of menace is good, the helplessness of a child in a house where something is wrong. But the old news reports you describe are all American, aren't they. Were you brought up in America?'

She continued to look at me over the coffee bowl. Then her eyes hardened, she lowered the bowl with a thump, and she once again scowled. So the pert elf with butterfly eyes was evanescent, too. It occurred to me that her sulks began, and reverberated, within the web of her own associations, each filament of her psyche quivering with this or that private grievance. And her joys would be the same, thrumming through some internal structure of her own.

It frightened me a bit; nothing I could do would, ultimately, mean anything to her. Yet why did I want to leaven her discontent in the first place? I remembered explaining to Léon and Max that I was feeling conscious-stricken about my mother, and that they had issued a kind of warning. They'd seemed, last night, to have Ursula's number, as well as my own, but now I could not remember their words.

She said ungraciously, 'What does it matter, where I was brought up? If you must know, my father is American, but I haven't seen him in about a thousand years. Anyway, it doesn't *matter*. The story is not autobiographical.'

'Yet it is about a child who feels imperilled at home, within her own family. And I gather your father was abusive, or at least negligent?' I paused. 'You know, I have no memories at all of my father. He died when I was an infant.'

She nibbled on a grape, head tilted like a blackbird. 'I do know. I mean, I suspected. It's in some of your novels. Boys without fathers. I *wish* I'd had no father. My dad was . . . ' She stared down at her plate.

'Do you have any brothers or sisters?' I asked gently.

'One brother. Married. His wife's dead gorgeous. They live in London. He's a *banker.*' She pronounced this word as if it smelt like a rotten fish. 'We aren't really in contact. That's what I meant last night, when I told you I have no one left. There's nothing for me in Dublin. My brother and I never got on. I can't be party to his standards, which I suppose are the standards of most people, their need for *things*, and all their compromises. I had to get away.' She seemed to hesitate, then blurted, 'I didn't go to my mother's funeral.'

Clearly this hadn't been easy for her to say, for as soon as she'd uttered it her face blanched, and she grew very still. I divined immediately that she had presumed that her journey to France, and to me, would free her from whatever demons had dogged her in Ireland. But of course they had travelled with her. I thought of that cool journey to Dublin I myself had made, not long ago, to attend my own mother's funeral. I'd been so correct, greeting the mourners in her gloomy parlour over the whiskey and baked meats, my face suitably solemn. Oh, I'd done my duty, all right, apparently unlike Ursula – but had I really *been* there?

'Why?' I asked. 'Did you have a falling out with your London brother?'

She swallowed. 'We always fell out. He's a real tight-arse, you know. He always slights me, makes light of my life. He confuses being an artist with being a wastrel, as though I'm irresponsible instead of just different from him.'

'That doesn't quite explain why you didn't go to your mother's funeral.'

She stood to make more coffee, and we were silent for a while. After she had poured it out, she said wryly, 'How *prim* you can sound!'

I acknowledged this with a small smile. She continued, 'My father liked my brother well enough, but he was really bad to me. And mum never protected me from him.' She sighed. 'When she died, my brother bustled back from London all aloof and pompous. I couldn't bear it. I mean, I'd looked after her in hospital even though she'd always been so cold to me. And then my brother arrives *at the last minute* and takes over. So I left him to it. I got out my rucksack and went away, the day before her funeral. I stayed at a friend's flat in Cork for a while before catching the boat to France.' She paused, then finished weakly, 'I did leave a message on the hall table for him.'

Once more we were silent, as I spread honey on warm bread, and considered what it must have cost her, to flout the conventions of grief. Had the rituals surrounding my mother's death salved my pain, or eased my guilt? I was not sure; as for Ursula, it was grand for her to declare that as a writer she must challenge the laws that govern most people's lives, but in practice it could be unendurably hard to do so. She seemed to confirm my thoughts by murmuring, 'It's an awfully dirty secret, isn't it? I mean, I bet you've never come across it before, someone who stayed away from their own mother's funeral?'

I suddenly realised why she had almost certainly, and indeed brutally, cut her own hair before coming to Nice. 'It doesn't mean you did not mourn.'

She lifted her coffee bowl, then put it down again. 'Do you think my brother understood? Do you think he knows why I had to get away?'

'He will in time,' I answered, taking her hand across the table. It was the first time I had ever touched her.

*

True to my word, I brought Ursula to a posh salon where a lookalike battalion of willowy young men cut the hair of wealthy *niçoises* and upmarket tourists. It was splendidly situated across from the promenade, so that I could gaze out at the sea while someone called Fabien worked on Ursula's little head, clucking disapproval as he lifted tufts of her ragged hair.

'My dear girl, who has been looking after you? This is shocking,' he cried in charmingly accented English. Ursula merely grinned; she seemed quite pleased to be so pampered. After he had finished, she did look much better, with a fetching *garçonne* hairstyle to go with her narrow black trousers.

We strolled homewards along the promenade, which was more crowded than usual for October, perhaps because the day was so mild, the sea glossed with a silvery light, like smoked glass. Gazing ahead towards the curve of the chateau, I saw Léon and Max, together with an American lesbian couple whom I knew, walking towards us. The lesbians, both in their fifties, were called Trudy and Alice. Trudy was plump, almost burly, with large sleepy eyes, while Alice was small and slight. They were said to be appallingly rich, though they dressed shabbily and gave an impression of being not altogether personally clean. Because Trudy wrote 'literature', they conducted a kind of salon in their cluttered flat, which involved cups of weak tea and plates of shop cake, to be followed, after about an hour of 'literary' talk, by wine, whiskey and cigars. Then the real talk started – which was mainly of money. When writers gather, they almost always discuss money. Or else subjects attendant upon money, like where to go for a good cheap meal in the evening, that sort of thing. Generally, the literary exchanges were conducted to please Trudy and Alice.

Léon saw us first. 'Ah, Sebastian, our new dear friend!' he cried in his over-animated way. It occurred to me that he, Alice and indeed Ursula were similar types, diminutive and excitable, whereas Max and Trudy, both heavy-limbed and slow-moving, could be brother and sister. (No one amongst them seemed to conform to my own tall fairish type.) We exchanged greetings; I saw Léon take Ursula in, and then give Max a significant look. They had of course instantly recognised her as the girl I'd described last night. Trudy and Alice were also observing her closely, but for another reason: I could tell by the glint in their eyes that they were speculating about her sexuality, especially given the piquant new hairdo and those black trousers. Also, I supposed that a community of eccentric expatriates would naturally show interest in a new arrival: fresh meat, as it were. Anyway, after we'd commented on the fine weather, Léon proposed a drink at a café in the Cours Saleya. We all agreed to this, Ursula giving one of her highly gracious grunts of acquiescence. I had already detected that she was not pleased by this meeting with friends. She'd stiffened at their approach, as though they were an encroachment on our day together. I, on the other hand, was feeling relieved by the chance encounter.

The sea light shimmered along the Cours Saleya, where the market was just closing, men hauling barrels of olives and *cageots* full of lettuce, fennel, radishes and fruit into vans. Bedraggled spinach leaves and some oranges lay scattered on the wet stones, and the air still smelled of cheese and herbs. We settled on the *terrasse* of Léon's café and called for pastis. Ursula, trying hers cautiously, hissed in my ear, 'Jesus, it's fecking *liquorice*.'

Perhaps it was the smells from the market, but we decided that we should have lunch. There was a menu: spinach salad with eggs; then red mullet in a Provençal sauce, with the chips made from chickpea flour that are called *panisses*. We all took this menu, except Ursula, who sullenly asked for a ham sandwich.

Neither here nor in Ireland had she ever seen me like this, chatting affably with friends of my own, and I had hoped it would temper her emotional avarice. But she was appearing at her worst in front of these people. I remembered that after Claudia, certain friends and even acquaintances had appeared eager to shoulder some of the burden of my grief. I was a rela-tively famous man who'd become suddenly vulnerable, and those who wished to be the satellites of sorrow, who yearned for confidences, for a kind of custodianship, had materialised then. Each had seemed to believe that he or she was the exclusive recipient of my stories of love and woe; each had seemed con-vinced that he or she alone *understood* me. And now here was Ursula, who also believed that she understood me, and was doubtless wondering why these others were bothering us. Who were they anyway?

Trudy looked up from her plate to cry, 'Sebastian, you must come to our flat next week. Katherine will be there.' She gave

Ursula a kindly smile. 'And you must come, too, honey.'

'Katherine' was a delicate woman who wrote fairly interesting stories about her years at university in England, but truly exquisite stories about being a little girl in New Zealand, full of the exact, unsentimental, ardent truths of childhood. Despite Clive's dismissal of her, she was a wonderful writer, and Ursula should have felt extremely grateful for Trudy's invitation. Yet she barely muttered a thank-you. And at one point, after I had placed my cutlery down in order to have a swallow of wine, she took up the fork and helped herself to a bit of the fish, in its spicy sauce, from my plate. I saw Max fasten his heavy-eyed gaze on her, and knew he was thinking, in his psychoanalytical way, that this ostensibly trivial gesture was an example of Ursula's offhand, probably pathological intrusiveness. I myself did not mind, since her sandwich looked forlorn beside our ample meals, though I supposed she should have asked me first; I must have been growing inured to her bad manners.

*

Her eyes were dark green. Of course the unoriginal comparison with emeralds occurred to me, along with bottle glass; but images of moss, and certain green fronds after rain, and the outer leaves of a lettuce, passed through my mind as well.

She was just a woman, perhaps thirty-five or forty, wearing a mackintosh and walking along Avenue Georges Clemenceau as Ursula and I returned home. Black hair, pale skin – and those eyes.

Ursula said, 'All your friends seem to be gay.'

'I don't believe that you have met *all* my friends.'

'Well, the ones I *have* met. You aren't gay, are you?'

'*You* are a very bold girl.' I hesitated, wondering if I should tease her, then decided to reply honestly. 'At university, I was drawn to the homosexual students because so many of them were artists. It struck me that nearly all that lot were painting pictures or writing poetry, whereas most of the heterosexuals seemed to be fledgling businessmen. My gay friends are still bohemian compared to the average straight person, I suppose. Also, I like louche places, ports and so on. And I enjoy camp.' I explained that I did not – could not – dismiss gay flamboyance as arch or affected; on the contrary, I considered it a genuine political position. 'Only I myself am not queer. I wouldn't have minded if I was, but I'm just not.'

She seemed to reflect, then announced proudly, 'I have gay friends, too.' I was reminded of how young she was, surely only twenty or twenty-one.

'What age are you, Ursula?' I asked impulsively. We had arrived back at the hotel, where Hervé favoured us with his usual glaucous look before muttering '*Bonjour*' and returning to his newspaper .

She surprised me by saying, 'Twenty-seven, though I know I look younger. I was a "mature student" at Trinity. Got my BA only last spring.'

When we were in the flat, she continued, 'I could give you something else to read, Sebastian: a story I wrote that's about two sisters, though really it's sort of modelled on my brother and me. I wrote it after I returned from Mexico last year. It may explain more about me.'

I took these pages into my bedroom, to read before the siesta, and speculated whether Ursula realised how lucky she was, that I had agreed to consider her callow efforts so closely. Usually if I contracted to read people's stories, it was for money. Yet now I had accepted, for the second time, to offer her a kind of unpaid private tutorial, and simply because she had appeared, uninvited, on my threshold. Just as I had given her meals and wine, and a room of her own. And as usual, she seemed to regard my generosity as her due, placing the foolscap into my hands with a tranquil smile, and not a word of thanks.

Closing my shutters against the luminous day, I wondered also about Ursula and money. What had she lived on during her vagabond twenties? I myself had been around long enough to know that a hippie life can be expensive, that those unkempt kids trudging with their rucksacks through Mexico or India or Sicily are often quite well subsidised by mum and dad. In other words, a certain kind of poverty, or apparent poverty, is actually a luxury. Trying to picture the Ursula I had first met, at Trinity the year before, I recalled that her clothes had been frumpy: heavy skirts and serviceable shoes, like her costume of last night, as if she hadn't quite managed to make the transition from convent girl to university student. I had assumed that she was very young, and perhaps so poor that she had had to press her old uniforms into service, but she had been at least twenty-six, and I was beginning to smell money in her background. Her years after school, and her sojourn as a 'mature student', had been supported somehow. She had been to the States and Mexico, and had got here without too much effort. No doubt she'd grown up close to where my mother had lived, or in another quietly prosperous part of Dublin. I imagined a solid Victorian house in a street of similar houses. And I pictured a younger Ursula walking home from school with her books and hockey stick, or sprawling on her stomach in the back garden to read a novel. I suspected that when she did, finally, contact her brother, he would tell her of a legacy, with a handsome portion for herself.

*

Maggie thought, *Their voices are so dark and rough, like cigar smoke in the air.*

She and her sister Nora were encircled by noise, dust and food. So much food: peaches reddening in the sun, papayas, mangoes, enormous cheeses, tortillas draped like laundry over wooden tables. A man smiled at them while chickens squawked at his feet.

'Don't smile back,' Nora whispered fiercely, but Maggie liked the man, with his brown face. The chickens were flurrying so thickly about his legs, he looked suspended in feathers.

Nora tugged at her sleeve and they walked on through the market. A boy was crouching in the dust, surrounded by fruit. Smiling, he extended an open papaya to her. Her mouth watered, but she murmured, 'No, *gracias.*' *It's too bad,* she thought. *It's too bad that I must be a fastidious* gringa *and say no to this boy who has offered me a papaya like a jewel – and it is a jewel.* She had wanted to say yes, to be unlike most visitors to Mexico City, with their fear of the open markets and their suspicious questions in restaurants and hotels. She thought it wrong to travel so far without venturing into the life of the place except to buy gee-gaws at some tourist shop or to ask a waiter if the tomatoes had been washed in mineral water. So she had wanted to say yes, only she was afraid; she had to admit it. The guidebooks had got to her too.

A woman was on her knees, crushing cornmeal in a blue bowl with a blue pestle. Three small children stood beside her; they had such beautiful eyes, vast, dark and full of a wine-coloured light.

Nora cried delightedly 'Oh, Maggie', because all the children had suddenly thrown their arms around each other and were kissing. Maggie and Nora laughed in unison, gazing at each other, and something, some tension, loosened between them; for a moment, Maggie loved her sister simply, as she had when they were small. Nora said, 'Hey, let's eat. Let's go to that place the concierge said.'

Their hotel concierge had written the name of a restaurant on a sheet of paper, which Maggie took out of her bag before approaching a young policeman. '*Por favor, señor. ¿Habla usted ingles?*'

'I speak English very well,' he said proudly.

'Could you tell us, please, how to reach this restaurant?'

He laughed quietly, looking at her, and not at the bit of paper. His eyelashes were very long. She could feel Nora glaring at her from a short distance. The policeman asked, 'Do you enjoy this market?'

'Oh, yes. There's no market like it at home. It's all new to me, and lovely.'

He gave his soft laugh again. Then, reluctantly, he lowered his eyes, with their long lashes, to read the name on the sheet in his hand.

'C'mon, Maggie,' Nora called. 'Let's go.'

He raised one eyebrow, smiling regretfully, then gave directions, and she and Nora walked away. Maggie did not look at Nora, who muttered, 'God. Why did you bother? He was just a stupid Mexican policeman.'

'Oh, Nora. I can't bear it when you talk like that. When you're so disdainful of people.'

Nora stopped in the street and began screaming. 'What do you mean? I'm not disdainful. Were we supposed to have a long conversation with him, and invite him to lunch? I wanted to go, and he was just a stupid policeman.'

'All right. Forget it.' Maggie was looking down at her shoes. *No one in this decorous city shrieked in the streets. No one but my family*, she thought miserably.

They trudged on to the restaurant. The meal, served with Mexican wine, was delicious, but they barely spoke. Maggie, trying to understand Nora's outburst, thought, *Nora believes I'm a flirt. She sees something frivolous in the way I exchange light talk with men she believes are unsuitable, policemen, or peasants with chickens at their feet. Only she doesn't realise how new and lovely this is to me – that phrase I used with the policeman: 'new and lovely'. Not only Mexico, with its policemen standing in dusty markets, and its layers of history and exotic things to eat and drink, but the kind of flirtatious banter she doesn't approve of. I was so shy, growing up. Now I'm twenty-six, but the world of flirtation is still 'new and lovely' to me. Can't she understand?*

Some three weeks later, back in Dublin, Maggie was looking out of the window of her flat. It was that uncertain hour, just before dusk, when the street lamps have come on although it is not yet dark.

She had begun to eat a bit of cheese when, suddenly, her whole body thrilled with happiness. Suddenly the street lamps became soft and blurred in the twilight; the city noises, the flavour of cheese, were almost unbearably sweet. Why, she wondered, am I so wildly happy, all of a sudden? Of course the feeling vanished then, but something of it lingered, like a scent in the air.

She walked into the bathroom and regarded her reflection: rough brown hair; oblique, greenish eyes. She looked younger than her years. Nora said that this was because she was too naive, but Maggie disagreed. It was simply that she was twenty-six years old and at the beginning of her life. Only who would believe her if she told the truth: that she had been asleep until now; that it had taken her this long?

*

I stopped there, dropping the pages to the floor beside my bed, and putting out the light. But I couldn't sleep: I kept thinking about Ursula's revelations in that fragment of a story. Clearly something, or someone – perhaps the father about whom she loathed to talk – had made her so sexually timid, she was only now awakening from a kind of slumber. I remembered how sexless she had seemed to me at Trinity, with her urchin's face and flat-chested figure. But I also recalled how that very morning her eyes had shone teasingly over the coffee bowls. She did seem to be learning how to flirt, all right. I wondered uneasily if she was still a virgin, and if I had been unwittingly recruited to tutor her in more than the art of fiction.

*

That evening she offered to cook us a meal, so I gave her some money and she went out to the Monoprix. In the meantime, I once again prepared two kirs, which, upon her return, we drank on the balcony. It was a beautiful evening, the air scented with lavender from the mountains, the sky darkening from pearl to lapis. Below us the oranges glimmered from beneath their thick leaves, and a bird began to sing. Ursula said, 'I love the colours of this hotel. Like being inside a painting.' For some incomprehensible reason, this observation moved me almost to tears. I suddenly wished that my mother was beside me in the twilight – a sentimental wish since, during her lifetime, her visits had driven me nearly daft . And hadn't I dreamt of her transformed into a monster? But she had been my mother; I had known her inside myself, with the animal knowledge of a child, and now I did feel that something was missing: I did miss her.

Ursula disappeared into the kitchen, from which she produced a pleasant dinner served in the French style. She had bought good wine, fresh bread, a ripe Camembert, and small bitter chocolates to go with the coffee. Remembering her dissatisfaction with last night's apple tart, I was impressed by how quickly she was learning European ways. Whatever her faults, she was clearly bright and imaginative: she had adapted to at least some of the customs of this country in little more than a day.

That night she came into my bed. I had half expected it, listening as she moved around the suite. Actually I had been thinking about the woman with green eyes whom I had glimpsed in the road earlier, but I was uncomfortably conscious of Ursula just outside my door, walking to and from the bathroom with what seemed an exaggeratedly heavy tread. Then there was a knock.

I lowered my book. 'What is it?'

'Are you asleep?'

'Absolutely.'

'May I come in? Just for a minute?'

I mumbled 'Yes' but she had already opened the door. She was wearing what seemed to be a man's white shirt for a nightdress. It drooped to her knees, which looked extremely vulnerable and bony. Altogether she was a remarkably skinny girl. She said, 'Thanks for the haircut. I saw it in the mirror just now and it really startled me. I mean, it's brilliant; it makes me look nearly elegant, you know?'

'You're welcome. Now I suggest we get a bit of sleep.'

But she had come into the room. 'What are you reading?'

Before I could reply, she had sprawled beside me and plucked the book from my hands. 'Graham Greene. He's really Catholic, like, isn't he? Really old-fashioned?'

'Perhaps. Now why don't you give me back my book and go to your own room, where you can read something more modern than poor old Graham Greene?'

She spread herself out full length, cheek nestled on her palm, and regarded me. I was relieved I had thought to put on pyjamas; unconsciously, I must have been preparing myself for this. For the first time, I was sorry the hotel had furnished my room with a generous double bed instead of some stern monk's pallet.

She said, 'You ought to read me bits. Some good bits, to convince me that he's a good writer.'

'I don't read aloud unless someone's paying me. And I'm tired. Shall we be sensible and go to sleep in our *very own* rooms?'

'Oh, *sensible*.' She reached over and kissed me hard on the mouth. She smelled lovely – of clean skin and clean cloth, and something like apples. I tried to move but she had thrown a surprisingly strong arm across my chest. 'Ursula . . . '

Now a leg was thrown over too. Her lips found mine again, and then, mainly out of curiosity, I moved my hands over her body – which was as angular as a boy's. I searched for a bit of softness, but met only hip bones, and virtually non-existent breasts. Yet she was so sweet-smelling, I thought I might be able to muster some ardour for her; only all of a sudden she stiffened and rolled over onto her back. I hoisted myself up and looked into those immense eyes, which were shining with an appeal I could not read. She said, 'I've never done this before.'

'Oh, Jesus.'

So my suspicions were right: she had travelled here not only to pursue the literary life, but also to learn the sexual ropes from me. I felt, simultaneously, a tremor of laughter, which I managed to suppress, and a kind of weary impatience. But mostly I was still just curious.

'Ursula,' I asked, 'why have you had so little experience, at your age?' Fearing one of her scowls, I continued, with a hasty attempt at gallantry, 'You are not unattractive. Surely you've had boyfriends?'

It took her a moment to reply. 'I was devoted to someone for a really long time. Someone older and successful, like you.' And she mentioned the name of a well-known Dublin playwright, who was actually (I thought indignantly) about ten years older than me. She went on, 'I sort of . . . He befriended me, like, and helped me a bit with my work. He recognised me, my gift. And he needed me. I understood him like no one else; I could almost read his mind, and I knew what he was trying to do nearly before he did. He wrote that last big play, the one they made into a film, with my help.'

I remembered the term Max had used to describe her: 'stalker'. Had she dogged this other man as she had me, misinterpreting his probably perfunctory sympathy as a deep rapport between the two of them? 'Were you in love with him?' I asked.

'We were in love with each other, only he was, you know, conflicted. Because of the age difference.' She paused. 'Also, he was married. The wife was sick all the time. One of those dissatisfied people who are always ill but not really, you know? Anyway, he couldn't . . . ' She sighed. 'He wouldn't make a move. Though I loved him, and I also loved being able to help him write. I inspired him; it was like an electric current that flowed from me to him. So I just waited. I waited for him to make up his mind. Like a nun, serving him and getting nothing much in return. And then one day he took me out to Mulligan's, and after he'd drunk three or four whiskeys, he finally mustered enough courage to tell me that he couldn't bear it any more. The conflict, he meant. He said he would have to break with me completely. After years and years of nothing physical except some kisses on the cheek. I took it hard at first, especially as my mum was beginning to get ill at the same time. But I got over it. Meeting you and taking your writing class really helped. Anyway, here I am, nearly thirty, and still a *maiden*.' She grimaced.

I smoothed a hand through her newly cut hair – more a gesture of sympathy than a caress. For I could not, would not, make love to her, despite the fact that I did like her. We clearly got on well enough, in our own eccentric way. After all, as I had observed before, I was fairly anonymous here in Nice – which had its advantages. On the other hand, there were few people to whom I could really talk, despite Trudy and Alice's salons, and the promising arrival of Léon and Max. Mostly I communed with myself in this hotel room – a solitude leavened only occasionally by letters from my agent or editor or an old Dublin friend. Yet now Ursula the Virgin Elf had appeared in my life, and I was compelled to acknowledge that our chatter about writers and books pleased me almost as much as it evidently did her. Not since Claudia had I actually lived with a kindred spirit, someone who fairly ate and drank books, and it was sweet, I had to admit.

Then why could I not initiate her into the physical intimacies in – let's face it – time-honoured fashion? For centuries, young women and men had emerged from affairs with older people more confident, better able for love – as long as those affairs were conducted with sensitivity and tact. So why could I not take

Ursula in my arms? Why was I denying her that chance, and myself the pleasure?

Looking into her eyes, I knew the answer. This girl harboured a need that had never been fulfilled. Her hunger was too great, and I did not love her.

She did not try to embrace me again, thank God, but merely continued to lie on her back gazing up at me, with some light in her face that I had never seen there before – a kind of candle glow behind those eyes. She actually looked serene, and almost beautiful. Softly she said, 'You told me you were in love once. When was that, Sebastian? Recently?'

'She was called Claudia. I met her when I was about your age. Her eyes were dark like yours but more a kind of chestnut. She walked into a room – into the Bewley's in Grafton Street to be specific – and I fell in love. "Love at first sight" sounds so mawkish; it's hard to say it without laughing, or apologising. But it's the truth. It's what happened.'

I paused. Ursula remained still, for once emanating none of the fractious energy that one usually felt crackling out from her. I found myself saying things I had told nobody in a long time. 'She was quite brilliant. A scholar of eighteenth-century Anglo-Irish literature at UCD – though she gave that up later to work as an editor. At first we lived in Dublin, though she was often able to arrange to come with me when I went to teach abroad; or I would accompany her to some foreign university that had invited her for a term. So we spent interesting periods in New York and London and Sydney. Then, after I began to make a proper living from the novels, she gave up her job and we came to live abroad, first Paris, then southern Spain, and finally here.'

'What happened to her?'

'She died.' As soon as I'd uttered those words, something I can describe only as a shawl, or veil, of sadness fell upon me. I was used to it, for of course it had fallen before, dropping through the air, light as smoke and at the same time a solid thing, settling on my shoulders and along my arms, pressing on my throat: a shawl of sorrow. I squeezed Ursula's hand. 'My dear, I do not wish to talk about this any more.'

We were silent for a while, then Ursula murmured, 'I feel so guilty sometimes, about my mother. Though at times I think guilt can be good. Seriously. For an artist, I mean. Can't it be like that bit of stone or whatever inside an oyster, which irritates it but also creates the pearl?'

I smiled down at her, this strange girl who could be a scrawny, unscrupulous spider one moment, and a diminutive sage with shining eyes the next. I was still marvelling at the strange alteration in her face, that luminous stillness, as if our verbal intimacy just now had fulfilled her more than if we'd had the sexual exchange she had tried to initiate. I found myself saying, 'Ursula, you may sleep here, if you'd like.'

'I *would* like that,' she replied, with a childlike honesty. So I put out the light, and soon heard her breathing deeply. She really was like a child, with her smells of clean cloth and green apples, as if a gawky little sister or daughter was sleeping innocently beside me.

As for myself, I could not sleep for thinking. And not of Claudia, but of my mother. I had thought I'd be relieved when she died, since no matter how many books I published, or how much the outside world seemed to respect me, she had never stopped clinging to me and making her querulous demands on me. But now I kept remembering trivial, ordinary things. Her rather silly raincoat, for instance, which was an unflattering greenish-yellow. Like all her clothes, it was often rumpled or buttoned wrongly, as if she had put it on absentmindedly. And now, remembering such an inconsequential thing as my mother's mackintosh, what I felt was that my heart was breaking, breaking in two with exasperation and pity, with fury and with love.

IV

The 'Clive business', as Claudia had taken to calling it, was dragging on. I had realised, after that unsavoury exchange in the café, that I disliked the man, but I was still loath to give him up as our driver. In the month or so since we had engaged him, I had got used to having a car at our disposal. This was especially convenient since the taxis of Nice are the most expensive in all France. But I think there was another reason. Claudia was probably right: it made me feel like a character in one of my own novels. I could ask at breakfast: 'Wouldn't you like to see those paintings in the castle at Carros? I'll ring the driver to arrange it.'

One evening over an aperitif on the Place Rosetti, Claudia tried to pursue the subject again. It was a lovely time of day, in autumn, so close to the sea; the light turning to honey, glowing on the old houses; children playing on the porch of the church. It was warm enough to drink on the terrace; we found ourselves surrounded by couples like ourselves, taking the *apero* before night fell, in the swift way it does in southern places. Claudia said, 'I'm feeling the danger precisely because I *am* in danger. He thinks you're meant to look after him. He thinks you and he can have a beautiful future together. Except for me. *I'm* the impediment.'

I remembered his proposal that he and I should collaborate

on a best-seller. But then I dismissed this thought, squeezed Claudia's hand across the table and said, 'Surely you're exaggerating? Anyway, I've agreed already. We *will* tell him to go. I'll take him aside and tell him; or you can do it; or we can do it together. We just have to find the right moment.'

'How about now?' She gave me a sidelong look. 'We could go home after this drink. I have a casserole in the oven anyway. We could go home and ring him up on his mobile and tell him. Tonight.'

'But you're going to Cannes tomorrow morning. D'you really want to take the train?'

This was clever of me, I thought. Claudia had begun to wear her hair in a crisp, nineteen-twenties Louise Brooks style, cut straight across her forehead and straight across at the chin, so that it swung with every tilt of her head. But the only hairdresser she had found who could cut it properly was a podgy little man with glasses who worked out of an atelier in Cannes. And Clive was meant to drive us there the following morning. I was coming along merely because I liked Cannes in the low season, and thought I would wander through the town while Claudia had her hair done, and then take a pleasant lunch with her in one of the cafés along the Croisette. Now she gave me a half-amused, half-grim look. 'All right, Sebastian. We'll discuss it again *after* tomorrow.'

*

Before I'd ever been there, I would have imagined that Cannes was a vulgar town thronged with rich tourists and mover-and-shaker types attending the ubiquitous festivals and conferences. But in autumn it was nearly a village, despite the glossy shops. Waiting for Claudia, I walked along La Croisette in the sheer light, to the basin where the yachts were tethered like large pampered animals in an open-air kennel. I strolled beside them for a while, then gazed across the harbour at the houses of Old Cannes. It was a very still, bright day. I thought I would look into the casino, because such places at once appalled and fascinated me. Besides, Claudia wouldn't be done for another half an hour at least, given that her hairdresser was an *artiste* who took his time. And our money.

The entrance hall was hushed as a temple, and indeed it was presided over by immense caryatids, grandiose and absurd in their gilded draperies, a number of them on either side of the corridor that drew one into the central gaming room. This was no plush enclave where men in dress suits and bejewelled ladies played roulette; that section would open much later. This was the province of the hoi polloi, with old-age pensioners, chambermaids, spotty adolescents, middle-aged couples – anyone and everyone, in fact – playing at machines that bleeped hysterically, and occasionally belched out a cascade of coins. It seemed Dantean to me as I walked along, or like some realm beneath the sea where creatures lived in a lurid gloom, silently foraging. No one looked at anyone else; they were too intent on the one-arm bandits, applying themselves with a gesture that struck me as onanistic. As if they were all desperately wanking for money.

I turned a corner past three elderly women whose faces, in the unnatural darkness, glowed crimson from the reflected light of their poker machine, which displayed a grinning Joker with its tongue hanging out. And then I saw Clive. He was ensconced before a machine with a bucket of *jetons* between his knees and a cigarette in the corner of this mouth. It occurred to me that all through Cannes, at that moment, men were standing in the cafés, in sunlight, playing *quatre cent vingt et un* and drinking pastis – such a different form of gambling than the joyless activity taking place around me. And Clive could have been out there, at the corner of some light-rinsed *comptoir*, rattling the dice and laughing with his companions. Instead he was here, looking so tense and alone even amongst these tense and silent people. I continued to stare at him: that stony face, the eternal cigarette, the hand steadily feeding tokens into the maw of his ridiculous machine. Then I turned and walked out, since I didn't want him to see me. It was almost as if I had stumbled on him sitting on the toilet.

I went back to the rue d'Antibes, where Claudia was standing at the entrance to her salon. We decided to stroll along in the direction from which I had just come, and to have lunch at the Caffe Roma, across from the harbour. As we walked, I looked at her narrow feet on the footpath – which was much cleaner than the footpaths of Nice, I had to admit, despite being a Nice patriot – and smelled some pleasant balm that the *coiffeur* had put in her hair. *Well*, I thought, *here we are, two Irish people who have made a new life, through love, in the south of France.* And at the moment of thinking this, I felt a rush of love for her: for her narrow feet in their brown shoes, for the smell of her hair, for everything great and small that she was. This love ran so deep in me that it seemed to make me more fully myself, as if it were a light flaring on in some forgotten room, illuminating corners that would have lain in darkness forever without it. We walked along, chatting about nothing, while inside I was fairly bursting with an unexpected and, I suppose, quite ordinary joy.

In the Caffe Roma, I was once again gazing out at the yachts, the houses of Old Cannes, and the bulk of the casino. I chose not to tell Claudia that I'd seen Clive in there. She was saying, 'When we're in Cannes, I sometimes play a kind of child's game. I pretend I've got loads of money and that I could have any one of those yachts I fancied. So I survey them, with their silly names, and I choose one.' She looked up from her salad to smile. 'But you know, I think that if we did have loads of money, we wouldn't change our life, would we? I wouldn't want an ostentatious old yacht. I would always like to go on living just as we do.'

I clasped her hand across the table. 'My dear, actually, we *do* have nearly enough money. Not as much as the yachting set.' I tilted my head towards the boats with, as she had said, their silly names: *Queen of the Sea, Happy Haven.* 'But between my novels and the film, and your parents' estate, we are better off than most.' I thought of the glum-looking people I'd seen in the casino, desperately trying to woo Lady Luck. Including Clive, of course – on whom luck had not smiled that day, as far as I could see. 'We're fortunate,' I said slowly. 'It's true that we're not rich, but then we don't want a luxurious life. I agree with you that what we want is precisely the life, and the love, we have.'

'Yet we must protect it,' Claudia murmured. 'We must protect those things.'

'Protect? From what? From whom?'

She gave me a strange look, but the waiter distracted us by removing our plates in that abruptly graceful French way. Then she said, still in a low voice, 'I think we must be true to those whom we love, to those who *belong* to us through love.' She looked round. 'Like . . . like being with your beloved in a restaurant, just the two of you at a table, while everyone around you is concentrating on their own food and conversation. They don't care about you. But in all that indifferent swirl of the restaurant, you care about each other; the two of you are looking after each other. And if the waiter is rude or the wine has gone off, you help each other through it.' She seemed to hesitate. 'The whole world may be uncertain and even perilous, but you and this other person have a compact, called love, and it protects you from harm.'

'It sounds a bit selfish, though, this magic circle that you describe. What about the others, who need our help? One feels sorry even for Clive, after all.'

Once more she gave me a curious look that I could not decipher. The waiter returned and we ordered coffee. Then she said, 'It seems to me that you are confusing compassion with pity, Sebastian. And pity can be dangerous.'

'Dangerous?' Again I was thinking that her language was uncharacteristically extreme, even grandiloquent. 'How can an impulse of mercy be dangerous?'

She answered bluntly, 'Pity is *not* mercy, though it often masquerades as mercy. With pity, one needn't feel too deeply. One is superior, aloof, feeling *sorry* for another, as you do for Clive.'

'Still,' I said stubbornly, 'there are those who are pitiable, who do need our help. Sometimes I have an image in my mind of a child, a lost boy, crying helplessly by the side of the road. Am I meant to just avert my head from him, and walk away?'

She looked steadily at me. 'Perhaps your heart is too easily wrung by those who appear at your door in the guise of that lost child. It seems to me that compassion simply means trying to fathom another person, and the nature of his or her experience. It certainly isn't pity. Nor is it some need to help another person as a form of penance, because you don't feel entitled to your own happiness.' Dropping her eyes, she murmured, 'Anyway, surely that child is you?'

I was a bit thrown off balance, and drank my coffee in silence. Once more, she was regarding me thoughtfully. 'What?' I heard myself ask – though I was not sure that I wished to pursue this exchange. She did not look like an oracle; she looked like a lovely woman with a stylish haircut, but I was finding her words rueful and sobering, and a little dark. I listened apprehensively as she continued, 'At night, lying in bed, we sometimes hear the scream of an ambulance, or someone hurrying along the road, in need or in flight. We read of heartbreak in our own local newspaper every morning. And I agree that those things *must* concern us, since we are, all of us, woven into the living fabric of the world. But, Sebastian, our hearts cannot be rent by every scream of every ambulance, by every death and every catastrophe. We must love those whom we love, in the practical sense, protecting *them* as best we can.'

*

Clive was waiting at the appointed corner, standing slouched against his car, a plastic carrier bag dangling from his wrist. I looked surreptitiously inside; it seemed to contain a chunk of meat or pâté wrapped in paper, along with a couple of oranges. Perhaps his machine had produced a shoal of change after all, and he had bought lunch to celebrate. But where would he eat it? In the car, I supposed. But what about napkins, utensils? Did he keep a picnic hamper concealed in the boot? I did wonder about the *dailiness* of his life. Not only where he slept, but how he ate and drank, cleaned his teeth, went to the toilet. He remained an enigma to me – or was he just a kind of cipher?

*

After that day in Cannes, I resolved to dismiss him as soon as possible. But as before, my resolve wavered. First of all, Claudia's troubled dreams had ceased, or at least eased. Also we were both working hard. Claudia was editing a children's Christmas book for her old publishing house in Dublin, which sometimes engaged her to do a project (and paid her well) at busy times. And I was revising my Malaga novel, which was resisting me, as novels can do. So we laboured long and were not free to drive anywhere, and days passed without us even catching a glimpse of Clive's hard, impassive face; we even forgot, from time to time, that he existed in our life.

Then Trudy and Alice called one day to announce that Alice had written a cookery book, which she hoped Claudia would edit. It was a volume of not only recipes but anecdotes and reveries connected to them, descriptions of towns where she and Trudy had first eaten a particular dish, or of markets where they'd bought a certain type of cheese, as well as accounts of dinner parties and restaurants.

Some of our other friends were astonished to hear that Alice had produced a book about cooking, since the dry shop cake and thin wine offered at their salons seemed evidence enough that both she and Trudy were indifferent to the pleasures of the table. But Claudia and I were not surprised, for they had invited us to dinner at their flat two or three times. Those meals had been served without ceremony, books and papers pushed to the side of the cluttered dining table to make room for mismatched plates and glasses. But the food cooked by Alice had startled us: delicate starters of seafood; then a dish of the region, a *boeuf en daube* or a local fish like *rascasse* or *rouget*. So Claudia agreed to help out – only she learnt soon enough that Alice's prose style was not equal to either her lively stories or her inventive dishes. And recipes must be written out in a very precise way, with exact measurements and an awareness of the difference between 'boil' and 'simmer' and so on: all of this was a challenge, and kept Claudia too occupied to worry about Clive for long.

About a fortnight passed, and then Claudia booked him to take her, Trudy and Alice to a *librairie* in Grasse that specialised in cookery and restaurant books. When she came back in the evening, I thought she was looking troubled, although she said they'd had a pleasant time, with Alice chattering in her usual way and Trudy smiling her customary slow, tolerant smile and saying little.

Then Trudy asked me to come out and have drinks with her at the Ruhl Plage, in the early afternoon, while Claudia and Alice were working on the book, writing and revising, as well as cooking up all kinds of dishes in Alice's kitchen. 'I can't stand the smells,' Trudy explained on the phone. 'They're too delicious, and then those awful women *throw the food away* and start over again.'

'You could offer to eat it,' I suggested.

'Ha! I'm fat enough. Anyway, sometimes the cooking really does go wrong, and the stuff looks all weird and curdled. It's beginning to seem like a lab in there. I'd rather get out and have a cocktail with you on the beach. And I have something to discuss with you, Sebastian.'

It was yet another lovely day, and lovely to be at a table on the *plage*, with the distances like gauze in the brine-washed light, the sea calm and the sky truly azure. Trudy looked summery in a floppy hat, cotton frock and sunglasses, though I was surprised to see her in such beach-resort gear. Generally she favoured sober clothes, and wore her hair scraped unceremoniously back from that brooding face. Now I said, 'Trudy, I hope you haven't abandoned your stern, old-fashioned dresses? I rather like them.'

'I'm just celebrating the weather. Hard to believe it's autumn. They're freezing their asses off in Paris.' The waiter came, and she ordered a pastis. I took a Campari-soda, mainly because I liked the colour. 'How are the cooks?' I asked.

She groaned. 'I looked in before leaving, but they didn't even notice me. They were huddled over a pot of tripe or something. I swear, Sebastian, they're like a couple of witches out of *Macbeth*. It's nice to get away from both of them for a while and be among sane people in the sunlight. Anyway, like I said, I need to talk to you.'

The waiter brought our drinks – which gave me a minute to wonder what she wished to say. Then she took off the dark glasses and I saw that her eyes were sombre. She said, 'It's about that creepy man. Your personal taxi driver.'

'Did something happen when he drove you to Grasse? I thought Claudia looked a bit upset when she came back.'

Trudy sighed. 'He didn't do anything *too* terrible, I guess. Mainly it was just a feeling. I say "just" but, you know, sometimes a feeling is a feeling is a feeling.' She poured water into her pastis. 'He was almost *acrid* behind the wheel, like a human version of gun smoke or something. Insolent and angry, behind that super-cilious smile. And when Alice was in the shop, figuring out which books to buy, he actually came in and told her to hurry up. Who is this guy?'

A gull flapped down, settled on the next table and stared impudently at us. 'Ugh,' shuddered Trudy. 'Look at that brazen thing. It's acting like it wants to have a drink with us. Make it go away, Sebastian.'

I waved my hands and the bird flew to another, slightly more distant table. 'I really don't know who he is, Trudy. He seems to have no resources beyond his Citroën and the jobs we give him.'

'But that's *bizarre*.'

'I know,' I said shamefacedly. 'It's as if he were a limpet, or some other kind of parasitic creature that draws strength from those it attaches itself to. Even his face gives me that impression. Don't you find he has a bloodless look, with those colourless eyes?' I paused, fiddling with my glass. 'I'm no expert on such matters, but I would guess that, psychologically, he's caught at some period of infancy. What I mean is, an infant cries until a breast materialises to feed him, but of course the baby doesn't know that the breast is part of a separate whole other person. He doesn't even know that the breast is separate from *him*, if you see what I mean.' I laughed uneasily. 'Though I don't suppose I look like a breast to you.'

Trudy usually chuckled at my clumsy jokes, but now she did not even smile. After a moment, she asked in a subdued voice, '*Why* have you let that man into your life? Why do you allow it?'

Once more I swirled my glass. 'I suppose his colourlessness, his adaptability – those things that strike one as so eerie in him – are also a temptation to keep him on.'

As I spoke I was reflecting, as often before, on my curious isolation in Nice, mine and Claudia's, our happy exile. We attended Trudy and Alice's once-a-month salons, and just a few weeks before, Anton, our sweet-tempered Russian playwright friend who lived in a hotel in the rue Gounod, had come to our flat for dinner. But while these literary friends delighted us, they were almost all ex-pats like ourselves, with reputations in some foreign country, and books written in a language other than French. Even the *maison d'éditions* that published translations of my own novels was up in Paris. So there was no real literary life down here. We foreign writers moved almost like ghosts through our adopted city, amongst a populace that did not know us and had not read us, and we seldom called on one another except for the salons. (Although since Clive had come into our orbit, Claudia and I did find ourselves going out more, and of course Claudia was seeing a lot of Alice these days.)

But the point was that we did not wish to live like Fitzgerald and Zelda, who, aghast at the idea of eating garlic or fraternising too much with the natives, had surrounded themselves with Americans on the *plage* at Juan-les-Pins. They could just as easily have sprawled on the beach at Cape Cod or Long Island, so indifferent and even hostile had they been to the life around them. Whereas Claudia and I felt happy amongst the people of our quarter – the newsagent, the baker and his wife, those who came to our favourite jazz bar – although perhaps I'd been harbouring a secret unfulfilled desire all along. A desire for fame, recognition? Why else would I let an obscure and perhaps dangerous Englishman turn my head? I remembered how, that first night on the drive to Monte Carlo, he had said, *I've read all your books, Mr Clare. I'm a real admirer.* We are all, I thought, susceptible to flattery, but I was beginning to think I was more susceptible, or more vulnerable, than most.

Trudy said, 'Sebastian, I've got to tell you that Claudia is deeply concerned. And it's not only that she feels menaced by that scary driver, she's also hurt that her misgivings about him, her *pleas*, haven't convinced you to fire him. I mean, if Alice were upset like that, I'd tell the man to get lost just to comfort her.'

Now it was my turn to sound sombre. 'Has Claudia been telling you – '

'Oh, don't get all pompous. She hasn't been betraying you with unseemly confidences or anything. She's just upset. And she and Alice are in that kitchen all day cooking up who-knows-what, so of course she talks about what's on her mind.'

'Did she ask you to speak to me?'

'She doesn't even know I invited you out for drinks. But I'll let you in on one thing. She's afraid to press you too hard. She thinks you'd get angry if she insisted that you dismiss the driver.'

I flushed, remembering a conversation we'd had the week before, at breakfast on our terrace. Claudia had brought up Clive again, reminding me of how he had sauntered into the flat that first morning, and how she had served him a *tartine* and a bowl of coffee. 'Why were we so docile? Why did we give him breakfast like that? And *why* did we accept his weird proposal?'

I had answered sharply, 'Perhaps it *was* a weird proposal, Claudia, but it was also tempting. You complain about him the whole time, but it is convenient, after all, having a driver. If you feel so strongly about it, why don't *you* learn how to drive?'

Trudy said, 'You're looking so damned grim. Don't beat yourself over the head. That's not the answer either. It's just . . . ' She gave a loud sigh. 'Where I'm from, we see guys like your driver more often, maybe because American society is so vast and unformed. Which can be exciting, I guess, but it can also be like there's no *there* there. And it makes some people desperate. They feel like they have no anchor, they feel *empty*, so they try to devour you.'

I looked out at the horizon, where a handsome ship – probably the Corsican ferry – was making for the Port of Nice. And once more I thought about our modest literary society. *We're in the same boat*, I said to myself. And to Trudy, 'Thanks, my dear. I'll sack Clive as soon as I can. You were a great help today. I suppose that Claudia and myself, and our friends, like you and Alice, and Katherine and Anton, are a kind of artistic Foreign Legion. We have to protect one another, since we are all we have.'

She grinned. 'Welcome to bohemia.'

*

When Claudia returned that evening, I said, 'Darling, you've been working in a kitchen all day. I'd make us a meal but I'm a dreadful cook. Let's go out to dinner.'

She had a quick shower, then put on a long grey dress. We went to La Merenda, where we were the only guests, since it was not yet eight o'clock. Immediately she said, 'You know, I was really upset by a remark of Clive's on the drive back from Grasse. It may seem inconsequential to you, but it stays in my mind. We were stopped at a red light, and out of the blue he looked over his shoulder and said pointedly to me, as if Alice and Trudy weren't there, "It feels like destiny, how you and Sebastian and I have found each other. Your name is Claudia and mine is Clive, and Sebastian's surname is Clare. That couldn't be coincidence, could it?" I didn't answer, and then he said, "Our names have almost the same sound, as though we were three parts of the same person. It's like we're meant to be together, isn't it?" Then the light changed and I told him to drive on, but, oh, I was shuddering, Sebastian. Absolutely *shuddering*.'

Trudy hadn't told me this bit. I was about to speak, but at that moment the waiter arrived with the *carte*, which was chalked on a blackboard in true French folkloric style. He made a fuss of balancing it against a chair and standing to attention while we considered and ordered, and then there was the ceremony of opening and pouring the wine. When he had finally gone back into the kitchen, I told Claudia about my meeting with Trudy.

'I'm sorry that it's taken so long,' I said bluntly. 'And I'm sorry that it took Trudy's strict words to sober me up. Your distress alone should have been enough.'

'Well,' she answered slowly, 'it was nice, sometimes, being driven about.' She gave a soft laugh. 'Oh, but what a strange man he is! You know, there's another story I haven't told you. Remember how he drove me to Nice Étoile last week? He had a bird on the seat beside him, a little brown bird like a thrush, lying there swaddled in a handkerchief.'

The waiter served our first courses: onion tart for me, a salad of rocket with a chunk of ricotta and a scattering of olives for Claudia. She went on, 'He explained that he'd found this poor little bird in a field, unable to fly. It had fallen or bumped into a tree or something. I asked him how he was trying to revive it and he said he was feeding it milk, so I asked did he have a dropper.

And he said no, but that he moistened his finger with the milk and the bird was somehow managing to gather it into its beak. "It seemed to be working," he said rather proudly. "This bird may seem frail to you," he said, "but you should have seen how weak it was when I found it."' She put down her cutlery, looked at me and shook her head. 'I thought of him being tender and painstaking with that creature, and I marvelled at how complicated all of us are. How complicated human beings are. I would never have imagined that man being tender with anyone or anything, but there he was, proud of rescuing a little thrush who was lying wrapped in a handkerchief on the seat beside him like an infirm aunt or a sick child.'

'Complicated or not,' I said, 'it's time to let him go. As you tried to tell me in Cannes, we can't rescue every wounded creature who comes our way. Some birds are just too broken. And therefore dangerous. Anyway, maybe he was just fattening up that thrush. Perhaps he'll cook him and eat him, ere long.'

Claudia laughed, uneasily. I continued, 'I'll do it myself, if you'd like. I could ask him to come to the flat while you're over at Alice's.'

'Oh, no.' Once more she shook her head, swinging that lovely hair. 'No, darling. We got ourselves into this together, and we should dismiss him together, too. Only, to be honest, I don't think we should do it in the flat.'

'I see what you mean.' I swallowed a morsel of onion tart, though suddenly I was not hungry. Some other people walked in: three young women with shopping bags; a tall Nordic-looking couple. I felt marooned from them somehow, isolated from their ordinary gaiety. I supposed that I was finally feeling how sinister Clive was, or could be. But why had I not felt it before, this sense of menace that was all of a sudden turning the food to dust in my mouth? I had thought him peculiar and even unpleasant, but

I hadn't actually been scared until this moment.

Claudia took my hand. 'Let's arrange to meet him in a café. We'll ring him up tonight, and make an appointment for a coffee tomorrow, in that café where the cat snoozes on the *zinc*.'

I gave her hand a grateful squeeze. 'Yes, we'll tell him in the café. That would be more sensible than doing it at home.'

'And safer,' she said.

V

In dream, I visit my mother in heaven, which is a ramshackle house. Many people are bustling about, but they do not disturb my mother, who is relaxed and smiling. In fact she seems popular with the others, who are amorphous to me as they shamble through the house, but whom she clearly recognises, and greets with affection. She tells me that she is not permitted alcohol, which pleases her because her mind is more focused now than in the past, when she tippled sherry and took wine with dinner. Yet there is an exception: each afternoon at three o'clock, she and all the others are meant to drink one tumbler of some delicious, searing whiskey. 'Is it really nice, the whiskey?' I ask sceptically, since my mother, in life, never liked spirits. 'Oh, it's *heavenly*,' she replies, and we both laugh. But then she frowns and says, 'If only you lot realised that dead people must eat. What we do is this: we scavenge after the funeral feasts, and gobble all the leftovers. Oh, but we are all so tired of baked meats and pastries!'

When my eyes opened, I immediately realised there was someone lying beside me, though for a good few seconds I did not know who it could be. About six months before, I had slept with an eccentric American dancer whose body had been supple and lovely, but whose febrility had discouraged me from contacting her again, after our one night of overly acrobatic lovemaking. And since her, there had been no one: so who was this deeply breathing bundle on my other pillow? My mind pitched in confusion; then she farted impressively, and I thought, *Oh, Ursula*.

She insisted on hurrying out to the boulangerie and making breakfast again – which was very pleasant, I had to admit. I would miss this kind of pampering when she finally left. And she had not been abashed to discover herself in bed with me, but had yawned like a cat before declaring, 'Boy, I really had a brilliant sleep.' Once again I felt like an older brother, or a father whose child had clambered into his bed. As a little boy, I myself had loved to burst into my mother's room in the morning and throw myself, giggling, onto the bed beside her; it had never seemed to make her grumpy.

After breakfast, I put on my figurative teacher's mantle and told Ursula to organise her story fragments. She had shown me, so far, only unfinished pieces on pages of foolscap, some written in pencil. 'I'd like to see a *complete* story,' I said sternly. 'And if you produce a full draft, I'll let you use my computer.' I sent her to the desk in the small bedroom and told her not to emerge for at least an hour – a command that seemed to please her, as the scandalised cluckings of Fabien the hairdresser had pleased her yesterday. Despite her sharp temper, she evidently liked being scolded, at least if the chivvying was friendly; I presumed it made her feel properly looked after. I settled down to some neglected correspondence for an hour or so, until Ursula appeared at my elbow with a cup of coffee and a biscuit.

I took her out to lunch in the café where I had met Max and Léon, and where, at this time of day, the usual drunks, eccentrics and layabouts had gathered at the *zinc*. I explained to Ursula, 'See that man with the black curls? I call him *Monsieur Bricoleur*, which means "Handyman", because he wears those paint-splotched trousers. Only I don't think he works at all; he seems to be here all the time, standing at the *comptoir* and drinking pastis. Probably he is the most dedicated barfly I've ever seen. In fact, I'd go so far as to say that the drinking of pastis is his real job, despite the *bricoleur* gear. Once he had a wife, whom I called *Madame Bricolette*, only she got disgusted with his laziness and came in one day carrying a toilet roll which she scrolled around his shoulders – to the amusement of the other customers – before leaving for good.'

'Who is that funny plump old lady with the red high heels?' Ursula asked.

'Ah, *La Belle*. She always wears short dresses and those bright red shoes, and she caresses her hair coquettishly. I think that in her day she was a lady-of-the-evening, and even now there seems to be a small coterie of loyal clients, local working-class men of her own age, with whom I gather she has a civilised arrangement.'

Ursula looked astonished. 'You mean she was – is – like, a *prostitute?*'

'Dear girl, don't forget that Nice is a resort. And resorts are full of people who make their industry from the pleasure of others.'

'Like writers,' Ursula grinned. I could tell that she was genuinely enjoying the theatrics of the café, with the hungry curiosity of a fiction writer, though I was glad that Léon and Max had not come in. I wouldn't have wanted to see her turn morose and possessive again.

After lunch, we once more strolled along the promenade. In fact, a positive aspect of Ursula's arrival was that I was seeing more of the beach than I had done since moving out of *vieux Nice*. Nowadays I was often too lazy to venture down, but the crescent of the Bay, the *belle époque* hotels, that backdrop of verdigris mountains and vaulting sky, were all beautiful in any weather.

And almost uncannily, as we walked, a flash motor car caught my eye, a Bugatti I thought. It was coursing by at alarming speed, but of course the driver of such a car *would* disdain ordinary caution. I barely glimpsed the man at the wheel, who was wearing a leather coat and seemed to have a fleshy, laughing face, because the woman beside him had caught my attention. It was my American dancer of last year, wearing a long red *crêpe de Chine* scarf that streamed out behind her. How strange I should have thought of her only that morning, and now here she was, laughing in her exuberant way, with that flamboyant scarf billowing out in the wind. I felt a burst of irritation: clearly the extravagant gear and laughter were calculated to impress, but the recklessness of her companion's driving, and something ominous about the too-long scarf, unsettled me. I recalled her hectic lovemaking during our only night together. At that time I had dismissed her as a narcissist, but now I remembered what had drawn me to her in the first place: the hard intelligence behind her histrionics, and also her beauty – each of her movements charged with a dancer's electric grace. So why would a woman of such style, and with such gifts, feel she must swoop along the promenade in the company of that florid man, wearing vintage clothes and flaunting their vintage motor car, as if they were characters in a film about the 'Riviera' (a word no one but tourists used)? I almost wished to extend my arm and cry out; I almost thought that I could save her.

*

Ursula gave me yet another few pages of a story, which she said she considered her 'most important work so far', since it concerned the kind of helpless, yearning love she had felt for her playwright. She promised that if I liked it, she would finish it.

That first morning, everything is liquid: her fountain throws a silver spume into the air; the garden shimmers. And his first night, he has a strange dream, of people wandering through a green-gold forest.

His second morning, he walks shyly into the kitchen, which smells of turpentine, but Isolt, his cousin, has not yet come down. He takes his coffee out to the terrace, encircled by that lush garden, dew glinting on the rose petals. The air smells of eucalyptus and oranges. He is far from home.

Isolt appears. She is about forty, tall, with a narrow, rather beautiful face and astonishing hair that floats around her when she walks. She settles in the second garden chair, and places her hand on the table between them. 'Good morning, Matthew,' she says formally. 'How did you sleep?'

'Very well, thanks. It's so quiet here.'

He follows her back into the kitchen. The sunlight warms her cat, asleep by its bowl. She puts a sourdough bread, butter, a pot of honey and a square of some soft cheese on a board in the middle of the dining table. Then, pouring out more coffee, she begins to talk.

'I love this old house, even though people say I'm mad, living here by myself. I love the trees and the fountain, and I like being alone. Although . . . ' She gives him a small smile. 'Although it is very nice to have you here. I can discover you now, learn you. You were always simply my little cousin . . . ' She butters a chunk of bread. Matthew worries that he has committed some breach of politeness by eating too much; already he has demolished the lovely cheese and his fingers are gleaming with butter and honey. But he couldn't help it: he is twenty-one, very thin, and hungry the whole time.

As though reading his mind, Isolt says, 'How fat you were as a child! And no one understood. They couldn't see your courage and dignity. I could tell that you suffered in your heavy body, but the other children just laughed, and the adults shook their heads and disapproved. And then you grew up, and how the family marvelled! You became tall and slender, and your eyes darkened to this strange yellow-gold colour – the eye colour we all have in our family – even my cat's eyes are the same honey-yellow. But you were still full of dignity. You suffered under everyone's admiration as you had under their disapproval. I saw this, only you were my little cousin and so far from me. In another country, really, another country of the spirit. Yet now you are here, by yourself, and we can finally talk.'

He smiles, flattered. 'I never knew you as just yourself, either. It wasn't only that you were my big cousin. It was also that I was a little boy and you were a grown-up woman. But I remember you were always nice to me; you talked to me seriously, not in a condescending way, and you would let me play with your paints. You didn't mind when I made a mess.' He looks sheepishly at the crumbs on his side of the table.

She asks, 'What is your first memory of me?'

He closes his eyes for a second. 'You had come back to visit us. You must have been about as old as I am now. It was, you know, a family gathering, and your mother was

angry because of your clothes.' He could still recall it clearly, a younger Isolt with even wilder hair, glaring at her
mother across the dinner table. He himself had thought
she looked cool, in her offbeat gypsy gear.

She laughs. 'My mother always hated my clothes. And
she still disapproves of my painting. She still says, "Isolt, if
only you would behave like a normal person . . . " At first
it pleased her when I came to live here, I suppose because
she thought I might marry a nice professor and finally settle down. But then, alas, I disappointed her again.'

They both grin. He hesitates before saying, 'My father
was difficult, when I was growing up. Did you know that?
I feel like our whole family, even you, thinks my father is
kind and understanding. He has a talent for presenting
himself well, so everyone is taken in. But, you know, his
wisdom and kindness, it isn't really true, it's like a myth, a
family myth . . . ' He sighs.

Isolt extends a hand, palm up, across the table. 'I
could tell he was a bit of a tyrant. He never deceived me.'

They are both silent. A panel of sunlight, chalky with
motes, falls across the table and touches her hair. He is
deeply pleased to be in a faraway place. She smiles faintly,
her chin in her palm, those caramel eyes gazing out at the
fountain. He notices that she is wearing a loose white
dress, with two big pockets, and demure shoes, also white.
Like a little girl, he thinks – and feels a deep tenderness for
her.

Later, he walks past her studio. The door is open; she is
inside, painting. The light streaming in once again catches
her hair, igniting it so that it is brighter than her face. She

wears another loose dress, although this one is black, old and paint-spattered.

He emboldens himself to come in. She is intent and has not heard him. He looks at the canvas and recognises his dream.

There is his forest, full of light in the foreground, darker in its depths, with figures moving beneath the trees. His heart gives a kind of thump: how uncanny, to stumble on your own dream-vision, in a painting! Of course he wonders could he have glimpsed this image before, absorbed it unconsciously and then dreamt it as his own? But he knows he has not. This is his first time in her studio. And since she is, after all, his cousin, he has followed her career, and knows that no picture even remotely like this has ever appeared in any of her catalogues. No, the dream came first.

She still has not heard him. Her eyes are narrow with concentration; there is paint in her hair. All of a sudden, his mouth is dry with love.

All his dreams flutter like moths around her. The whole time, he thinks about her: her voice, her long medieval face, her body within those loose dresses. In her cloistered garden, insects weave a glinting floss from leaf to leaf. He listens to the fountain, and he is sick, sick as a dog, drooping about the house. No longer is he animated and forthcoming at breakfast; now, stricken with a ferocious shyness, he munches his bread silently and stares at her while she speaks, or moves through the kitchen. It does occur to him that he is probably boring her to distraction, but there is nothing to be done.

*

Once again we took our kirs out to the *terrasse*, in yet another soft dusk. The clouds were marbled pink and white, and in the failing light I saw the gleam of her large eyes. 'Well, did you like it?'

I hesitated. 'It is well written. But actually I liked it the least of your pieces. It is terribly romantic. Even calling the woman Isolt, and giving her that tranquil Madonna's face straight out of a painting. And the magical house and garden that seem to exist beyond time. It's all so earnestly romantic, Ursula. And it isn't *funny* enough.'

She stiffened. I went on gingerly, 'You should laugh a bit at that clumsy boy, not cruelly, but lightly. His kind of puppy love is potentially very funny. I mean, as you observe, he must be a terrible bore, staring at his cousin with worshipful eyes and saying nothing all day long. She must feel completely exasperated. You could write a very funny scene about that.'

Ursula was silent a moment. Then she said in a high, tight voice, 'It might interest you to know that I modelled this story on *your* style. *Your* writing style is rather formal and . . . ' She smiled thinly. 'And even *prim*. And let's face it, you aren't famous for your sense of humour. You write about places and people in a very old-fashioned, *sentimental* way. But your style is elegant. I'll say that much for it. So I tried to write in an elegant way. I thought you might *like* an elegantly written, old-fashioned, *prim* story. Like one of your own.' And she glared at me.

I was astonished by how deeply her words seared me. Instantly I remembered a review of my fifth novel, by a bombastic yet witty Oxonian. (A writer always forgets the good reviews, while the negative ones haunt him or her forever.) The Oxonian had written, 'While Mr Clare's early novels are endearing portraits of intelligent young men out and about in Dublin, and while his more recent books are shrewd chronicles of our society and its foibles, he writes in a stilted, old-fashioned way. In this latest effort his style is once again overly formal, wooden, and, by definition, without humour. I should like to admonish Sebastian Clare to *loosen up*.'

I had a sudden, brutal picture of how others might see me. A pompous man, his attenuated face once handsome, but now grown too taut, too guarded. A slightly prim man, halting in his manner, and dry as a bone.

On the other hand, I did not see why Ursula should be so angry. I had not derided her story. All I had done was to proffer some mild criticism, as a professional novelist to a beginner – something she should have been glad of, it seemed to me. Instead, my well-meant advice had provoked one of her unfathomable rages. For she was indeed much more than hurt or vexed. Her face was white with anger, the eyes narrowed to glittering points. How absolute these furies of hers seemed, how out of proportion to what some other person might have said or done, having to do basically with some cable that lay coiled in her psyche, ready to pull taut at any moment. Her cheekiness was the same, I thought. She could allow herself to be so rude, and to encroach on other people's lives as she had on mine, because she was essentially oblivious. Nobody else really existed; there was only herself, and us, who were merely extensions of herself. Her past was a mystery, with those references to Mexico and America in her stories. Her character, Isolt, had referred to marrying a professor. Had she grown up, at least partly, in some American college town? Perhaps she had lived in California, amid eucalyptus trees, with her shadowy American father. I surveyed her while she glowered. Who was she, after all, this sloe-eyed guttersnipe, this gawky virgin? I could not fathom her. She was, simply, beyond my understanding.

'Ursula,' I tried, 'if you wish to be a writer, you must be able to accept criticism without getting so angry . . . '

'Oh, be quiet, Sebastian.' She was still speaking in that tight, sibilant voice. I was nearly frightened by her. She went on, 'Please, don't *lecture* me. It's so boring. What do *you* know about the modern world, anyway?' She made a sweeping gesture. '*You* live in a magical garden, like the people in my *old-fashioned* story. What do *you* know, with your boring, totally uncool novels?' She stalked into her bedroom, and emerged with her rucksack. 'I'm going out. I can't stand it here. It's too fucking *genteel*. You say you like louche places, but the truth is you are too sedate for words. See you later. *Maybe.*' And she left, banging the door behind her, like an angry child quitting its own home.

I lingered on the balcony until night fell in earnest. I was shaken, and also hungry: I had expected her to make a meal for us again. Everything seemed forlorn; not even a bird fluttered below. Eventually I ate some cheese and an apple, and went to bed, though I found I could neither read nor sleep.

And as midnight approached I began, reluctantly, to worry about her. Late at night, Nice was a dangerous town – more dangerous perhaps than even the wildest parts of Dublin. One glimpsed the underbelly of resort life after midnight on, say, the promenade or in the rue de France: hollow-eyed junkies standing in doorways; the strangely tall and deep-voiced prostitutes walking naked, or nearly so, beneath glittering coats; their clients skulking along the streets. I pictured Ursula wandering through that world. With an irritable sigh I rose, got dressed and went out to look for her.

At first it seemed an enchanted journey. Up in my quarter everything was closed and dark, but as I made my way south I saw, behind an art deco house, a small garden that I had never noticed before. Lamps shone here and there, powdering the trees – olives and gnarled fruit trees – with a golden light like pollen. A pair of gardening shears lay on the grass beside a lichened fountain, and I imagined a woman, a rather stately woman, moving amid those boughs that would be shadowy even in full daylight, pruning flowers, gathering pears. I stood gazing for a while, then pushed on, towards the Cours Saleya.

It was there I realised how futile this search was. The cafés, bars and clubs were still open and full of revellers; how could I hope to find little Ursula in such a throng? On impulse I went into the Pub Opéra, because it was an ordinary place whose prices even she could afford.

I looked around; there was a table of elderly German ladies, another of American young people dressed absurdly in shorts and flip-flops, as if they were determined to have a Riviera beach holiday despite the weather. A small, wizened man stood drinking beer at the *comptoir*. But no Ursula. I asked the barman, 'I am looking for a girl, an English-speaking girl, very thin with dark hair. Perhaps you have seen her?'

He smiled, not unsympathetically, and said, 'Monsieur, they all look like that.'

I trudged along the *cours* for a while, feeling lonely and out of place. Ursula was right, I told myself bleakly. *This* was the real Nice: this garish and slightly sinister atmosphere; these waiters standing, arms akimbo, at the entrance to their silly restaurants; these clumsy-footed tourists; these gangsters in shiny suits; these confidence tricksters, whores, pimps, drunks, mendicants; these scavengers that feed on a beach town at night. Had I thought I could escape? Had I thought I could be free of it, old-fashioned me with my precious, enchanted gardens? Was it because I felt somehow invulnerable that I'd let Clive into my life? And now Ursula?

Presently I gave up and began to walk home. But as I turned up avenue Jean Médecin, a deeper sense of foreboding assaulted me. Of course I'd walked this street before, at just such a late hour, though always accompanied – as when Ursula and I had strolled downtown after her dinner in my local restaurant. Yet now I was alone on the silent avenue, with the buildings seeming to lour on both sides, and the sound of my footsteps my only companion. I made sure to walk directly under the streetlamps. Suddenly a figure detached itself from the shadows: a bearded *clochard*, wearing nothing but a filthy blanket. His body was emaciated and grey, with a long grey penis dangling between spindly shanks, and he exuded the rank sweetness of unwashed flesh. Abruptly he extended a hand, and I rummaged for a coin to drop into it, while he stared at me through small gleaming eyes and said nothing.

I was overwrought by the time I got home, and dismayed to find that Ursula had still not returned. *Why the hell should I care*, I chivvied myself. *She's just an unpleasant, angry girl who means nothing to me.* I fairly threw myself back into bed, but once more could not sleep.

I heard her come in after an hour or so. She rattled in the bathroom for a while, then tentatively opened my door. I pretended not to hear. She hovered there a minute, before settling softly beside me. Her breath smelled of toothpaste, and her hair of French cigarettes.

'Hi, Sebastian,' she whispered.

I sighed. 'What did you do, after you left?'

'I went to your local café. They gave me a few beers and two of those big baguette sandwiches.'

'*Two* sandwiches?'

'You know how hungry I get. And then, afterwards, I just walked around. I went down to the prom . . . ' Her voice grew fainter. 'It was . . . a bit scary. A man wanted me to buy drugs, and there were other men, standing about in dark suits, and loads of, you know, girls.'

'Some of them are not even girls,' I murmured.

'I know. Those were the more gorgeous ones.'

Something occurred to me. 'Ursula, how could you afford two sandwiches and a few beers? You'd only a few centimes to your name.'

'I said to charge it to you. I knew you wouldn't mind.'

'You are too much!'

I turned away, resignedly, and presently it seemed that we both slept, chastely, side by side, like the night before.

*

Towards dawn, I dreamt again about my mother. In this dream I am a child of about ten, and she is keeping an eye on me while I play with some other boys in Herbert Park. It is one of those rare hot summer days in Ireland. And I am happy enough as I tussle on the grass with my friends, except for the awareness of my mother standing at the periphery of the lawn, with her bright hot gaze fixed on me. Clearly she is anxious, worried about how I am getting on, which makes me irritable. I feel acutely that in some way she *pities* me, which is why she is keeping such an unseemly vigil, standing there with that glassy smile, compromising my boyish dignity.

The dream stopped there. I opened my eyes and gazed at the ceiling, careful not to move for fear of disturbing Ursula. I was not being solicitous; I just had no wish to speak to her just then, for the dream had upset me.

It had made me realise that I was the child of two mothers. The first had caressed my hair and praised me for my charm. But the second had pitied me – perhaps, ironically, for the very dependency she encouraged.

She herself had been a pale, shy child. 'I had an artistic temperament,' she'd explained once. 'Which of course made me unpopular. The other children didn't understand.' And I was thinking now that the qualities she had decided were the reasons for her own social failure – her 'artistic' nature, her 'sensitivity' – if those very qualities were, in myself, not a weakness but a source of promise and power, well then I would undermine all of her justifications for self-pity. And it seemed she had needed to pity herself, as she would need to pity me.

*

Naturally both Ursula and I overslept. But at lunchtime she was cheerful, even giddy, full of prattle like, 'Isn't it brilliant living in a hotel, how they give you clean towels every day?' Or, 'I think they should change the name of the Promenade des Anglais to the Promenade des Irlandais, in honour of us, don't you?'

It was as though nothing had happened last night, as though she could shake off a quarrel like an old coat. But I could not be so blithe. For me, rows left an acrid smell in the air, a lingering smoke of hurt and baffled rage. When I was small and my mother was displeased with me, she'd sulk for days, as if she were the child, while I, sad and desperate, had to keep petitioning her for forgiveness; perhaps this was why I could never manage quarrels very well. Nevertheless, Ursula's buoyant humour this morning astonished me. Even though I knew how mercurial she could be, I still marvelled that there was no rue, no apology for how her insults might have hurt me, or for how she had flounced out so rudely, to eat a café meal at my expense. (I did not let on that she had so worried me, I'd gone out searching for her.)

In any case, it seemed to me that in the aftermath of her sudden rages, she was like a drunk in the morning, remembering nothing of how he had shouted or smashed a bottle the night before. But I did remember.

In the middle of the morning, while she scribbled next door (I did not know if she was still working at the same story, or if she'd moved on to yet another fragment), I shamefacedly read through my file of good reviews. My agent had sent them on a few months before, yet I hadn't felt like looking at them – until now. I read: 'Clare's Dublin, peopled with clever young men whose adventures ring so *true*, it could be called "Clare Land" or perhaps even "County Clare", so vividly does he create an atmosphere, a milieu, indeed a world.' Or, 'As Clare has matured, his novels have grown from finely wrought accounts of young urban men and women, to a broader exploration of Irish and indeed international society on many levels. In fact he has become a master of the social novel, interweaving individual psychology with problems of class and culture, all in his own fine and intelligent way.'

So much for Ursula, thought I triumphantly, closing the file, but I was blushing to think how deeply she'd managed to fluster me.

*

I was not working well in this period, the aftermath of my mother's death. But I have always needed to work, in an actual physical way, like needing to eat. And the absence of work in my life, like the absence of food, has always afflicted me with a hollow feeling and a general sense of malaise. So over the next few days I began to cobble at a short story. I didn't know where it had come from; I think I had dreamt it, or bits of it anyway, shortly after the arrival of Ursula.

The story was about a young boy in Dublin who befriends another boy, the child of Italian immigrants. Of course, there weren't very many of those in my day. One can forget, now, how homogenous Ireland used to be, with nearly everyone blue-eyed and pink-cheeked and the cousin of everybody else. On the other hand, at least half a dozen families of Italian origin had flourished in the Dublin of my youth: I had been at school with a boy called Pietro whose people were from Calabria.

In my story, the Irish boy takes to having lunch every day at the home of his Irish-Italian friend, whose mother serves them exuberant meals *à la calabrese*. Only when he arrives back at his own house, his breath, skin and hair are redolent of garlic – which becomes a source of consternation to his traditional potato-eating family. His grandmother goes so far as to wonder if he has been drawn into a coven of witches; why else those *foreign* odours that surround him like a miasma?

I wanted to explore the mixed feelings of the Irish boy in the face of his family's censure. He is ashamed of their ignorance but at the same time feels guilty, as if those lavish lunches at the table of his friend are indeed somehow wicked. Is he betraying his mother by secretly preferring the cooking of Mrs Alvito? And is it *wrong* to relish not merely her food but also the atmosphere surrounding it, the grown-ups drinking red wine from squat glasses and waving their arms and arguing in loud good-natured voices over the many serving plates and the big bowl of fruit? Is he, in fact, being corrupted by foreign ways, and is this why he comes home stinking to high heaven of garlic? And what will he do, in the end? I hadn't yet decided if he would remain loyal to his friend and his friend's family, or if he would succumb to the pressure of his own family.

'May I have a look at that?' asked Ursula one afternoon, emerging from her own workroom. I had been writing, or trying to write, at the dining table.

She settled in her chair. 'I can tell you're having problems. I mean, you're really frowning, like. Perhaps you could use another eye?' She smiled timidly: she had been 'good' Ursula, considerate and soft-spoken, ever since her outburst of a few evenings before.

So I pushed my few sheets of paper towards her. 'I haven't got very far. And it's an early draft. I always do the first couple of drafts in longhand. You'll find the writing clumsy, I fear. For some reason I'm just not *getting* it, this time.'

She didn't bother to answer – which I rather admired, since I myself never replied to students or fellow writers when they apologised nervously for the poor quality of their work. And while she read, pencil in hand, I felt a shudder of melancholy, and said to myself, *Oh, how I have been missing my editing sessions with Claudia! How lonely I have been, without fully knowing it . . .*

Presently, she raised her head and regarded me seriously. 'It should be a first-person narrative, Sebastian. The *child* should be speaking, you know? And look, these paragraphs are muddled. This one should come *first*. And this sentence here is a bit *dead*, don't you think? You could find a better way of saying the same thing.'

I swept my eye over the text and realised she was right. Of course the boy should tell his own story in his own disarming voice! The pages almost seemed to thrum into life in my hands, and I found myself smiling warmly at Ursula. 'Thank you, my dear. This is good advice.'

I was remembering how self-confident, even arrogant, she had seemed when assuring me that she *understood* me. I hadn't thought she could be right – that her love of words, and of my novels in particular, could give her certain sympathetic powers, enable her to fathom my intentions more accurately than I could do myself. She seemed suddenly once again like a little flame to me, burning with literary promise and ambition, and I felt at once grateful for her help, and deeply unnerved for needing it.

*

We received one of Trudy's embossed cards, inviting us to a salon the following week, but Ursula's clothes were as dreadful as her hair had been. So I took her to a shop in Nice Étoile and insisted on buying her a simple black dress with a mandarin collar, since I had divined that strict, modest styles would suit her best – though she was drawn to flounces and floral patterns. On the day itself, she was somewhat subdued, which became her; it was pleasant to see her both well-dressed and well-behaved.

While we walked along Boulevard Victor Hugo, she said hesitantly, 'I like the way you use language, Sebastian, because I remember how my dad spoke, ages ago when he was still living with us. A certain American way of speaking, you know? So *jagged*, full of jargon and catchphrases. Flippant, I suppose you'd say. I prefer your European style.'

'Not all Americans speak flippantly,' I answered mildly. 'Trudy and Alice are very well-spoken, and so are some of the other Americans you'll doubtless meet today.' But I acknowledged to myself that her timid praise was meant as an apology.

We walked on in silence for a while, past a rouged elderly lady walking a poodle, a gaggle of children, people hurrying home for the evening meal with baguettes in their hands. Then I asked, 'What kind of flippant things did your father say?'

I spoke tentatively, since previous allusions to her father had provoked only scowls, but I thought that anyone who loved words should consider language closely. And now she didn't glare, but answered dryly, 'He was sort of a hippie type, so he'd make really profound statements like, "Don't be uptight" or "Hang loose". You know, those hackneyed hippie expressions. And he had a way of *flattening* language. If something wasn't working, he'd say it was a "non-starter". And he preferred awful words like "utilise" instead of "use", always choosing technical names over the nice simple ones. Really abrasive, I always thought, even when I was small.'

I smiled, remembering the letters of an American lawyer I'd had to engage some time ago over a contract dispute. And once more I pondered this nebulous father. So he was a 'hippie' type. I pictured a hairy student sauntering through Dublin in the 1960s. Ursula's mother had probably considered him romantic. I imagined her as a demure convent girl, for whom some hippie with grubby feet in sandals would have seemed exotic. She might even have thought that he resembled Jesus Christ. Or at least one of the disciples.

*

The first guest I noticed, with a bump of the heart, was the woman with green eyes. She stood by the window, talking to an old man whose gaunt northern European face looked vaguely familiar. Her own face was a pure oval, with fine black eyebrows. She had copious, rather stylishly messy black hair; in fact, her whole aspect was pleasantly, stylishly rumpled, from the white jumper with pushed-up sleeves, to the wool skirt and plain shoes. While I gazed at her, she glanced idly at me, and once more, those eyes! Immediately they spirited me to Ireland, to the ferns that flourish along its lanes, behind stone walls, in summer. I realised this was a romantic image (I remembered Ursula deriding my 'sentimental' style), but I couldn't help it. On the other hand, it also occurred to me, perhaps cynically, that she might be wearing green contact lenses.

I dragged my own eyes away, to survey the room, which was its usual cluttered self. Dust swirled in the air above the too-heavy furniture and the piles of books on which plates of the inevitable yellow cake and cups of tea were balanced. Through the window, beyond the green-eyed woman, one could glimpse palms and a ribbon of sea, but within it was all carpets and arm-chairs and books, books everywhere.

Trudy and Alice must be pleased, I thought, because the place was unusually crowded. I noticed Katherine, wearing a cream-coloured dress. She appeared slightly tense, balanced on the dreadful brown sofa, drinking a cup of tea while talking to her earnest husband. Her eyes in the heart-shaped face looked brilliant – too brilliant, I thought. They seemed to glitter with a dry heat, and below them her cheeks burned bright pink. Even from a distance, one had the impression that her skin would be dry and hot to the touch. There was clearly something fierce beneath that flower-like composure, some kind of incandes-cence, but whether it was the illness burning away at her, or her determination to overcome it, I could not know.

Beside her on the sofa, talking to little Alice, was the Russian playwright, Anton – though he preferred 'Antoine' in France. He was about forty, with a sensitive face, and slender hands, with which he caressed his little beard. Once, I had told him that while others extolled his plays, I myself especially cherished his short stories. Giving me a limpid smile, he had bowed with an Old World courtesy I had only ever seen before in films. I found him mannered, like most people connected with the theatre, but he was charming for all that, with some glow about him that I could only describe as sweetness.

Trudy swooped over, extending her hands in welcome. She was wearing a loose brown garment – a kaftan, I supposed. It bellied out behind her and made her look even larger, though I was also struck by how handsome she was, with that heavy, intelligent face.

'Lovely to see you both,' she cried, before taking my arm peremptorily and muttering, 'Sebastian, you must go over *tout de suite* and speak to Phebus. He's a little gloomy. And he's been saying how much he wishes to talk to you. Go on, introduce your friend to him. *Please.*' And in an even lower voice, accompanied by a 'significant' look, she continued, 'Loulou is with him. You know what *that* means.'

Phebus was reclining on a settee, cheek cradled on his hand, like that famous photograph of Oscar Wilde. In fact, he bore a faint resemblance to Wilde, though Phebus was handsomer, with gentler features and a tiny explosion of curls around his brow. He was a poet, of course. Anyone who sprawled on a settee while sighing *had* to be a poet. And indeed there was Loulou beside him, heavily painted, wearing one of her hats, and sulking. I did not know why bossy Trudy had selected me to intervene in one of their rows, but since she was my hostess, it seemed I should oblige. So I took Ursula's elbow and guided her to their corner.

As we settled on chairs across from them, I noticed that Phebus' large head was partly covered by a red kerchief, which I hadn't noticed because it lay over the ear that was facing the window. It made him resemble at once a buccaneer and a wounded soldier. 'Don't be so *turgid*,' he was saying in French to Loulou, who stared at him like granite before smiling brightly at me and crying in English, 'Why, hello, Sebastian! How *well* you look!'

'Thank you. And how splendid *you* look.' I also spoke in English, for Ursula's benefit, although in truth Loulou was not looking terribly well. Tendrils of her auburn hair had fallen down from the hat, and her face was very pale. She gave a general impression of being dishevelled, sweaty and angry. Now, still in English, she hissed, 'My dear Sebastian, it is *such* a relief to see *you* here, after this Polish upstart of a pseudo-poet has been *torturing* me for *ages*. I do not know why he even bothers to come down from Paris. I was much, much happier before he arrived and decided to *immure* me in that *sordid* hotel – you know which one I mean – for *days* and *days*. There isn't even any proper *room service*. And it was *extremely* awkward for me to arrange to slip away from my own *quite comfortable* domestic arrangements, only to be subjected to the most . . . ' She broke off, with a shudder of revulsion.

Phebus said mildly, in English this time, 'Come, Loulou. Don't be hysterical. You know that you adore our meetings. You *know* that in love, one must journey to the depths; one must become a child again, experiencing the caresses and also the harsh hand of love.' He abruptly flung out an arm, as if in salute. 'All is possible in love!' The large smiling face turned to me. 'Our friend Friedrich has observed that when a man calls on a woman, he must not forget to bring a whip. Quite right, too. Only what if *she* has a whip, as well!' He gave a shout of laughter, and touched the cloth on his head. 'Oh, my dearest Loulou. My wanton girl! Why must you fall into the arms of another? Why must you succumb to the empty lures of that bourgeois, with whom you shall never know real rapture? Why should we not spend all our days in our glorious hotel room, sequestered from the rude crowds below, beating each other's tender flesh in rage and bliss? Ah, violence is the salt of love!' He sighed, and closed his eyes, as if that ardent outburst had exhausted him.

Loulou regarded him scornfully. 'It is your *mother*, Phebus. It all goes back to your horrid, Polish, *demi-mondaine* mother. You grew up with the smell of cigars in your nose and the rattle of the gaming tables in your ears. All you ever knew was the glitter of the casinos, and all those dreadful people, you mother's dreadful *friends*, who spoilt you and then forgot about you once the games started up again. You became *impossible* quite early on, and you shall *always* be impossible.'

But all of a sudden she smiled at him, and he opened his eyes and smiled brightly back. I realised that I'd fulfilled the mission Trudy had charged me with, by doing absolutely nothing. Those two needed to quarrel, preferably in public, especially after one of their hothouse sessions in the decaying grandeur of their station hotel. And then they needed to make it all up, as ostentatiously as they had rowed – also preferably before an audience. Now Loulou suffered him to take her little hand, which he pressed against his heart while giving her an adoring look.

Ursula was staring at them with a thunderstruck expression, her mouth actually half-open. I touched her arm, and we silently rose, leaving those two to their swoon of reconciliation. Phebus' cry, 'You are my only joy!' was the last phrase I heard before we were greeted by Léon and Max, who informed us that the tea things had been taken away (thank God) and we could finally have a glass of whiskey.

They were flushed as if they had been walking on the beach. And they were clearly in an expansive party humour, better disposed towards Ursula, who, after her dumbfoundedness before Phebus and Loulou, was once more looking shy and fetching in her black dress. So I left her to their benevolent attentions, and made my way through the thicket of tables, books, bottles, cigarette smoke and people, to where the green-eyed woman still stood before the window, alone now. I considered this extreme good luck; everywhere throughout the room, guests were talking in pairs or groups, while this woman gazed out of the long window, still and solitary, the evening light glinting on her hair.

'I have seen you,' I said, my voice low with nervousness. 'I saw you the other day, walking along Georges Clemenceau. You were wearing a mackintosh.' *Oh, God,* I thought, *why did I say that about the mackintosh?*

She turned. I almost couldn't bear to look into those eyes. She spoke as bluntly as myself. 'You are Sebastian Clare. I have read many of your novels. And that very good story you published some years ago in the *New Yorker*, I think.' She had a pleasant voice, but I could not place her accent.

Little Alice suddenly appeared, thrust one glass of whiskey into my hand and another into the hand of my companion, then vanished just as suddenly, like a pixie. Bless her, I thought, praying that the drink would relax me. I said, 'You must be a writer, too. Nearly everyone here is a writer, except for the psychiatrists and Loulou.'

Before she could answer, Anton (or Antoine) approached us. He had taken off his spectacles, which now dangled from the long fingers of his right hand. I'd noticed that the eyes of myopic people are often lovely, all soft and wondering, and Antoine's were particularly clear, with crinkles at their corners. 'Dear Julie,' he murmured in his Russian-accented English, clasping the hand of my green-eyed girl. (Ah! Julie!) Then, 'Sebastian,' he cried, 'I must speak to you. And to you, too, my dear.' He touched Julie's white sleeve. 'I have just received a most distressing letter from Livia. You do remember Livia, Sebastian?'

I had to think hard, because Antoine was usually in the company of some girl or other, probably because he loved to flirt – in a mild, avuncular way – and he was charming. More crucially, of course, he was an influential playwright, so that actresses and would-be actresses often hovered about him, brightly coloured and tremulous as butterflies. In fact, I had thought once or twice that perhaps Antoine was a bit irresponsible with those girls, flirting with all of them, apparently oblivious to the insistent beating of their wings. Though perhaps I was just jealous; anyway, who was I to talk, with Ursula in my bed?

I seemed to remember Livia, a very young Russian girl with slightly insipid looks, but beautiful manners, like Antoine himself. She had been, I recalled, one of his most devoted hangers-on. 'What does she say?' I asked. 'You look a bit upset, Antoine.'

He sighed. 'She writes from *Switzerland*, of all places. You know, the poor girl, she was in love with me, only I'd no idea. Perhaps if I'd . . . ' He sighed once more. 'Anyhow, she was just a child, though a dear child. But after she saw that I could not respond to her as she would have wished, she tried to overcome her infatuation by going off with old Potty. That second-class scribbler! That opportunistic goat!'

I had never seen Antoine so agitated. 'Isn't old Potty married?' I asked.

He made a gesture of disdain. 'My dear Sebastian, *of course* he is married. His intentions were never honourable, that *dog*. And now he has left the child, left her in a Swiss hotel, all alone, and . . . ' He touched the fingers of his left hand to his brow. 'And now the girl is *enceinte*. That insufferable Potty! Not only an arrogant devil and a bad writer, but a cad! He has seduced and forsaken poor Livia, leaving her pregnant and penniless, in *Switzerland.*'

I did not know what Antoine had against Switzerland. Probably it was just that he hated to picture a forlorn and pregnant Livia marooned in some antiseptic hotel, surrounded by cuckoo clocks. Julie asked, 'What will you do, Antoine?'

His shoulders drooped. 'I don't know. I thought I could go over there, to comfort her. To rescue her.' He smiled wanly. 'I feel responsible, you see. Surely I cannot abandon her?' He made this appeal to Julie, who took a swallow of her drink before saying carefully, in her pleasant voice, with the accent that I could not place, 'Antoine, you mustn't confuse pity with love.'

Suddenly I was eating lunch in Cannes with Claudia, her eyes worried as she says, *It seems to me that you are confusing compassion with pity* . . .

Antoine sighed. 'But I *do* pity her. I was unable to love her. But I *do* pity her, poor girl.'

Julie continued, still in the measured way that reminded me so disturbingly of Claudia, 'Yet pity is insidious. I think that we love those who have come to reside in our hearts, if you see what I mean. We love those whom we are meant to love, and they are our charges and our equals. But surely pity is different; it means you are standing apart and feeling *sorry* for her. Pity contains an element of judgement, even contempt.' She shook her head. 'Oh, Antoine, if you travel to Switzerland, *you* will probably feel better. But what about *her*, this girl whom you cannot love? What about her, afterwards?'

Antoine looked perplexed. 'Only what else can I do? She is appealing to me. I must do *something*, mustn't I?'

Julie gave a soft laugh. 'You could send her some money. Has she family in Russia, or somewhere? You could send her a bit of money, and then she'd be able to travel to her people?'

He considered. 'She does indeed have family. And closer than Russia. There is a cousin in Paris, an older woman. Quite sympathetic, I believe. Perhaps I could send Livia some money, as you suggest, and a ticket to Paris?' He sighed. 'Ah, but I remain so troubled. I have muddled things so badly. I encouraged her without knowing it; I teased her and flirted with her, until she was driven so mad that she flew into the arms of that scurrilous Potty. Poor little bird!'

I put my hand on his arm. 'Antoine, there is only one answer.

You are a writer. You must write about it.'

He looked doubtful for a moment, but then seemed to brighten a bit, squaring his shoulders. 'That is true, Sebastian. Only writing it out would restore me to sanity. Excellent advice, my friend. I shall begin straightaway tomorrow morning, after I have made arrangements for Livia to travel to Paris.' Suddenly he began to cough in a soft but urgent way. I saw it in his shoulders, which shook heavily as if absorbing a fiercer blow than the discreet coughing showed. I was abruptly aware of how thin he was, and how he was ill as Katherine was ill, with that same burning affliction of the lungs. Like her, he had come to live here for the climate, although our famous climate was something of a myth. The winters could be sharp enough; on the other hand, they were certainly balmier than St Petersburg. Or even Dublin. Now Antoine swiftly recovered his poise, touching a handkerchief to his lips. Then he kissed Julie's hand and shook mine in his formal way, before wandering back into the crowd, looking more jaunty, despite the coughing, than the dolorous figure who had saluted us only moments before.

Gazing after him, Julie finally answered, 'Yes, I am a writer. I have published four books of poetry, and I do some translations as well.'

I registered her small smile. People often give you a rueful smile when they admit to writing poetry, as if they fear you may think they live in a garret and scrawl on vellum with a quill – unlike shrewd journalists and novelists.

We continued to stand by the window, while the light deepened outside, and the conversation grew warm with whiskey inside. Trudy was floating about in her kaftan, replenishing people's glasses. I thought that Katherine and her husband were preparing to go home, but I could hear other guests discussing the possibility of dinner at a nearby restaurant, or further drinks in the café below. I was glad to glimpse Ursula across the room, talking to an American novelist called Noel something-or-other. When I turned back to Julie, it seemed that I could identify her after all. 'I think I know who you are,' I said slowly. 'You are an English poet, aren't you? Though didn't you move to Nice quite recently? And you were given a poetry prize last year, I believe. It was in the English papers. But wasn't there some controversy?'

She grimaced. 'Yes, it all became a mess. You were meant to be born in Britain or you couldn't receive the prize. I carry a British passport, but my parents were French Jews, and I was born in America. So the prize committee wanted to take it back, only ultimately they didn't. But by the time they decreed I could keep it, the whole experience had soured for me, as you can imagine. I returned the money.' She laughed. 'It wasn't very much, or I mightn't have been so principled. But as it was, the whole thing had come to feel grimy. So I gave the money back to the prize people – who were happy enough to take it.'

'It sounds cynical. And sad.' I was going to say more about the charged world of literary prizes, but instead I surprised myself by blurting out, 'Your eyes are very green.'

'Yes, aren't they?' I was pleased by that simple reply, neither coy nor coquettish. She laughed again. 'People accuse me of wearing coloured contact lenses. But my eyes are simply this deep green colour. They are my father's eyes. My mother's were grey, like yours.'

We spoke more, though afterwards I would not remember most of what we said. It was not personal, however, that much I could recall, despite my gauche homage to her eyes. I would have liked to ask about her French-Jewish parents, why she'd been born in America, and whereabouts in Nice she was living now. But I must have been too shy – as perhaps she was, as well, for after that exchange about eyes we talked only of publishers and prizes, and people we both knew in London.

Also, I could not stop thinking about her advice to Antoine, which had disturbed me not only because it was so like the wisdom of Claudia years ago, but also because of my encouragement of Ursula now. Julie's words recalled me to some Hollywood film I'd seen as a boy, at the Stella Cinema. The beautiful but frail heroine had died in the arms of her beloved while the audience wept, making me feel as if I were in a wood surrounded by dripping boughs. And it was occurring to me now that pity and sentimentality were related in some way; both an excuse to *not feel?* Were my reactions to Ursula merely sentimental, and full of hollow pity? Why had I let her into my home, and into my bed – where we continued to pass our weird, sexless nights? Claudia had cautioned me about the danger of succumbing to shallow pity eight years ago; was it possible that I still had not learned, even after everything that had happened in the meantime?

Presently, Julie said, 'I must go. I've got letters and things to write.' She paused before saying abruptly, 'I live in *vieux Nice*. Would you like to come to my flat for dinner? Next Thursday, perhaps?'

'Next Thursday would be fine. Thank you.' I was trying not to sound childishly enthusiastic.

She scribbled her address and phone number on a bit of paper, and we said goodbye. My eyes followed her as she moved towards the door, a slight, straight figure, pausing to kiss Phebus and Loulou, to clasp Alice's hand, to say farewell to others whom I did not know. Trudy materialised at my shoulder. 'You are naughty, Sebastian,' she said sternly. 'You didn't *mingle* enough. Lots of people wanted to talk to you, but you never moved from this window, and so they went forlornly home.'

'Ah, Trudy, they must be bawling into their handkerchiefs as they trudge off to some expensive café, all because I did not speak to them.'

She gave a wry laugh. 'Well, I guess you shouldn't have left your little friend alone. She's standing over there, glowering at you.'

I made my way to Ursula, who was indeed wearing her sulky face. 'I tried to speak to people but I didn't *know* anyone,' she wailed. 'And you spent the *whole evening* talking to that middle-aged woman, and the thin man with the beard.'

'Ursula, it is customary to greet people politely when they approach you, to say, "Hello, Sebastian, did you have a nice evening?" or something of that nature. And you certainly did know some of the guests. What about Léon and Max? And I noticed you talking to that American novelist.'

'You're sounding very pompous,' she said, but then grinned. 'He was cool, the novelist. He said he'd like to read one of my stories. Isn't that cool?'

'Quite cool,' I answered obligingly, though I felt concern for the American, who probably did not yet know how relentless Ursula could be. On the other hand, it would be a relief if she began to press her half-finished stories on someone else for a change.

VI

We had arranged a rendezvous with Clive for Monday evening, at the café where I had looked at his story fragment. But just as we were preparing to go out, my mother rang.

'Hello, Mum. Listen, I've got a crucial meeting and I mustn't be late. I'll ring you back.'

'Oh? How nice. With a publisher? What is it about?'

'If I explain now, I'll be *late*. I'll ring you afterwards, all right? You'll be in all evening, won't you?' A kind of panic was rising in my throat. I swallowed hard. She said, 'Well, why don't I talk to Claudia then? You go out to your meeting, and ring me back later, but in the meantime I can talk to Claudia.'

'Mum, Claudia is coming with me.'

'With you? To a meeting with your publisher?'

'I never said it was a meeting with my publisher. Actually it promises to be a rather difficult meeting, and I would very much like *not to be late*. I'll talk to you in a couple of hours, Mum.'

A sigh. Then in a forlorn voice, 'All right, dear. Good luck. Bye for now.'

She often phrased her farewells like that: *Goodbye for now*. As if to assure – or threaten – that she'd be back in contact all too soon.

Ringing off, I grimaced. 'Sorry. That was graceless.'

Claudia shook her head sympathetically. 'Oh, darling. Not at all.' She seemed to hesitate; then, with a soft smile, 'You know, when you have those exchanges with your mother, one would never guess that you were such a big grown-up boy who had written all those nice books.'

'All right, all right.' I seized my coat and opened the door. 'At least she didn't tell me not to forget my umbrella. Generally she thinks the weather everywhere is just like Dublin.'

*

In fact, the evening *was* a bit like Dublin: dove-grey, the air slightly damp. At the *zinc*, four elderly men were playing *quatre cent vingt et un*, while, beside them, a young man was talking softly to a young woman while the cat, oblivious, slumbered at her elbow. Nearly all of the tables were full; Clive waited at one close to the door. He was drinking a light beer or perhaps a *panacheé*, and reading the *Daily Mail*.

When he saw us, he closed the paper and raised a hand in greeting. As usual, he seemed offhand to the point of insolence. He made me feel like a schoolmaster or a sergeant major; I wanted to tell him to stop slouching and stop smirking *this instant*. Though I only said 'Hello', and then we joined him at his table. Claudia called for a kir and I took a whiskey, since I thought this encounter might require strong drink.

But I was wrong. I don't think we said much, and what we did say was probably clumsy, things like, 'We don't think this is working out' and 'We're a bit disturbed by your growing attachment to us, and anyway we really don't need a driver.' We mentioned our friends, I think, how they were also growing troubled by his increasingly free-and-easy presence in our lives. At this he gave an unpleasant laugh, and said, 'Your snooty friends? Who cares about them?'

He said only two other disturbing things, although one might actually have contained a kernel of truth. After we had finished with our cumbersome explanations, he was silent for a moment. Then he tilted back in his chair and observed, 'You know what your real problem is? You, and probably all the Irish? You just don't know how to handle servants.'

'Perhaps you're right,' said Claudia. 'Or perhaps we simply don't want a servant. One can become too dependent, you know.' She paused. 'And you, Clive. This is no life for you, sure-ly?'

For the first time since I'd known him, he looked discomfit-ed. He played with his moustache, then said, 'I think I'll go back to England. The French don't suit me, really. Perhaps I can go to one of those writing schools in England; you know, those uni-versities where they have workshops with famous writers.'

So he still clung to his novel-writing dream. I considered how to help him; I could write to my contacts at the East Anglia pro-gramme and elsewhere to suggest that they take him on as a mature student, if he applied. He did have an interesting subject matter, after all, with that sinister, sorrowful family. Perhaps all he needed was some structure and discipline. Anyway, I was feel-ing a little bit responsible for him.

But then he said the second disturbing thing. 'I wouldn't enrol, or anything. Why bother? I'd just hang about, go into the lecture halls and so forth. They couldn't throw me out, could they? I could talk to one of the teachers in his room or while he was walking home, offer my services. I'd say, "Why not Drive with Clive?" Something clever like that.' He gave a low laugh. '*You* know what I mean. I could work as the bloke's driver in exchange for being let into his workshop. That kind of thing.'

For the second time that evening, I found myself swallowing hard. Neither Claudia nor I spoke.

And then he left. But first he actually paid. He was ungracious enough about it, ignoring the saucer put out for coins, throwing them instead almost disdainfully onto the table as he stood up. But they were enough to cover all our drinks. Next he folded his newspaper and said, 'Well, sorry it didn't work out. Perhaps we'll meet again one day.' And before we could speak, he had gone.

I don't know why we were so astonished. What had we expected? If he was, as I had surmised, a kind of parasite, then his reaction made sense. Once the host body dies or is exhausted, or becomes in some way inhospitable, what else would the parasite do but look for another one? In other words, Clive had been down this road before, and knew when he had been found out, when it was time to leave a place and search out a new target. I pictured him standing on the lawn of some university campus, his hands in the pockets of that leather coat, his bleached eyes gazing narrowly at the tweedy professors and book-laden students as he wondered whom amongst them to move in on.

We stared at each other. I listened to the click of dice, the chatter of two Italian men at a nearby table; the cat suddenly sprang down from the *comptoir* and glided beneath our table, circling round and round our legs. Claudia said, 'Well.'

'Well,' I echoed. 'What an anticlimax! Anyway, I suppose that's that. Our first stalker.'

'Not our first. There have been others, Sebastian. Generally girls, but not only.' She gave a half-smile. 'So many people are hypnotised by fame these days, irresistibly drawn to it. Like moths round a fire. Only they aren't *admirers*. Not in the old-fashioned sense, anyway. They have this glittering look about them, a glittering rapacious look, like they want to eat you. Or else use you up and then push you aside.'

I thought of what Trudy has said on the beach. Claudia went on, 'I suppose the difference is that Clive has been the most blatant. Maybe even the most honest.'

I laughed, picturing his seagull eyes and tense body, his incomprehensible life, which seemed to contain nothing much beyond the little Citroën. 'Don't grow sentimental about him, darling, now that he's gone.'

*

But he was not yet gone. About two weeks after we dismissed him, and just before vanishing from Nice altogether, he called on Trudy and Alice. We did not know about this call until later, because Claudia and Alice had finished their work on the book and were no longer in daily contact. We learnt of it only when we received this letter from Trudy:

Dear Claudia and Sebastian,
Just to let you know that yesterday your ex-chauffeur Clive rang our doorbell. It was about three in the afternoon and Alice didn't want to let him in since generally she takes a snooze at that hour and anyway it just seemed brash of him. We don't really know him, and he hadn't phoned or anything. Also, when the bell rang we thought at first that it was Henry M. and April, because they're supposed to arrive any minute, cycling down from Paris. So we swung the door open, but instead of Henry's face with those funny round glasses, who did we see but your Clive. As I said, Alice was for turning him away but I was curious about him despite finding him creepy, and besides I was a

little relieved that it wasn't Henry after all because I hate the fact that he's an anti-Semite, though I can tolerate April well enough.

Anyway, because as I say I was curious about him, I whispered to Alice, 'It's all right; it'll just be a minute', so we let him in and gave him a cup of tea. He explained that you two had dismissed him 'because of pressure from friends'. Next he said he hoped those friends weren't me and Alice. (He looked almost sinister when he said that.) And then he told us he would probably go back to England now but that he'd decided to sound us out first to see if we might want to take him on as our driver. Or else as our cook. Can you imagine? Alice would rather chop off her foot than let someone else cook for us.

So of course we said no, no, thanks very much, etc. I was still intrigued by him in a kind of dark way. He looks like he's not one person, as if he's composed of many sides, all fractured, somehow. It's those glacial eyes, I guess – they don't show any feeling. But he accepted our refusal pretty well. He said he didn't really like France anyway: the cigarettes are too pungent, the natives talk too much, the money is impossible to figure out, the restaurant menus are written in French (imagine that, in France!) and the food gives him indigestion besides.

He reminded me of certain Americans when he offered that catalogue of grievances. (Being from those parts myself, I give myself leave to criticise American attitudes.) Just a couple of months ago my sister's kid, a college boy in California, came over to visit us. He wouldn't stop talking in this booming voice, you know? I kept telling him to modulate it, that in the cafés and restaurants here people generally speak softly. It's a form of courtesy to others, I explained. But he just threw up his hands and grinned (actually he's a nice kid, quite engaging, with that smile, and smart as a whip at college), and he said, 'But Aunt Trudy, this is the way I am. I'm American. This is the way we talk.' And I realised that a lot of Americans, a lot of my American friends, feel the same as he does. They think that if they engaged with another society on its own terms, they'd be compromising their integrity. As if honouring the customs of a foreign country, adapting to its ways, means you are lying or being phoney. 'Hey, Aunt Trudy, this is the way I am. This is the way I talk.' And he said similar things when we took him to a restaurant and he ordered a *café au lait* for his aperitif and then complained to the waiter about the salad being served after the main course. Anyway I guess old weird Clive reminded me of my nephew because I think his attitudes are almost the same.

They're the attitudes of empire, of imperialists in the colonies. What I mean is, the Americans are the imperialists now; their language (our language!) is the supreme instrument of commerce. Only of course the English-speaking hegemony that came before ours was the British Empire, so that's probably why Clive has this sense of entitlement also. When he complains about the menus being written in French, he's being dead serious; he really is offended.

I know I'm digressing. I think I need to let off steam about Clive because he did unnerve us. Even before yesterday he had upset me, as you know. Last week Alice and I took that little train up into the mountains, all the way to La Brigue, in fact. It was really cold up there but the light was gorgeous, hard and pure and nearly silver. It had already snowed on the higher mountains. Everything felt very still and nearly mystical. In the evening we went to the big *tabac-café* on the square. It was very crowded, which was not surprising since it's the only show in town. Children were scampering around and the grown-ups were playing cards or gossiping with the *patronne*. Everyone looked almost the same, the same slightly coppery complexion and eyes spaced a little too close: there must be a lot of intermarriage in these remote villages. Also they were not exactly unfriendly but they didn't say hello to us, as the French usually do when you walk into a café. Some of them just gave us this sidelong once-over, although a couple of them smiled. But as I've said, I don't think they were being hostile; I think that's simply the way of isolated mountainy people. Anyhow, there was one man standing alone at the zinc and fingering his moustache, and for a minute I thought he was your driver and my heart almost stopped. That's what happens with weirdos like Clive. They fasten onto your psyche in a funny way and you feel almost haunted by them, so that your local butcher or the bus driver or the man sweeping your street begins to look like them. Another point in all this is that both Alice and I really liked that sweet little mountain train. Who needs a driver, when there are trains like that?

I have two more things to say, though I know this letter is sprawling all over the place. The first is that I was only half-serious in my diatribe above, about America I mean. I actually love America, in the way one loves their very first place. For me it's a hot summer night alive with crickets or the umber sky at dusk in Oakland, where I grew up, or my mother's voice, singing to me. Such fine points of memory are so deep, and they are sources of recognition for me and Alice, and others who are from that country. I also like how positive Americans can be, how they are always inventing new medicines or some clever new diet. And I like the tough style of Henry and April, with their Brooklyn sense of irony and that salty accent (even if I do disapprove of Henry's politics). Only I left America, of course. I left because I feel more at home here in France than in the States, but I am divided. I do live between worlds, between my first place (and my mother tongue), and the life and language that I have chosen through love. I guess I am trying to say that I – that all of us ex-pats, maybe – are a little bit like your Clive, after all. Maybe it was ourselves we caught a glimpse of in his peculiar uneasiness, even though Alice and I and you two are happy in our life here.

My last point. Despite what I have just written about there being a little bit of Clive in all of us, I also experienced, yesterday, something very low, very dark in him, unlike anything I have ever come across before. Which is saying a lot, since I have been, in my time, a frequenter of every lowlife dive from San Francisco to Budapest. But something he said just as he was leaving really disturbed both me and Alice. In fact I wasn't sure I should even mention it to you, but then I thought, *Why not? They should know.* Anyway, he's gone, or at least we hope so. He had gulped down his tea and had risen to leave, but then he turned back and said, 'I think I'll contact my brother, once I'm home in England. We've been estranged, but I think I'll look him up, after I return and have settled a bit.'

'Well, that sounds nice. That sounds a positive thing to do,' we mumbled vaguely – and rather inanely, I guess, but we didn't know anything about this brother. Alice and

I had risen too, since we were growing anxious for him to leave; in fact, I was beginning to feel pretty jumpy. But he just stood there, with this slightly impertinent smile. And after a minute he said, 'My brother doesn't like bullshit, you know. If he were here, he wouldn't be impressed by all you pretentious artist types.' He gave a snort. 'All you lot probably think your lives are quite glamorous here on the exotic Riviera. But you're all quite grubby, actually, quite poor compared to my brother. He drives a solid-gold Rolls, and he fucks film stars and models.' He laughed nastily then, as if he had wanted to offend our lesbian sensibilities. Finally he said, 'And he wouldn't stand for nonsense. Like "pressure from friends". If he thought that certain "friends" were bad-mouthing him or driving him out of a place, he would just pay them a discreet visit, you know, and silence them once and for all. No bullshit, like I say.'

I had stiffened with apprehension, and I could hear Alice breathing in this ragged way she has whenever she's scared. I mean, we were all alone with him. Everything felt so quiet, and the neighbours were probably not at home. What if he drew a gun from the pocket of that dirty leather coat of his? But he just laughed again, and opened the door and walked out.

So there it is. I've told all. I did think you should know, especially you, Sebastian, since we all kind of felt you were not aware enough of that unbalanced, sinister thing in him. It was a pretty terrible meeting yesterday, and last night I had dreams where I was trying to protect Alice from some vague threat but always losing sight of her. Anyhow, enough is enough, and we hope he's gone for good. When Henry M. and April do arrive, I'll arrange an impromptu salon. Henry really likes your books, Sebastian. I kiss you both, and Alice sends love.

*

I said slowly, 'I hope they don't think we were really so craven as to tell Clive we were sacking him because of pressure from friends.'

'Well, we did mention our friends, but no, I think Trudy and Alice understand.' Claudia moved from the dining table, where we'd been reading the letter, to a chair beneath the window. Lowering herself onto it, she pushed aside the curtain, and the midday sunlight struck her face. I saw, suddenly, that she was tired. My beloved's face was tired, with bluish shadows scalloped beneath her eyes and a pallor in her cheeks I had never seen there before. My throat closed for a moment with an irrational fear. Presently I said, 'It's funny. When we had drinks on the beach, Trudy gave me this sobering advice about Clive, about how dangerous he possibly was – and then she lets him into her flat, where she and Alice are alone and vulnerable. It's as if he throws a spell over people.'

'I know.' She turned to me, smiling, and the fear lifted. 'Thank God he didn't harm them. Oh, Sebastian, I *hope* he has finally, truly left.'

'I'm pretty sure he's gone, darling. He's played his last card here.' I recalled his greyish face surrounded by red and blue casino lights, that Joker behind him with its tongue hanging out.

She said, 'What Trudy wrote, about certain smells and sounds spiriting her back to her first life? And how she and Alice

have those things in common, those particular points of refer-
ence? I suppose it's true for us as well. Dublin, I mean. The way
the city used to feel on a summer evening, or certain pop songs
on the Irish radio from when we were small. You and I have that
together. Yet I am beginning to feel rather wistful about Nice
also, whenever we go away for a while. When we're up in Paris,
even, or back in Ireland, I remember the way the light looks, and
the shutters on the houses. I do love our life here, Sebastian.'

Suddenly, for no reason, I asked, 'Would you like to have a
child? Do you think we should have a baby?'

She looked quizzically at me, then gave a light laugh. 'Oh,
dear. Don't turn all conventional on me. We decided ages ago
about babies and marriage and so on. Besides, I'm too old.'

I walked over and put my hand on her shoulder. 'You're only
forty. Lots of women have babies in their forties.'

She laughed again. 'My darling, what in the world has got
into you?'

I pressed my face against her hair. After a minute I said, 'I
don't know. I think I just want to give you a present. To say sorry
perhaps, for all that Clive ordeal.'

'Our life is my present. In both senses,' she said.

*

Early the following spring, I was in London to promote the
Malaga novel when my mother fell ill and I was summoned to
Dublin. This did not surprise me. When Claudia and I were still
living in Ireland, my mother had shown a remarkable talent for
getting sick precisely when we were leaving on a holiday or for a
reading tour abroad. I had never known a mother so desperate
to rope an adult child to her side: always, or nearly always, an illness called me back just when I was about to celebrate some

aspect of my separate self, my writing self or my love life. Not that her illnesses were invented; nevertheless the timing was extraordinary.

And when Claudia and I made our new life on the Continent, my mother would become ill, sometimes going into hospital – not while we were at home, but whenever I was relatively nearby in England, in London to see a publisher, say, or to read at a literary conference. Of course this was extremely thoughtful of her, since swooping to Dublin from London was far easier and cheaper than a journey from faraway Spain or France. Once, her crippling headaches made the doctors fear that she had a tumour of the brain; another time she suffered such alarming pains in the region of her heart that they kept her in hospital for a week, just to monitor her. In fact she did have a genuine heart complaint, which would finally be her undoing. But while we were living in Paris, her doctor had phoned to report a stroke – the day before I was to fly to London for a book launch. 'Quite slight,' he'd said. 'On the other hand, you had better come over. It would do her good to see you.' Me being me, and her being her, I'd half-believed that I was to blame for this stroke, and also for the fibrillations of her fragile heart: I had forsaken her, and made her ill.

When Dr Nugent rang our Nice number this time, and Claudia called me in London, I groaned, 'Dear God, not again. What is it now?'

'Apparently the driver of a number ten bus was being rude to a black man – which your mother found racist and unacceptable, so she rose to protest. Only she fell back at once. "Blacked out," Dr Nugent rather coarsely said, in an unfortunate attempt at humour, I'm afraid. They think it's a fault in the brain.'

'She's done the brain thing already, Claudia.'

'I know, darling, but that's what Nugent thinks. A bleed, he said. A *slight* bleed. But, you know, it is the brain, after all, so they put her into hospital straightaway. They do think it's slight, I promise. She's completely lucid and in no pain now. Only it is the *brain*, so they must be careful. She'll be in hospital for a week . . . '

'And she'd *love* to see me. Why is it always a major organ? Why couldn't it have been her big toe this time?'

'Well, I'm afraid it does seem to be her brain . . . '

I felt bitter and angry, yet I would go. I would go because I was bound to her through duty and love, but also by this dark other thing. It was hard to talk, even to Claudia, about my mother's cruelty – although cruel she had been. Her reluctance to allow me even the humblest measure of ordinary freedom, her wounded silences and scalding reproaches, her harsh criticism of my character when I was only a child: these things had been meant to devastate me, to keep me fastened to her as a part of herself. And she had nearly succeeded, since her husband was dead and I was the only male in her life. Oh yes, I'd had to fight hard for my freedom, yet that very day I would travel to her.

And when I saw her, the terrible pity returned. She was so small, and frightened-looking, in the cold hospital light. And the way she brightened when I came into the room at once moved and angered me. Pity and anger and love; I pushed them all down and forced myself to smile.

Afterwards, grizzled old Nugent said, 'You know, it's probably nothing, but one never knows, and it would be prudent to keep an eye on her.' We were walking along the main corridor and he stopped abruptly, swivelling his head in a curious feral way and fastening his own rheumy eye on me. 'It's hard for her, you know, living all alone.'

Was I meant to feel guilty? I *did* feel guilty, but also annoyed. *Why don't you marry her then?* I thought peevishly, but what I said was, 'She has friends, Dr Nugent. And I can always fly over if I'm needed. But I have made my life abroad.'

He grunted, perhaps in rough sympathy, though I doubted it. More likely it was a censorious grunt: how could I be so self-indulgent, scribbling stories in the south of France while my poor mother endured phantom maladies in Dublin?

*

Well, presently I returned to London to resume my promotional tour. I half-expected to glimpse Clive's imperturbable face in the bookshop crowds, but he was never there.

As for my mother, she was not sick after all. But when I came home to Nice, Claudia told me that she had been feeling off form and so had gone to our doctor, who had given her very bad news indeed.

VII

Ursula was, as I had feared, perpetually hungry. Her favourite food seemed to be bread; she loved the *boulangeries* with their stalks of baguette; the blackened, rugged crusts of their *pains de campagne*; their vast ovens smelling of yeast and flour. Sometimes she'd volunteer to buy our bread, only to arrive back at the hotel with an empty sheath in her hand, since she'd eaten the whole baguette on her way home.

'It was warm,' she'd say apologetically, 'and it smelled like heaven.'

All day long, she went to and from the various local bakeries, so that she could munch croissants, brioches, *tartines au beurre*, pâté sandwiches, and bread and cheese, while working at her stories in the small bedroom. (It was I, of course, who supplied the money for these impromptu morsels.) And this was in between meals; she still managed to consume full lunches and dinners in that haphazard way of hers.

Yet she remained so painfully thin, I worried about her health. Anyway, it seemed to be a part of her character, this relentless eating that did not soften her jagged figure, or satisfy her need for long. Even so, food – especially bread – did appear to be her major need apart from writing.

We still slept together, reading our books, then putting out the lamps with an affable 'Goodnight'. But she never reached out to caress me, nor did I try to arouse her. It was a bizarre situation, but I had grown used to it, as I had grown used to regularly brushing crumbs off the sofa, the dining table, and the top of the television.

A few days after her first Trudy-and-Alice salon, she gave me another story fragment.

Because her friend, Joe, worked as a waiter in a certain bar, Maggie visited it often. And gradually Joe's friends among the other waiters, as well as Marco the barman, and the 'regulars' who drank there, started to accept her as one of their own. In fact soon they were welcoming her warmly when she sidled up to the counter, making sure she was served her usual drink of white wine, and asking her about Ireland, since this bar was in New York.

The bar part of the establishment was different from the restaurant, which extended out behind it. In the restaurant, rich young downtown types ate posh meals while pretending to be bohemian by dressing all in black. Sometimes sedate people from uptown visited the restaurant, but they looked out of place, as did the couples who had driven into Manhattan from the suburbs, and who seemed uncomfortable surrounded by all those cool, taut Soho-ites smoking French cigarettes. Joe and his colleagues expressed an airy scorn for all the customers, referring to them by table number: 'Isn't 18 a total bitch?' Or 'Jesus, look at E4; this is his sixth margarita.' The bar area was a world apart because, unlike the restaurant, with its air of studied cool, it truly was bohemian. Toby the local drug dealer drank there, and a jazz musician from Sweden called Christophe, and Isis the transvestite prostitute, and Kitty the female prostitute. Maggie liked to go there partly because she was separate, 'in' the world of the bar but not 'of' it. The place to her was nearly like a sea – swirling, dark – while she, an island, could observe everything.

These two paragraphs intrigued me; I continued to marvel at Ursula, who, despite being naive and virginal, had clearly ventured into lowlife New York. And it seemed that she had behaved like a real writer there, absorbing the inflexions and cadences of people she did not know, but whose lives she grew able, by and by, to imagine. In it but not of it, as she herself had written. And she might even have made good writerly use, within this fragment, of her solitary journey into Nice's 'night town'. She had been scared, when she'd ventured down to the promenade after our peculiar quarrel, but still she had managed to *observe*, like Maggie herself. Also, her style here was indeed looser, more lively, than in her account of the lovesick boy. More lively, perhaps, than my own style.

But the story also baffled me: once more she had shone a fitful light into the shadows of her own past: Dublin, Mexico, a lush garden in some American college town, and now New York. Where *had* she grown up, gone to school? I gazed at her one day as she moved through the suite, eating a ham sandwich. She glanced back with an insouciant smile, and I thought that while she looked frail, there was also something truly implacable about her. Yet when I remembered the American novelist who had apparently promised to read one or two of her pieces, I did not feel relieved this time, but jealous. If she really was gifted, then surely it was I who should be her mentor, especially after going to all the trouble of housing and feeding her? It would be extremely annoying if some interloping American tried to take the credit for polishing her, I thought peevishly.

*

One morning over the coffee bowls, in exchange, perhaps, for her fragments, I told her this little story of my own.

When Claudia and I lived in Dublin, I used sometimes to walk through Stephen's Green, especially in spring or autumn, when the light was a particular tender gold, and the children would play on the lawns or feed bits of bread to the ducks. There, I came to follow the adventures of a certain little boy whom I christened 'wee Charlie'. He must have been only five or six, with wondering eyes and loads of soft hair the colour of bog water. He came to the Green with his mother, a placid-looking young woman who wore spectacles and who would settle on a bench to read while he played.

Why did I find the child so arresting? He was certainly adorable, caught up in his webs of fantasy, talking solemnly to a leaf or a single flower in the grass, or to the small stuffed rabbit that he was always clutching. But I think the real reason for my fascination lay in this: although too young to be let out of her sight, he still seemed to fear that his mother might vanish if he didn't keep an eye on her. Every so often, he would look over his shoulder to make sure that she was still there reading her book (always a popular book with a bright cover, a film star's memoir or a romance novel). Or else he would scurry over to touch her arm, as if she were a talisman. And once, after playing for a while with two blond boys, he approached her breathlessly. 'I didn't see you,' he said in his piping voice. 'I didn't see you, for a minute. I thought you'd gone.'

She lowered the book, giving him her serene smile. 'Now, pet,' she said mildly, 'do you think I'd do that? Do you think I'd ever go away and leave you?'

He was silent, but then his face broke into a luminous smile. 'No, Mammy. I don't think you'd *ever* go away and leave me.'

He changed after that, asking his mammy for permission to accompany other children on their expeditions to feed the ducks, laughing and tumbling over the grass with them, like a puppy. It saddened me slightly: he was no longer the strange solitary boy, talking to the butterflies, weaving spells, with whom I had fallen in love. He was now just another healthy child playing with other children. He even abandoned the rabbit! But it was good for him, that much I knew. He had realised that he could be brave in the world, that he could carry his mother's love inside him. He need no longer touch her for a talisman; the talisman was within himself. It was grace that he was learning.

Of course I glimpsed the ghost of my former self in wee Charlie; I had also been a slight boy with bog-brown hair. Only my own mother had not tutored me in grace. I would have clung to her while she read on her bench, and she – ah! she – would have wanted it so.

Remembering that dream of my mother hovering over me while I played in Herbert Park, I said to Ursula, 'I used to imagine, as a child, my mother dissolving, the way a scarf of smoke will spiral up and up, to dissolve in the air. Of course, that fantasy terrified me when I was small, but now I wonder if I'd also secretly *wished* for it, wished for the wearisome bulk of my mother to finally dissolve like smoke and leave me free.' I paused. 'And now, in a way, she has, hasn't she?'

Ursula did not answer, merely staring at me, those vast eyes limpid with sympathy. I suppose my story was sadder than I'd thought. And of course Ursula must have been thinking of her own dead mother. How they madden us, our mothers, though I suppose most of us triumph naturally, simply by outliving them. Why had I continued to see mine as some large formidable thing, even after she had clearly grown frail and was preparing for death?

Suddenly Ursula said, '*Smoke?* She wasn't *cremated*, like? I mean, I wouldn't mind it myself, but Irish mothers of that generation . . . '

I began to laugh, perhaps too shrilly, for Ursula extended a *petit pain* across the table. I accepted it, though I was not hungry. Given her peculiar obsession, it made sense that she should try to console me with bread.

*

Thursday morning broke grey and chill, with a contrary wind that blew dust in everyone's face and made us all irritable, like animals with their hackles up. It felt like one of those winds with romantic menacing names, the mistral or the sirocco, except that it seemed to be blowing every which way at once. At my café, the locals stared gloomily at *Nice-Matin*, which declared that these terrible gusts were pelting us from the mountains, where snow had already appeared. (The *niçois* are not used to cold weather and complain elaborately when it comes, bundling themselves into overcoats and shuddering theatrically, even if the temperature has fallen just a bit. But these current winds, combined with squalls of rain, were in fact remarkably irritating. *Monsieur Bricoleur*, for example, was a louring presence at the bar, refusing even to say good day: very peculiar in a French café, where that ritual exchange of '*Bonjour*' and '*Bon appétit*', melodious as a dovecote, nearly always prevails. Even *La Belle* looked morose rather than saucy, perhaps because the weather had compelled her to wear regulation green wellies instead of her customary crimson high heels.)

I had come out to buy the *Guardian*, for which I had written a review, and a baguette for Ursula, since she had eaten only two *pains au chocolat* at breakfast and by this time was probably ravenous. When I returned, she called to me from the bathroom, where she was ruffling her wet hair with a towel. She had decided to go out as well, to buy some *jambon cru* and a bit of cheese for our lunch, along with a pot of *sanguins*, the delicious local mushrooms that are harvested in the mountains and marinated in oil and garlic. As usual, I wondered at her strange blend of thoughtfulness and tactlessness, consideration and selfishness. Of course I paid for the food; still, it had been kind of her to venture out to the *charcuterie* on such an inclement morning, and there was always something careful, even gentle, in the way she prepared our little meals. Yet she could be so irascible – and of course so greedy, devouring the delicacies she brought home with her own peculiar offhand gluttony – I supposed the only word for her was 'quixotic'.

We both seemed a bit despondent at lunch, probably because of the weather. Ursula kept sighing, and I was not inclined to talk much. Mainly we stared out at the rain-blurred garden. I realised, as well, that I resented having to tell her I would be dining out that evening. Why should I feel obliged to give an account of myself to Ursula? On the other hand, surely it would be discourteous to simply vanish?

I plunged in. 'Ursula, I am invited out to dinner this evening.'

Her pensive look changed to a smile. 'Brilliant. I can wear my new black dress. Is it Max and Léon?'

I was truly shocked – which was, of course, stupid of me. I was not too thick to realise that I had found, in Ursula, a version of my possessive mother. Hadn't Léon and Max suggested as much? Yet her intrusiveness still had the power to bowl me over.

'Ursula,' I tried again; then paused. Rain spattered against the window. 'Ursula, we are not attached at the hip. A friend has invited me to dinner. *Me*. Surely you don't think I am bound to bring you with me wherever I go? We aren't married. You aren't even my sister!'

Her face turned white, and her eyes, grown suddenly hard as obsidian, measured me, but she said nothing. On the other hand, I was beginning to feel nonplussed – once again – by her abrupt fury. I fancied that I could detect it not only in her face, but even in the air, which seemed to be darkening around her as if the clouds had come inside. And although I knew it was craven, my impulse now was to placate her. Perhaps my rebuke had been too blunt, too harsh, after all? I nearly extended a hand in apology, only at that moment she spoke.

'If you think . . . ' she said slowly. 'If you think you can just *shit* on the deep understanding between us, then you are more fucked up than I thought you were. You *chose* me. You *recognised* me, when we met in Ireland. I suppose you *do* remember how you touched me on the back, in praise, after I read my story in class, and how you would invite into your office for *private* talks? That day when you said, in an almost puzzled voice, "Why do you amuse me so, Ursula?" That was a *declaration*. And here in France you *welcomed* me and took me in. You know that I'm your best chance, Sebastian. And if you think you can take a spiritual connection, like the one we have, and simply *tear it up* . . . ' She drew a shuddering breath. I was feeling so tense that my temples ached. I also felt powerless to move or speak.

She went on, still in that level voice. 'Who the fuck do you think you are, with your twee novels and your affected manners? Do you think anyone takes you seriously any more? You write like a prim English schoolboy, or a *eunuch*, with all your sick-making flowery descriptions and your pretentious, unnatural dialogue. *Nobody writes like that any more.* Your prose has no *balls*. And neither have you.' She took another breath.

I should have said something then, but I merely kept staring at her, my eyes and mouth dry, the skin of my face tingling strangely. Was there an element of pleasure in my dread? Was I a masochist, at once breathless with fear and longing for the sting of this girl's lash?

'Don't let's forget,' she said. '*I* know your secrets, don't I?'

And then she said it, finally, the accusation I had half-consciously known was coming. I felt light-headed as the words slithered like a snake from her mouth.

'*I* know that you killed Claudia. You could have saved her, but you let her die. You let the woman you loved rot with disease before your eyes, didn't you? And no doubt you killed your mother as well. You didn't look after either of them. Your cowardice killed them both.'

Suddenly her voice changed, became offensively wheedling, a parody of baby talk. 'And we know your other little secret, don't we? Poor thing! We can't get it up any more, can we, poor thing? We have a young lady in our bed but we can't offer her a nice shag now and again, can we? Because we are secretly a *pansy*, aren't we? We're just a blithering *poufter*. Just like our fey, affected, glutinous little novels.' She spoke harshly again. 'No *spunk*. No fucking *balls*. Why, in a couple of years I'll be out-writing you *and* your whole boring gelded generation.'

For some reason, I focused on her choice of the word 'glutinous'. Why glutinous? Was she picturing congealed semen, or some kind of verbal porridge?

She fell silent. I realised grimly that the rain had turned to hail, which was making a loud clatter as it bounced off the shutters. A detached part of my mind hoped it would ease by that evening, since naturally I would prefer to walk through the labyrinthine streets of the old town rather than take the bus or a taxi. And I must remember to buy wine.

I rose stiffly, without looking at Ursula, though I could hear her heavy breathing, and walked into my bedroom, closing the door behind me.

I looked about with a growing sense of shock, almost terror. My room was altered. It had been changed, indeed soiled, by her presence. Her tattered Forster lay on the bedside table, alongside a pot of some unguent that she used each night to moisten her lips. The *femme de chambre* had folded her nightdress and put it on a chair. All so domestic and ordinary. She was here; she had come to live here, to leave these homely signs of her presence everywhere about. I had loved once, and afterwards I had made my careful life in these frugal rooms, with my books and my things for solace. In some way I had consecrated this little hotel suite, and my routines within it, to Claudia. Yet now I had let Ursula in, an impudent girl who meant nothing to me. But I had, of my own volition, let her in, and now her presumption of intimacy had become a real, physical, casual intrusion. Her nightdress, her pot of moisturising cream, her smell on the sheets. I had done it. I had let her in. I settled heavily on the bed, and stared down at my hands, wondering how, under heaven, would I ever manage to get her out?

*

I do not know how long I remained like that, staring helplessly at my hands, but presently the door opened and I looked up at a timidly smiling Ursula.

'I've been out again,' she announced. 'The rain has stopped, and the wind is dying down.'

'Ah, the weather girl,' I said dryly.

She gave a nervous, high-pitched laugh, clearly unsure if I was joking. Then, in a tentative voice, 'Sebastian, perhaps I might take myself out to dinner, since I'll be alone tonight? I mean, if you left some money in the bowl . . . '

'That's a sensible idea. I suggest you go to the little place with the funny murals. You know, where *maman* cooks and the shy son is the waiter. I'll book for you, if you'd prefer.' I heard my cold prim voice, and disliked myself. Though I certainly disliked her even more.

'Don't bother. I'll just play it by ear.' She continued to stand there while I said nothing, until, after a few moments, I heard her sigh and close the door.

*

The rain-washed sky glowed, and the stones of the old streets still shone, though now it was dry and fairly warm. In the *place* in front of the *Palais de Justice*, people were taking the aperitif outside, on the sprawling terraces of the three cafés – one of which was sedate and offered complicated ice creams, another of which appealed mostly to tourists, while the third was bohemian and raffish, with a hairy barman who served cheap, sharp wine. You could feel the presence of the sea just beyond the stone arcades.

As I walked, I thought of Claudia, could almost see her rising from one of the café chairs and moving towards me. All of *vieux Nice* was charged with her memory, and now my heart seemed to expand and I murmured *Claudia, Claudia* in a kind of paean and lament. Yet I was glad, too, that I had come here to see Julie, who had moved me as no one had moved me since the death of my beloved.

She lived along one of the narrowest of the narrow streets, in a very old, sagging, sun-scorched house. As I climbed up to her flat, I heard the cries of children, and a woman singing in *niçois*. Such things still happened there – people speaking or singing in the old language – and there were still some restaurants where the tourists never went, although those were rapidly vanishing.

Julie answered the door promptly; she had put her hair up, but bits of it were tumbling down in the attractively messy way that seemed natural to her. She was wearing a long black dress, which emphasised those wide-open green eyes, with their dark lashes. Ursula had dismissed her as 'middle-aged', but she looked young to me, or anyway ageless, though I supposed she was probably in her forties. It was just that a certain clarity about her, not just the smooth skin and bright eyes but something clear in her expression, made her age hard to determine, or else irrelevant, somehow.

She thanked me for the wine, and gestured me inside. The flat was surprisingly spacious, an airy room and a largish kitchen by French standards, with a corridor extending out to other rooms: the bathroom, no doubt, and a bedroom or two. A lovely painting hung above the sofa, of a woman in a translucent white dress standing on a sun-flooded balcony. It had been done, I could tell, by a fine local artist called Pierre, whom I had met at Alice and Trudy's. Generally, the place was modestly furnished and gave an impression of lightness, which was at variance with the romantically sombre façade of the house. There was lots of space for books.

Of course we seized on the weather, as nervous people often do. 'It hailed today!' 'Yes, and that bizarre wind!' both of us exaggerating our astonishment. I cannot remember most of what we talked about next. I vaguely remember the meal, which began with a plate of small things, artichoke hearts and roasted peppers, and *saucisson* with chunks of a hard cheese that she said came from Corsica. And then there was a stew, I think: veal or chicken. It was all very simple and pleasant. We drank her own bottle first, a red from Aix, and then moved on to one of mine. I sensed that we both wished to drink a bit too much, for our own reasons.

Raw from that day's exchange with Ursula, and without much repose, I preferred to talk about her. And she obliged, telling me that her parents, both university professors, had escaped to America through the intercession of academic friends there, just before the Second World War. But they had not taken to the States, perhaps because the war had so shocked them that they had grown into a cautious, insular couple, for whom adjusting to a new life in the New World had been just too hard. They'd had Julie when they were quite advanced in years. 'I remember them mostly as grey, anxious people, very tender but more like grandparents, really.' She paused, then went on slowly, 'They never stopped loving France, but they couldn't bear to live here after the war. So they retired to England when I was six, and I grew up in London, though France always called to me. Through their songs and stories, I suppose, but my own dreams as well.'

I observed, 'In some ways your story seems typically Jewish. I mean, your parents' love for Europe and then their flight during the Occupation, and finally your return. Yet you don't seem particularly Jewish.' She gave a soft laugh, and I amended hurriedly, 'The Jewish people I know here in Nice are generally intellectuals or artists, like your parents and yourself. But many of them give an impression of being more self-consciously Jewish, if you see what I mean.'

She considered. 'I am not a religious Jew or a Zionist or a

Bolshevik, those clichés people associate with Jewishness.' She paused again, then said emphatically, 'I am not ashamed of being Jewish. But I am not particularly *proud* of it, either. In fact, I loathe it when people display a jingoistic pride in themselves. It's very common in the States, isn't it? People declaring they are *proud* to be American. I am French and American and English and Jewish, all those things, I suppose. A happy mongrel.' She looked up and smiled. 'I love living here. It's a bit like Italy but very, very French. Don't you find you can work well in Nice?'

'I do,' I answered, trying not to stare at her. I was falling hard, plummeting down and down, a voice in my head saying, *I feel I have always known you. I love your messy black hair and your strong mind and the way you speak. I suspect you are a fine poet. I suspect you are the lady for me* . . .

She suggested we take coffee on the sofa. I was wanting more drink, and as if she had read my mind, she brought out a bottle of cognac and two glasses, along with the coffee things and a plate of petits fours. At one point, as we slowly drank the brandy (I taking considerably more than she) and talked of this and that, I realised that it would be all right to kiss her. So I turned and did so, gliding my hands up along her bare arms, and after kissing her lips and then finding her tongue with my own, I touched my mouth to her cheek and throat, and the top of her breasts above the dress. She was moving her hands through my hair, but then she lowered then to unbutton the dress so that I could caress her breasts, which were larger than I'd thought, and clearly excited by my ministrations. I was wild with desire for her, but suddenly I remembered my awkward secret – Ursula waiting for me in the hotel suite – and I drew back.

'Oh,' she cried, and made to do up the buttons, head turned away, a tendril of black hair falling across her cheek. But I placed my hands over hers to still them. 'Don't,' I said. 'You are so beautiful, and I want you so much. In fact, I think I am in love with you already. Please don't.'

So she dropped her hands and settled once more against the cushions, her face still, those green eyes large and intent. Her breasts were very white against the parted sides of the black bodice. I reclined beside her, and took her hands in my own and kissed them, and then I told her about Ursula.

When I had finished, she rose, smoothing her hair and doing up the dress. I stared at her back as she moved silently to the window, where she pushed aside the curtains and gazed out for a moment at the lamplit house opposite. Then she turned and spoke quietly. 'Sebastian, I think that you have put yourself in some danger.' She laughed dryly. 'I don't mean that this girl is a menace the way a large strong man might be. But she has encroached on you, and it may be dangerous. For you, and perhaps for her as well.'

She returned to the sofa, and I was relieved when she reached for my hand. I did not know what she would say next, but at least she was not recoiling in horror from my bizarre story. She continued, 'Perhaps I am too cautious. It is a legacy from my refugee parents. They were mainly gentle but also sometimes bitter and afraid. So I try not to be too much like them, convinced that the world is full of danger. But I gather that this young woman is something of a parasite, and therefore possibly dangerous.'

I said, with an attempt at flippancy, though her words had actually made me quite apprehensive, 'Do you think she might burn my manuscripts, or wreck the hotel room?'

'I don't know. But I meant emotionally dangerous. She doesn't seem to recognise the distinction between herself and other people. She seems to just want to feed off them. Or so I surmise. From what you've told me. But I don't *know* her, Sebastian. *You'll* have to decide what to do.'

I laced my fingers through hers. 'I do not feel that Ursula is my "care", in the Irish sense – meaning my charge, or responsibility. She doesn't *belong* to me in that sense; she does not belong to my heart.' I hesitated. 'Though I am moved by her. She has a certain courage, and I do think her gift may be real. But she doesn't *belong* to me, except that I have been her teacher, and should like to give her my blessing before sending her on her way.' I gave a dry laugh. 'But will she *go*? Will she go on her way?'

Abruptly, Julie asked, 'How is your own work going?'

I opened my mouth then closed it; I must have looked absurd, as if I were trying to impersonate a fish. But it was just that her question had thrown me off balance. I hadn't been working properly since that story about the garlic-eating boy. Still, I was used to fallow periods. Sometimes my imagination blazed after months of frustration, so why should the fact that I was not producing much material trouble me now, especially since I was bereaved? Though I thought that I knew what Julie was getting at. Did I unconsciously hope that Ursula's ambition would jump-start me back into a more fruitful kind of writing? Did I see her as a muse? More to the point, was I expecting her to counsel me again, as when she had rescued the garlic story, seeming almost to quicken it into life? Or was it simply that I had grown weary of myself, and had needed a change? Or perhaps I was deflecting an anxiety about my own writing into an absorption with hers, with those sometimes well-written fragments scrawled on foolscap. I had complained of her overly fierce devotion to me, but perhaps I was also exploiting her.

At that moment, an image of my mother floated, unbidden, into my mind, as often happened when I was thinking about

Ursula. My mother! From her reminiscences, and from photographs, I could picture the child she had been: a diffident girl, wanly pretty, but also somehow irritating, a bit *cringing*, bad at games and unable to speak up for herself when teased by other children. And once more I considered how she had decided that those things – her sensitivity, her shyness – had been a source of woe for her, and how it had followed that she would not, could not, endorse those very same qualities in me as my touchstone and my strength. She'd had to believe I was too frail for the world, as she was frail. She'd had to pity me. But had I also pitied myself? And did I pity Ursula now as my mother had me, as a form of protection against some hurt my spirit harboured for itself?

Instead of answering Julie directly, I said, 'My mother died recently. And coincidentally, so did Ursula's. I suppose my heart went out to her a bit.' I sighed, exasperated by my own weak-mindedness. 'Oh, I don't know. I really don't know why I've let her stay so long, except that she's not a bad cook, and her stories have potential, and she seemed so *helpless*, showing up at my door with nothing but a rucksack full of books.'

Julie gave a sympathetic smile. I squeezed her hand and said gruffly, 'You have told me a lot about yourself, your past, and I am grateful. I'd like to tell you things, too, or – well – one thing. I lived with a woman for a long time. Her name was Claudia and when she died, about six years ago, I thought my heart had turned to ashes. But now, with you, I feel that I am coming back to life. Does it scare you, to hear me say this?'

She shook her head solemnly. I continued with clumsy eagerness, 'Listen. Please let me see you again. *Soon.*'

She laughed. 'How soon?'

Recklessly I cried 'Tomorrow!' She touched my cheek and murmured, 'All right. Tomorrow. Come here again, and we'll go out to dinner?'

I brought her hands to my mouth and kissed them. Then I said, 'Julie, I'd like to borrow a book of yours. To read overnight, and also as a charm, to reassure me that you are real and that I didn't just dream you up.'

So she gave me a slim blue book of her poems. On her threshold I gathered up my courage, and promised that this 'Ursula mess' would be resolved by the following evening. I was really trying to say that I would not allow Ursula into my bed again – something I should have put a stop to long before tonight, Julie or no Julie.

'Oh, don't promise.' Once more her fingers touched my cheek. 'Please don't promise. You can't know. Just try, my dear.'

I was moved by her understanding, especially since my problem was fairly incomprehensible, even to me. I had been completely candid, telling her not only about our daft sleeping arrangements, but also Ursula's insolence, her sudden tantrums, her voracious appetite, everything. Yet I had not been spurned. So I promised myself that I *would* settle everything by tomorrow evening, not only for myself and Julie, but for Ursula, whom I should release from the crazy spell that she had thrown over us both.

VIII

For one and a half years after Clive left, we were exiled to a kind of netherworld of doctors' surgeries, hospitals and clinics, where lives are muffled in pain and waiting. But then Claudia experienced a reprieve, a 'remission'. Her hair had grown back but she was still keeping it short, in a kind of Jean Seberg crop that emphasised the lovely shape of her face and made her eyes seem even larger and more doe-like. Oh, she was beautiful all right, with the translucent beauty that in a certain class of bad novel invariably accompanies illness, as if afflictions like Claudia's were romantic instead of the truth – which is that they are shaming and evil. However, in that period, in her thinness and pallor and courage, she was in fact more beautiful than ever.

At that time, a married couple befriended us. They were from Australia, he a tall jocose fellow, altogether too loud, though bright behind the bluster; she a somewhat silly woman, concerned mainly with what used to be called the feminine arts, clothes and makeup and hairstyles, although she was bright as well. They were older than me, retired English professors who had bought a flat in the old town and who more or less fastened onto us after glimpsing us from time to time in the shops and cafés of our quarter. Myself, especially, they wooed, since they had taught my books at their college in Sydney. (On occasion, people who have read or lectured on my novels will go weak at the knees when they meet me in the flesh, as if delighted to find me still alive – surely all writers on university curricula are dead?) So it was with this couple; they were overly enthusiastic, gushing: 'It's *so* great to meet you, Sebastian, you are *such* a fine writer. You – and Claudia, of course – *must* come to dinner on Thursday . . . ' Et cetera.

They were sycophantic, possessive, though it took us a while to see this. He collected books, she was a good cook; they liked films. In short, we thought we had found kindred spirits. But slowly, obscurely, they began to let us down. At first it was just things they sometimes said – foolish or overly aggressive things. Then we gradually came to realise that they did not truly understand or appreciate artists; they did not, for example, actually bother to read most of the books that he collected. Claudia and I started to see, regretfully, that whatever rapport had existed among us had clearly come to its ultimate point and would develop no further. And if a relationship cannot grow, then surely it must founder?

Which is indeed what began to happen. Instead of relaxing, growing more expansive in their company, we found ourselves becoming increasingly guarded, fearing one of his angry pronouncements or one of her fatuous non sequiturs. Over the dinner or café table, while they talked on and on (always a bit too stridently), we began to exchange the glum looks of those who cannot make themselves understood and are giving up the effort. Yet the more we tried to discourage them, the more fiercely they clung, ringing us up the whole time, expecting to have drinks or meals regularly. One spring day, they asked if they could accompany us to Trudy and Alice's salon.

I was shopping when I heard them calling out to me. I turned slowly in the road, clutching my *panier de provisions* full of the usual things – a cheese, vegetables and a punnet of strawberries, bottles of olive oil and wine – and made myself smile.

'Hi,' said the husband, who was called Andrew. 'Nice day. How's Claudia? Lucy and I were wondering if we could come along with you to the flat of those ladies. You know, those literary ladies who have gatherings. How about it?'

'Um. Well, I don't know. I couldn't say, Andrew. Trudy and Alice would have to invite your themselves. It isn't really up to me.'

'That's okay,' answered Lucy confidently. 'We rang them up yesterday. Said we were great friends of yours. It's the day after tomorrow, right? We can all go together.'

'The brass neck!' Claudia exclaimed when I arrived home. We were putting the things I had bought into the cupboards and the fridge. I turned to see if she was genuinely upset or just mildly exasperated; ever since the Clive episode, I had promised myself never to dismiss her misgivings about people. But she caught my look and smiled. 'Not to worry. I mean, I suppose it's a fait accompli at this point. All we can do now is explain to Trudy and Alice that they invited themselves under false pretences. God, Sebastian, I'm starting to think some people get away with murder just because they're so brazen, everyone else is simply too flabbergasted to protest.'

'Or everyone else still has good manners. And good manners seem to be going out of fashion.'

'Darling, you've just put the red wine into the fridge. Don't worry; Trudy and Alice will understand. Anyway, good manners have been out of fashion for quite a while now.'

We continued to put away the food. But suddenly she stopped, cradling the wrapped cheese in one hand and a lettuce in the other. 'How long will it last, do you think?'

I looked at her, at the sunlight striking her cropped hair, the clear line of her cheekbone. I knew she meant neither the cheese nor the lettuce. 'I don't know. Perhaps forever?'

She shook her head slowly. 'Nothing lasts forever.'

*

Claudia said we might as well walk to the salon with Andrew and Lucy, since they wouldn't be sure of the way, but I put my foot down at this. 'They'll have to manage for themselves. If they come with us, it will seem we're sanctioning their intrusion. Trudy and Alice are probably already wondering who we'll drag into their lives next, after Clive and now these two.'

They were already there when we arrived, clutching bits of yellow cake and gazing around with the glassy, slightly wild look some people take on in the presence of 'celebrities'.

'Wow,' I overheard Lucy say to Andrew, 'there's Antoine something-or-other, the playwright. Shouldn't we go over and talk to him?'

So they made their way to where Antoine stood against a wall of books. He was wearing his habitual tender myopic expression: dear Antoine! Like many theatrical people, he was actually quite shy, and I saw him smile nervously at the approach of these people, to whom Trudy and Alice had not introduced him. Lucy said, 'Hi there. It's really great to meet you. We're Andrew and Lucy from down under, although we're living here in Nice now.'

'Ah,' said Antoine.

'It's really great to meet you,' Lucy repeated. 'You're such a famous writer!'

'Ah,' Antoine repeated. There was a silence. Presently he cleared his throat and said cordially, 'Is it my plays or poems you have read, or perhaps the stories?'

They both stood there, smiling. Finally Andrew said, 'Well, actually we're not – um – that well acquainted with the Russians. But now that we've met you, we'll be sure to read all of your books.'

'But only if you sign them for us,' Lucy shrieked coquettishly.

Claudia and I exchanged a look and went across to rescue our friend, who did not seem too perturbed after all; I supposed he was used to being gushed over at First Nights. Still, I considered it our duty to intervene.

Antoine clasped Claudia's hand. 'How is your health, my dear?'

She kissed him. 'Better. And how is your own health, Antoine?'

'Also better.' He gave her his sweet smile. 'We must have a party soon, to celebrate our improved health.' They looked at each other, and suddenly I feared that I might cry. Then Lucy said, 'Oh, *health*. Everyone talks about *health* these days. Homeopathic remedies and vitamins and herbs and spiritual therapies and so on: it's *boring*. Anyway, I think people are responsible for their own health. Like cancer. People bring it on themselves, in my opinion. They repress an emotion until it curdles up inside of them and they get sick.'

I had endured similar declarations from Lucy before. In fact, Claudia and I had privately christened her 'the Thought Police', since she had a way of expressing her opinions with such shrill vehemence that other people's responses buckled into silence. But never had I heard her make such an unfortunate faux pas as just now. We had not told her Claudia was ill, nor did she seem to know about Antoine's condition; nevertheless, surveying her foolish smile, all I could feel was deep embarrassment.

Antoine broke the silence, changing the subject in his calm

way, saying something innocuous. Anyway, Lucy and Andrew had begun to scour the room again and were barely attending. After a moment, Andrew noticed Katherine and tugged at Lucy's sleeve; she mumbled 'See you later' and they both plunged over to corner their new quarry. Looking on with dismay, I thought that at least they might be able to discuss Katherine's work with her, since she was a fellow antipodean; they had probably 'done' some of her stories in their Sydney university.

Antoine and Claudia were talking intently, so I left them to it and settled on the brown sofa beside the American consul, an extremely pleasant sixty-year-old man who belied Trudy's every harsh word about her compatriots. He bore the homespun American name of Wilbur C. Carver, and he was gracious, soft-spoken and very well dressed, with the elaborate good manners of an American gentleman of the old school.

He raised a finger to push up his spectacles from where they had fallen along his nose, and said, 'Good to see you, Sebastian. I very much liked that last novel of yours, the Spanish one.' He touched my arm. 'And Claudia is looking well, I must say.'

I tried to smile. 'Yes. That happens sometimes. There is a kind of respite, you know, and the . . . the patient looks blooming. We don't know for how long, in Claudia's case. But one hopes. One hopes and hopes.' I thought that I was talking in this honest way to Wilbur because he was American, with that particular New World forthrightness which invites a similar candour in others. Also, in the beginning we had asked him to find a doctor for her, since Claudia, along with Trudy, believed that Americans were admirably sensible about practical problems like health. And the doctor he found was indeed quite good, under the circumstances. Now Wilbur sighed. 'Ah, well, of course one hopes. Curious how so many people come here for their health.

Katherine, for instance, and Antoine, and that glum English writer, David something, the one with the hollow cheeks who lives in Vence.'

'Yes, I know the man you mean. A good writer, though a bit strict. I suppose consumption takes people differently. It has made Antoine more tranquil, I think, and Katherine, too, but it burns white-hot in David. He's so fervent and intent. Anyway, as we know, the Mediterranean climate is not always good for the health, despite its reputation.'

'Yes. That's the irony, isn't it? Antoine has been telling me how much *worse* he feels in the damp sea air. Yet they love it. We all love it, for the beauty of the place, and something magical, I guess, about this deep part of the world. Katherine was saying she doesn't notice that she's ill in summer, in her villa, with the vines and flowers and the golden light all around. My wife and I may come to live here ourselves, when I retire.' He gave a bashful chuckle.

We were silent for a while, drinking our tea and of course, as always, secretly longing for the booze to appear. James the black American novelist came in, wearing a beautiful blue shirt and laughing, his arms extended to greet everyone. He was an arresting presence, with his elastic face, out of which the extruding eyes shone. Wilbur murmured, 'And then there are those like James over there, and that sardonic English novelist who lives on Cap-Ferrat, and Trudy and Alice. The homosexuals, I mean, who felt constrained in their grey Northern cities. They can be themselves more easily down here, I guess.'

I could hear Lucy's high-pitched voice behind me, which compelled me to say, 'Just about everyone in this room, excepting Phebus and Babette, are not French. And only Friedrich and Antoine are not anglophone. I suppose we are mainly just a bunch of English-speaking francophiles who have left the grey

Northern cities you spoke of for the relative ease of life here.'

He spoke slowly. 'Although at a cost. Expatriates are more conscious, which is not always comfortable. You and I are perhaps overly sensitive to nuances in this society in a way that a native *niçois* would not be. We stand apart.' He gave his warm laugh. 'I include myself in this category, though I'm just a civil servant who goes where he's told. You, on the other hand, are a writer, and therefore used to standing apart and observing society – or so I imagine.'

'Do you ever miss America, Wilbur?'

Once more he laughed. 'Sometimes when I am out to dinner in Nice or Cannes with an entirely French group, I secretly wish for another American. Just an American man or woman to talk to. You see, at times I miss talking to people who grew up as I did, who have similar memories and would understand immediately certain things I might say.'

I told him about Trudy's letter, in which she mentioned her American past, impressions that were graven on her senses and her spirit, older than words. And Wilbur said, 'Yes, there is that. Also when I'm among Europeans, I sometimes miss people who cherish those famous American ideals. It's awful, isn't it? Believing in equality and freedom? It sounds so sentimental, but I was brought up to believe in equality and freedom, that they are possible. Anyway, we Americans are *supposed* to be all sentimental and earnest, aren't we? We would disappoint our European friends if we weren't.'

I laughed, and once more we fell silent. I had begun to ponder, while he spoke, his comment about writers, that they 'stand apart', and to consider how I had deepened my own solitude, had chosen not only to stand on the margins of my native world but also to become, literally, a foreigner. At that moment, Lucy spoke again, shrilling to someone behind us, 'Oh, yes, we *do* love

Nice. You get such good value for money here.' For the second
time that evening, I felt myself redden at her gaucherie, and
then, making a jump of associations, I wondered if my own
deliberate exile here really was, in some primal sense, driven by a
need to escape my mother.

For of course the pushy Lucy put me in mind of her, and
what I was feeling now was more than mere embarrassment. It
was a kind of revulsion, which that poor woman's silliness probably did not warrant. Anyway it was true, my mother had wished
to invade my most private precincts. She had at times exhorted
and at other times beseeched me never to leave her side, yet
despite my guilt I had come away. And when I had done so,
when I had lived first in our atelier in Paris and then in Malaga
and now finally here in old Nice, I had felt – still felt – free.

Or did I? How would I feel if Claudia . . . Here I halted. I
could not bring myself to think it, much less say it. Thankfully,
Alice appeared just then with a whiskey bottle in one hand and
a wine bottle in the other, causing myself and Wilbur to
exchange a smile of relieved complicity.

*

I kept remembering Trudy's comments in her letter, about her
American nephew, and I thought about other Americans whom
we knew, Wilbur and Alice and Henry M., as well as Lucy and
Andrew, who were also from the New World, though the other
side of the globe. I was trying to create a character.

Some of our New World friends adored France for its sen-
suous richness, how the eye and mind and body were delighted
every day, every hour, by the splendour of this older world. They
felt that France had changed them. And then there were the others who would not be changed, who seemed unable, as Trudy

had said of her nephew, to engage imaginatively with another country. It had become a cliché, the American tourist gazing stolidly at a European cathedral before saying, 'Our churches back home are just as big.'

So I wished to create a character, an American who comes to live in Europe, but whether he (or she) would be the defensive and suspicious kind, or the Trudy-Alice-Wilbur kind, I had not figured out. Over the days immediately following my talk with Wilbur, I decided that this character should be a woman, and I wrote in my workbook:

> She grapples. There is of course her involvement with America, her past, her parents, that sprawling Middle West which is at once familiar and foreign to her. How foreign she always feels when confronted with those plains, and those plain-spoken people! Yet she was born there, and while she may no longer call it home, it will always be a part of her.

I had written that paragraph almost automatically, and afterwards it dismayed me slightly. I thought that I could write with some confidence about New York, but I did not know the immense American Midwest. Yet something in me wished for this still-nameless character to come from that place. Perhaps I was thinking of Willa Cather, who had travelled from her home in the East to distant Nebraska? A few mornings later, I had settled to write in my study while Claudia worked at her desk in the bedroom. Again I was speculating on paper:

> One could start with either the lost Eden or the desolate place, either the verdant source or a barren cityscape. Perhaps that cityscape, the mean-mindedness which lies

behind it, a suburban shopping centre in all its tawdry glory, etc. Without yet knowing what it is or where it may lie, she thirsts for a richer source…

I paused, gazing out at the windows opposite while something, some frail thing, an image of this character, began to coalesce in my mind. I was ready.

Then there came a knock at the front door.

Wearing a yellow dress that swirled around her legs, Lucy walked in first, a hand extended in admonition. 'Stop!' she cried by way of greeting. 'Stop working at once. We must gossip about that lovely evening chez Trudy and Alice. Aren't those people delightful? We feel like we've made a whole lot of new friends, don't we, Andy?'

He had entered almost noiselessly behind her. 'Yeah, it was great. Thanks for inviting us.'

Claudia gave me just a quick glance but it was enough for me to register the near-panic in her eyes. Our apartment was not really open to casual visitors; we considered it to be an intensely private place, consecrated to work and to our intimate life. Perhaps it was selfish, but we cherished the morning hours of silent concentration, followed by lunch and a snooze, and then, in the changed light of afternoon, more work. Generally, no one called on us without an express invitation. Even Lucy and Andrew, in the earlier days of our friendship, when we were dining at each other's homes, had never blundered in unannounced like this. I presumed that their evening of hobnobbing with the literati had made them even more overexcited than usual.

'Would you like a coffee?' Claudia asked.

'Love one,' replied Lucy, settling on the sofa and arranging the folds of her yellow dress. 'You know, Claudia,' she continued, 'you look quite pale. You should get more air, should-n't she, Andy?'

Lucy and Andrew had the healthy, bronzed look of older people long accustomed to an outdoor life. But their skin, cured by the Australian sun, had also grown a bit leathery. Now, in unison, they turned their brown faces upwards to consider Claudia's complexion, and Andrew said, 'Yes, she should. She should walk on the beach more.'

They prattled on, though I barely listened to what they were saying. I was utterly distracted, still absorbed by my character, that woman from America who was taking shape in my head. And again I thought about what I had come to see as the two contrasting New World attitudes towards Europe: that which is bereft of curiosity, like Trudy's nephew and Lucy and Andrew. (And even though he was English, I supposed I would have to include Clive in this category, with his indignation at the French for speaking French.) As opposed to the attitude of Katherine and Trudy and Wilbur – those who felt that Europe in its wisdom and beauty had taught them how to live.

I remembered a man in a restaurant in Paris, an American eating dinner with his wife and her rather stern-faced sister at the table next to ours. Not one of them spoke a word of French, so Claudia had kindly helped them with the menu. 'It's really great to meet people who speak English,' the man had cried as Claudia explained *poulet rôti aux herbes*. He had seemed excessively grateful and relieved, as if the French voices encircling him in the restaurant were an aberration or even an affront. And then he'd gone on to describe his town in New England, how there was a singular attraction there: a nuclear submarine. 'People come from all over to tour inside it,' he had said. 'You should see the crowds. As many people as visit Notre Dame over here. Really, just as many.'

We had been silent then, though he had talked on and on, revealing his political views – which were appallingly, though not surprisingly, far to the right by our own standards. Meantime, the hard-faced sister-in-law had stared at us without speaking.

But I was also remembering the first time I had taught in the States, at a university in New York, and how the students there had been so ardent and bright. Intelligent young men and women full of promise, eager for life: through them, I had fallen in love with America.

So who – what – would my female American character be?

Andrew was saying that a mendicant, a young gypsy girl, had dogged them as they walked here, thrusting her grimy hands in their faces. Finally he had shouted at her, and she had melted away, 'as that lot do, once you blow them off'. It struck me that Andrew was a terrifically angry man. I wondered what his father had been like.

They had polished off their coffees and the biscuits that Claudia had served, and it was clear that they were expecting to be offered more. But Claudia, God bless her, gave them a smile as new-penny bright as their own and said, 'Well, thanks for dropping by. We've got to get back to work now, I'm afraid.'

Lucy gave her screeching laugh. 'Oh, of course. Do forgive us. We're just old retired people. We've been lazy for so long, we can scarcely remember what working feels like. Why, we could stay here chatting to you all day, couldn't we, Andy?'

*

Sometimes Claudia preferred to shop in the market up at Libération, in the quartier Malausséna, towards the north of the city. It was a different Nice, presided over by the corroding husk of the old *belle époque* station, and distinctly Italian in its atmosphere, with cavernous cafés and a little square with a fountain. One late Thursday morning, after walking up there to buy vegetables, we stopped at a brasserie in the avenue Malausséna for a pastis and to look at the passing crowd, as was the custom of shoppers in that district.

We were greeted at our table on the terrace by a marvellous fiction writer called Babette, a lady in late middle age with a mound of curly red hair and a theatrically painted face, chalk-white except for a circle of scarlet rouge on each cheek.

'Hello,' she cried in English. 'That Pernod looks delicious. May I join you?' Then in her rather histrionic way, waving her hands, she plunged into her native French. 'I must tell you about a decidedly peculiar phone call I received yesterday. Do you mind if I smoke?'

Of course we did not mind, and so from her elegant black reticule she produced an elegant black cigarette holder and a cigarette. After the small fuss of summoning a waiter to light it for her, she resumed, 'Most peculiar. It was an Australian lady. She rang in the middle of my working morning and gabbled on and on about how she and her husband had seen me chez Trudy and Alice. I could not recall an Australian couple chez Trudy and Alice and I told her so, but this, I am afraid, did not discourage her. She went on to inform me that she and her husband were "Sebastian Clare's best friends". And then she asked me to their apartment for dinner.' She paused, drawing deeply on her cigarette. 'I have no idea how she got my number. I assure you that I know neither of you gave her my number. Just as I know that you are not her best friend, Sebastian. She must have ferreted it out of someone during Trudy's soirée.'

As tersely as I could, I explained the identity of this mystery caller. I was embarrassed, and so, I could tell by her suddenly flushed cheeks, was Claudia. Babette went on, 'Do you know the most extraordinary thing? She wanted to engage me in a conversation about literature. She was an English teacher in her previous life, she said, although her discourse did not strike me as being particularly literate. Anyway, despite my attempts at a glacial silence, she proceeded to tell me all about my own short stories, and then she announced by way of conclusion, "Of course we all love the art of fiction, even though it is, as we know, basically a frivolous form." She actually said that: a frivolous form!'

'What did you answer?' asked Claudia, who seemed genuinely interested in how someone might try to counter one of Lucy's shrilly expressed and unfortunate opinions.

In a quiet voice, looking into her glass, Babette said, 'I told her the only thing I could. That there is nothing frivolous about fiction or any other art: no trickery, no self-regard or self-indulgence. That it is serious, utterly serious, and that when it works it is utterly true.'

I said slowly, 'It's weird, isn't it, how a former English teacher can be so vacuous about books, and express her rather silly views so passionately? She told us once that her father was a low-church Protestant clergyman. Perhaps that has something to do with it, coming from a world where strict notions of right and wrong matter far more than the life of the imagination. But the odd thing is, she isn't always like that. Neither she nor her husband. They can actually be clever and charming.'

'Pouf,' answered Babette, waving her hand. 'I found her neither clever nor charming, and I told her that I never dine out – which is of course a lie. Speaking of which, shall we three have dinner next week, before I return to Paris?'

So while Claudia and Babette discussed a rendezvous for the following week, I thought about Lucy and Andrew. They had told us in their forthcoming way that they were childless by choice. And like many childless couples, they seemed at times to be each other's children. Once when we were out to dinner and Andrew had grown surly, Lucy had murmured some tender thing and he had calmed down, and occasionally I had seen him temper her freneticism with an unexpectedly gentle word. And one Sunday morning not too long ago, I had been walking with Lucy and Andrew along the Promenade des Anglais, which had been crowded and festive-feeling in the exuberant light. Suddenly Andrew had stumbled before quickly righting himself, but I had been afraid that he would show a customary flash of anger at this betrayal of ordinary weakness amongst the children, young couples and cyclists who surrounded us. Only Lucy, clasping his arm, had smiled up at him and he had smiled down at her, a smile of full of rue and intimate knowledge – after which he had been all right.

I reflected now that if Claudia survived – this time I allowed myself to think it – we would probably be an elderly childless couple ourselves one day. And I hoped that we would be devoted to each other then, tactful and tender, that we would console each other for our increasing frailty, our diminishment, our fear of death.

And thinking these things, I could not condemn Lucy and Andrew for their pushiness, or at least not completely.

They did continue to press too much, to telephone nearly every day and to expect a long meandering chat each time, as if we had nothing better to do with our morning or afternoon than gossip with them. I felt harrowed enough by my mother's unceasing demands for telephonic attention without taking on Lucy and Andrew as well. Also my mother was my mother, and therefore a natural if annoying burden, whereas Lucy and Andrew we barely knew. Yet they remained oblivious to our dismay, even declaring every so often, as they had to Babette, that we were their 'best friends'. Or at least that I was. Clearly my name mattered more – which was a further source of dismay.

But no human being is simple, and we still glimpsed their other side. After weeks of declining invitations, we finally gave in and accepted their hospitality, strolling to their flat one evening for 'a quiet dinner, just the four of us', Lucy had promised. She had prepared an excellent meal, and instead of insisting on her opinions and crowding out other voices in her usual style, she was considerate, and her comments on books and films, and on life in Nice generally, were thoughtful. In fact she nearly glimmered with a quality that I had rarely if ever seen in her before: repose. And Andrew was so lively and droll that we were reluctant to leave. Finally, walking home late, our bellies full of good wine and Lucy's delicious food, we decided that we had been too harsh, had misjudged them perhaps. Claudia said, 'You know, Lucy's frantic manner and all that, maybe it's just her style. I mean, she may actually know that a lot of her comments are ill-considered. She may expect us to realise that saying aloud whatever pops into her head is just part of her nature. I bet she'd be appalled to learn that people take her prattle seriously enough to be offended by it.'

So we were once more well disposed towards them, as we had been in the very early days of the friendship, and the following week we invited them to our own flat for dinner. But the week after that, we received a card from Antoine. Generally his letter-writing style was as measured and contemplative as his discourse, and he had a beautiful hand. So the relative agitation, as well as the relative illegibility, of this message surprised us.

My dear Claudia, my dear Sebastian,
Yesterday evening, the Australian lady and gentleman who attended Trudy's most recent gathering called on me in my rooms. They wished, they said, 'to have a chat', and they

informed me that you had encouraged them to call on me in this informal way. I never (here something was crossed out) receive visitors in my hotel suite, which is a kind of sanctum. Also it is often untidy, since it is quite small and I like to work with all my papers and books about me, and at times to walk up and down the room, talking out loud in the voices of my characters. Moreover my tables and desks are forever cluttered with the medicaments that I am obliged to take for my condition: bottles and droppers and crumpled paper handkerchiefs and so forth.

I tell you these details in order to convey the intimate and vulnerable quality of my quarters and my habits of work within them. And to emphasise once more that I am always very, very reluctant to open my rooms to guests, to observe their eyes wandering hungrily over my working papers and my bottles of tablets or some personal garment that I might have thrown over a chair. Even in Russia I never held 'at-homes', nor was I inclined to attend those of others. Yet when the couple from Australia appeared at my door yesterday, I felt that it would be unseemly to turn them away, especially since they are your friends. I did manage to persuade them to leave after a cup of tea, but I remain afraid that they will disturb my privacy again.

I did not believe them for a moment when they said you had encouraged them to call on me, but I think you should be aware that they are exploiting your names in this fashion. And since I do not know them and feel quite helpless in the face of their bold conduct, I must ask you to please intervene on my behalf. Dear Sebastian, dear Claudia, please ask the lady and gentleman in question to desist!

Fondly, Antoine

This time I was not only embarrassed but furious. There was something about Antoine – his tenderness, his Old World manners – that made Lucy and Andrew's intrusion into his private sanctuary seem more serious than mere impertinence, more like a violation, a real soiling.

Also both Claudia and I were appalled by their unconscious humiliation of themselves, how they were letting themselves appear as buffoons. Babette, Trudy and Alice had endured their grinning and fawning, as well as the aggression that lay poorly concealed beneath, with a certain sang-froid. But they had also been astonished by the sheer social clumsiness of Lucy and Andrew, finally dismissing them as figures of fun. Only since they were, in fact, unconscious of their exposure of themselves, it was Claudia and I who bore their humiliation for them. It was our cheeks that burned with consternation when Babette or Antoine told of another importunity; it was we who suffered, since they did not suffer, were too cocooned in each other, too childish or narcissistic, to register the effect they had on others. 'It is,' I said glumly to Claudia, 'time to call a halt.'

I wondered how to go about calling this halt. I could write a wintry letter, or, for that matter, a mild though strict letter. I could telephone, or arrange a rendezvous in a café, as we had done with Clive. I realised that Andrew would probably be harder to handle than Lucy. She was, to put it unkindly, a bit of a fool. But Andrew was an angry man. Sometimes he showed this anger in sudden, jagged flashes, like a lightning storm. Other times he said something nastily provocative, or genuinely vicious. In other words, he could be extremely unpleasant in a macho, blustering way that I found tiresome. And I did not want him, or his wife, to trouble Claudia with either invective or tantrums, since she had enough problems of her own these days.

Speaking of Claudia, I supposed I had half-unconsciously

hoped that they would be surrogate parents for her. Her own parents had died years before, so that in her time of crisis she'd had neither a maternal breast on which to lay her head, nor a good father to protect his little girl. I'd been there for her, of course, as had her sister in Dublin, and our friends in Nice. But since Lucy and Andrew had no children of their own, and Claudia was just the age to be their daughter, I'd imagined that Lucy would mother her a bit, and that Andrew would offer her a paternal sort of affection.

Only of course that hadn't happened. Lucy, who had never quite grown up herself, seemed to regard Claudia as a kind of sister or school pal. She loved to sprawl on her sofa and gossip about the celebrities she had read about in *Hello!* magazine, or the new makeup tricks she'd seen in that month's *Vogue*. Claudia herself did not wear makeup; in fact she referred to it, rather endearingly, as 'paint', in the manner of her mother, who used to say things like, 'Mrs O'Flaherty's daughter paints too heavily'. She had looked at *Hello!* once, in her doctor's waiting room, and afterwards had declared that it was more nauseating then the chemotherapy. As for Andrew, he often spoke condescendingly to Claudia. Actually, on occasion he also spoke condescendingly to me, as if anybody who scribbled stories for a living couldn't possibly be a serious person. Yet they had taught English to university students!

I still felt sorry for them. The day after we'd received Antoine's card, I glimpsed them trudging through the *marché aux fleurs* in their outback hats, and I thought they looked horribly out of place, yet plucky for all that. How far they have travelled, I said to myself, and how brave they are, after all, to have made a new life on the other side of the world.

By the following Sunday, we had not yet figured out how to suggest they should cool their overheated engine, and back off a bit from us and from our friends. That morning we were shopping in the Cours Saleya, which was quite thronged with both locals and tourists. Bees hovered above those cunning marzipan fruits – peaches and plums fashioned from almond paste – which always made my lips pucker as I imagined filling my mouth with their terrible sweetness. We had stopped under the awning of the Corsican butcher to buy some of their extraordinary *saucisson* made of *sanglier*, or wild boar. But mainly we were lingering in the humbler part of the market, on the square behind the cafés, where people from the mountains displayed unkempt yet delicious vegetables along with new-laid eggs of various sizes, and simple cheeses made from the milk of sheep or goats. We were examining an enormous wine-coloured artichoke when suddenly we heard Lucy's voice, raised in argument.

'I didn't break that egg! You broke it,' she was screeching at a woman selling eggs and cheese at a nearby table. The whiteness of that table, along with the woman's white coat and her white porous cheeses and bowls of eggs, gave her entire stall the look of a pantry; I almost expected to see crocks of milk, as on an old-fashioned Irish farm. The woman was listening patiently as Lucy carried on. Finally she answered calmly, 'You break egg, madame. I no break egg.'

'Of all the stupid things! What do you expect, when you put something as fragile as eggs into a bag? Haven't you people ever heard of egg boxes?'

At this point a man in a beret, a mother with two small children, three Arab boys and a couple of Italian-looking tourists had positioned themselves beside Lucy and were grinning from her to the egg lady and back again.

'You buy eggs. You pay,' said the egg lady, arms akimbo.

I wouldn't have thought it possible for Lucy to raise her voice an octave, but she managed it. 'I will not pay! Of all the nerve! Do you hear me? I will not pay for your foul old eggs!' I guessed that she was quite unaware of her own play on words.

Claudia had left my side to stand beside her. 'Calm down, Lucy,' she murmured, touching her shoulder. Lucy turned, wide-eyed. 'Claudia?' She seemed slightly abashed. I supposed she had thought it acceptable to spend her fury on a simple woman from the mountains, only she had not considered that someone she knew might overhear.

Claudia said, 'Did you not know, Lucy, that these people gather the eggs when they are very, very fresh, and then they carry them down here to sell? It's all they have, really, things like eggs, and plain cheeses made from the new milk of their goats, and the fruits and vegetables that they grow. Even egg boxes are too expensive for them. One can save one's own old egg boxes and bring them here and she will fill them. But these are poor people.'

Lucy stared at her, pink-faced. After a moment she cried, 'Well. In Australia we wouldn't let our farmers scrape out such a poor living! We would provide for them. We would . . . ' She faltered, glancing wildly about at the people who had gathered to observe her, and at the egg lady, who was gazing at her with an expression of almost scientific interest. 'We would provide them with egg boxes! Free egg boxes!' At this she wheeled round and stomped off, looking, in her shorts, like an angry Girl Guide.

Claudia bought Lucy's six eggs, including the broken one – which was not really broken at all, only slightly cracked (like Lucy herself, I thought). And I blushed to think that these eggs cost only a few centimes, which would mean nothing to Lucy, so I asked for six more.

After that incident we concluded that it would be impossible to simply temper the friendship, to withdraw a bit without rejecting them utterly. Andrew was just too full of spleen, while Lucy was too hot-headed and profligate with her silly tongue. So we became determined to break with them, although we did not phrase the matter so brutally. I merely rang them up on the Monday, and when Andrew replied, I told him as gently as I could that perhaps he and Lucy were pressing too hard, presuming a solid friendship with myself and Claudia when in fact we didn't know one another very well. I said something oblique about Claudia feeling ill these days and needing privacy, and then I explained that I, too, savoured my private life and my work – on which they were, alas, intruding. Finally I observed, 'I suppose, Andrew, that friendship, like love, is quite mysterious. You can't force it.' I hoped I wasn't sounding too pompous.

I never learnt if he considered my little speech pompous or not, because he rang off without a word. But the next day we received a highly emotional phone call from Lucy, who declared that she and Andrew had been betrayed, and could not credit why their best friends had behaved so heartlessly.

Anyway, they did desist. We continued to see them shopping in the old town or strolling by the sea, but they cut us every time, marching past as if we were invisible. At first we tried to speak to them, but by and by we simply let the thing drop. Sometimes I felt relief that they were no longer clinging to us. But at other times I felt a tremor of regret. I would glimpse them walking along, swinging their shopping baskets and laughing like much younger people, or standing tenderly, arm and arm, on the Quai des États-Unis and gazing out at a ship in the distance. Who were they, after all? Stalkers, or just a rather lonely, rather gauche couple who felt out of place in a new country and were trying – a bit too hard – to make friends?

But they did leave Trudy, Alice, Antoine and Babette alone, too – which was an unalloyed relief. Then after a few months, they seemed to have disappeared. We wondered guiltily if they had gone back to Australia, but Babette stumbled on them one day in Antibes, where, they explained, they had bought a flat in the anglophone enclave beside the harbour. We wondered if they were happier in that British hothouse, just inside the walls of Old Antibes, surrounded by fish-and-chips shops, restaurants serving roast beef and Yorkshire pudding, English pubs, English newsagents, and English voices everywhere. (For Graham Greene, the only sanctuary in that quarter had been Chez Felix: a rather dilapidated café with indifferent food, but at least his compatriots never went there.) As for Lucy and Andrew, we would never know if they were more content in their new home, since we never saw them again.

*

Late spring the same year, Claudia observed one day that I had 'charm'. She did not say this to either flatter or reproach me; she stated it as a fact. At first I was startled. I believed that I was too old-fashioned and serious. 'Charming' was not a term I would have applied to myself. But on reflection I began to see what she meant. Something about me, perhaps a kind of bashfulness, attracted people, or at least certain people. And the problem with charm is that you can't really control it. You are bound to attract admirers you do not want, and to be confronted with the fact of their unwelcome attachment, and even to be told, now and again, that you had 'led them on'.

If I'd realised that I had charm, perhaps I would have handled Lucy and Andrew better, given them certain signals at the beginning of our peculiar friendship, as well as all along the way – signals which would have kept the boat of our

relationship from capsizing altogether. I concluded that I was
not very good at establishing 'boundaries' – that fashionable
term which seems to be on everybody's lips nowadays.

*

In May, an incident took place that confirmed my view of myself
as being poor at boundaries. It was a beautiful May, hotter than
usual. The tourists had appeared in their pastel finery and were
getting fiercely burnt. In truth they looked like iced cakes with
cherries on top, compared to the natives, who were continuing
to wear dark clothes and avoid sunburn, like sensible people. At
this time, Tobias, my very rich Dublin friend, descended on us
with his young wife.

He was tall and haughty-looking, and because his mother
was Moroccan and his father an Irish merchant prince, he was
handsome in an exotic way, with pale skin and black eyes and
fine eyebrows like black wings. His new wife, called Olive, was
also a sultry presence, with lavish dark hair and a drowsy smile,
but Tobias was not behaving well towards her. In fact he was
being overly gallant to Claudia, almost seductive, as if to taunt
Olive, and when we took an aperitif in an outdoor café he always
praised the passing women too volubly, again as if to deliberately wound his wife. And once, in a restaurant, after admiring a
lady in a chic black frock, he turned to Olive and said, 'Why can't
you learn how to dress?'

She tolerated this for a while, smiling her sleepy smile, busy-
ing herself with cigarette and lighter, saying nothing or almost
nothing. Then, by the third or fourth day, she began to flirt with
me in an arch, hectic way. Clearly she was trying to exact some
revenge on Tobias and also to save her pride, so I did not discourage her, although I could see that her exaggerated coquetry

was making Claudia uncomfortable. Anyway, the dinner table was becoming a very tense place, with Tobias ignoring Olive and flirting with Claudia more and more ostentatiously, and Olive beginning to smoulder wildly, to drape herself over me, caress my chest and bridle like a cat.

Their final evening, we were having dinner in a small restaurant close to the Port of Nice. As usual, Tobias was focusing all of his considerable charm on Claudia and ignoring Olive. Suddenly she rose from the table, came over, settled on my knee, and put her arms around my neck. I supposed that I couldn't push her to the floor, but the idea did occur to me, for we were still at our first course, and mine was a delicious seafood crêpe, which I wanted to eat before it grew cold. Also by this point, I had grown thoroughly bored by both herself and Tobias. 'You should visit me in Dublin,' she was murmuring into my ear. She had pressed her rather lovely upper body against mine. 'You seem tired, Sebastian. You should come over and visit me. I would look after you.' And she gave her slumbrous smile.

I said something neutral, I suppose. Presently she returned to her place and finished her meal, laughing softly to herself as if she had triumphed at some game that only she had been playing. Tobias remained indifferent, while Claudia drank too much – which was unlike her – and barely spoke to anyone – which was also unlike her.

When we got home, she asked in a tight, angry voice, 'Why did you let her do that? Why did you let her? When Tobias behaves in his disgusting way, I try to diffuse him and to be courteous to her. But you allowed her to almost make love to you in public.'

I sighed. 'I've seen this before. Tobias can be so cruel to women. He slights them or ignores them, and eventually drives them so wild with humiliation that they go a bit mad and try to make him jealous. I felt sorry for her.'

Claudia stiffened, and I thought that with her cropped hair and flashing eyes, she looked like Joan of Arc. 'So you were considering her feelings, were you? What about mine, then? Why were you considering her humiliation above mine?'

I thought a lot about that question. And finally I felt grateful to Tobias and Olive, because their outlandish behaviour had helped me realise something. The point was not that I had considered Olive's bruised feelings above those of Claudia. The point was that I had let her down by failing to consider the public face of our love. I realised that at some point in their life together, every couple must decide how they wish to present their relationship in public. It is part of their compact, the social part. Even if they do it almost unconsciously, in some way they must determine how to declare their alliance to the world. I thought that if I had understood this earlier, I would have done a better job of controlling people like Clive and Lucy and Andrew, as well as Olive.

And a year before, an ostensible admirer, an Englishman, had begun to send me loads of my own books to sign and return to him. His letters oozed gratitude and humility, were in fact almost nauseatingly obsequious. But behind that deferential display, he was as cheeky as they come, posting those awkward piles of books, all of which he expected me to sign, package up again and send back. He could have been selling them, for all I knew, although he kept assuring me in his letters that he cherished each signed copy since he was my 'most devoted reader'.

When he proposed to fly to Nice just for one day, in order to meet me and shake my hand, I finally said no, writing back that he was not welcome as we were very busy, very private people. Moreover, from now on would he please refrain from sending me books? He obliged, posting neither any more books nor any more cringing letters, but I must confess that once again it was Claudia who had insisted I put a stop to his excesses, who had begun almost to fear him. And over the years there had been other stalkers, people who would travel to every reading I gave, even if they were not enthusiasts of the novel. They were drawn to my fame or to my 'charm', I suppose. Anyway, I was never all that good at dealing with them. On the other hand, Claudia (who had far more beauty and charm than myself) had always been very adroit at gently letting down overweening admirers.

Why could I never seem to learn from her example?

*

That August we went one day to Carros and St Jeannet, mountain villages where the houses seemed to clamber up the slopes like sheep that had turned to stone. The weather was not too hot, and the narrow roads were quite still, nearly empty of tourists despite the season. I invariably felt, in these hill villages, the real Provençal lore, as if the very air were freighted with those ancient legends of heroes, maidens and dragons. We strolled through St Jeannet at dusk. The lamps had just come on, and a smoky gold light burnished the houses like the glow inside a church. We took a meal at the hotel there, despite the fact that Trudy had told us she knew they put cat food in the pâté. Over coffee Claudia said, 'What a lovely day we're having, everything so rich and lovely. And these flowers look so brave, how they seem to burst from the sides of the houses.' She paused then said simply, 'I am not ready to die.'

But a month or so later, her health began to decline again. When she died, we had been four years in Nice. Trudy and Alice arranged a small memorial service and then I flew back to Ireland with her ashes for the funeral. I had successfully repelled my mother from visiting; Nice was the one place to which she had not followed me . Yet when I saw her in Dublin, I was grateful to her. And she mustered some dignity as well as compassion, and comforted me then, and in some ancient place in myself I had needed this, had called out *Mother, Mother* in my distress, although I had not even known I was doing so.

*

My novel about the American woman, Jenny Smith, appeared three years afterwards. Henry James once said something about how only an American can become a true European. So my Jenny spends most of her childhood in England and on the Continent with her diplomat father, and is therefore fashioned into a kind of European early on. As an adult, she continues to love the richness, the diversity, of Europe, the various languages and literatures, the medieval villages of Provence, the Moorish opulence of Spain, the wild bustle of Italian streets, the serene loveliness of English university towns. 'Such accumulated beauties', in the words of Edith Wharton. Most of all, since she is an aspiring painter, Jenny loves the various styles and genres of art and architecture in Europe.

Back in the States, as a young woman at university in Boston, she is disappointed by what she considers the uniformity of her native country, its absence of accumulated culture and society and history. She finds life there flat and shallow, although her younger sister (whose memories of Europe are dimmer) adores the sense of possibility, of opportunity, which America embodies for her.

Later, when Julie told me about her parents, their flight to America, and then their return to Europe and her own homecoming to France, I thought about Jenny Smith, although I did not speak of the book. It was one of my most popular novels, and also a kind of private touchstone, since I struggled to produce it through a period of almost unendurable grief. In fact I remember very little of that time. What I recall most clearly is that Trudy helped the most. She concluded, quite rightly, that I could no longer live in our flat, or anywhere in Old Nice. It was she who found the hotel and more or less ensconced me there. In the course of *Jenny Smith*, the heroine's husband dies, and afterwards she finds some solace in life on the Côte d'Azur. In this way, I wrote out my story and leavened some of my grief, although it will always be a part of me.

IX

When I arrived home, Ursula had still not returned from her solitary meal, or wherever it was that she had gone afterwards. But she had left another story fragment on my pillow.

Isis, the transvestite prostitute, and Kitty, the female ditto, walk into the bar. Kitty groans, 'My feet are killing me.'

Isis says, 'Honey, if your feet are killing you . . . I mean, Jesus.'

Isis is tall, even for a man, and sinuous and beautiful, with very black skin and sherry-coloured eyes. Each one of her gestures is lissom and feminine. Only her height and her voice betray her.

Now Kitty sighs, 'I'm so hungry, I could die.'

A long-haired man, who has actually walked in with them, produces a bag of sweets. 'Oh, you darling!' cries Kitty, selecting a candy wrapped in silver paper.

'You know I like those caramels,' declares Isis, choosing one from the bag. The man says glumly, 'You should be more careful, you girls, the shit you eat.' He narrows his eyes at Kitty. 'You especially. How old are you, anyhow?'

Isis says to Maggie, 'Will you listen to this man? He is

a smack junkie, and Kitty and me between us are fucking this entire city, and he thinks sugar will kill us.'

Once, at about four in the morning, after the bar had closed, Isis invited Maggie up to her apartment in the East Village. It was just an ordinary New York flat, pretty shabby, actually, and not very clean. But Isis said, 'Come, honey, look at my clothes!' Then she threw open the door of her wardrobe, and it was like a dream, lovely dresses billowing outwards as if a wind surged behind them: taffeta ball gowns; crinolines; dinner, tea and cocktail dresses; embroidered shawls. And the colours: emerald, magenta, violet, shiny black and dull black, patterns of flowers and peacocks, and swirls of sequins.

Kitty asks for a gin and tonic. She must be only seventeen, maybe even younger, although Marco lets her buy drinks. Maggie remembers herself at seventeen, an earnest student in Dublin, clumsy and shy, afraid of boys. But Kitty is like a myth, like Aphrodite or the Sirens, with her wonderful hair and knowing eyes. Yet what do they know, those world-weary eyes in the very young face? Maggie thinks they can follow the threads that quicken invisibly in the air, the strands of yearning and desire that connect us, each to each. Sex, she means. She, Maggie, understood nothing about sex, its promise and power and danger, until recently. But poor Kitty knows everything; she is like a myth, only it doesn't seem to be serving her all that well.

Christophe comes in, and calls for a glass of white wine, like Maggie. She tells him that he looks pale and distracted, and he explains that his mother is coming to visit the following day. She's seriously crazy, he tells Maggie. She's convinced that the Bulgarians (why the Bulgarians?)

have encircled her brain with a kind of mesh through which they manipulate her thoughts; they do this with computers. He laughs a little.

Then he says, 'There are about ten homeless people living on my street. Tonight, when I was coming here, I saw one of them, this very fat man with a red face, standing up against my building and crying like a child, you know, with those loud gulps, the way little children cry. And he was peeing at the same time. So there he was, sobbing like a child, with the tears streaming down his face and the pee pouring down his leg. I offered him some money but he said, "No, no!" So I gave him a cigarette instead. And he said, "Thank you", still crying and peeing.'

Maggie remembers that once, a few months ago, she went to a late-night party at a downtown club. Walking out of that strident place into a soft drizzle, she realised dawn had broken; the rain looked like shards of glass against the pale street lamps. And then she noticed three homeless people crouching up against the wall of the club, all three bundled into loads of shawls and sweaters. They each extended a hand to her, three grimy hands reaching out in unison through the light rain. She looked at the hands and then at their faces, and saw that they were a family: a bearded man, a woman wearing glasses and a girl of about nine. She gave some money to the little girl, then returned and worked on a drawing for five hours straight, without stopping to eat or sleep. When she was finished, the drawing was full of faces; it could have been Calcutta, but it was home.

*

I knew I must wait up for her tonight, but I was growing quite tired. Finally she appeared, standing tentatively at the bedroom door, an echo of that afternoon, when she had stood there smiling despite her savagery of only a short time before.

I looked up from the side of the bed, where I had settled to read her manuscript. I was rather touched to see that she had put on the black dress after all, as if she'd been determined to make a celebration of her lonely evening. I said, 'Your new frock does become you. It makes you look pert, like an elf.'

She grinned. 'Thanks. Only that's all right for *now*. It's grand for *now*, looking like an elf. But what about later, when I'm old? Can you imagine an old, wizened elf?'

'When you're old, you'll be a distinguished, literary, elderly elf.' We both laughed. She did not hesitate before walking into the room, but of course she considered it *her* room now.

'Where did you go tonight?' I asked gently.

'To the restaurant with the funny murals, like you said. The son was surprised when I came in alone. And he kept calling me *Madame*.' She gave a half-proud, half-sheepish laugh. 'I suppose he thinks you and I are *married*.' A pause. 'Then I walked a lot. I had thought I might ring up Noel. You know, the American novelist. But my heart wasn't in it.' She plucked an invisible thread from her sleeve. 'I kept thinking I should be with you. That whoever you were with, it couldn't be as nice as if you and I were together.'

How childlike she is! I thought. Even her outbursts were like the tantrums of a child – except when they were all too full of an adult cunning. I touched the pages on my knee. 'Thank you for leaving me this. It's very good indeed. Funny, too. If you finish the story, I'd be glad to try to place it for you. Ursula, you have learnt something essential, something that eludes most young writers. You have learnt to avoid writing solely about yourself. And the dialogue is really excellent.'

She stood over me, smiling. I was pleased to make her happy, considering what I would have to say next. I paused before speaking bluntly, 'Ursula, I'd like you to sleep in your own room tonight.' Even this was an inaccuracy. The second bedroom was not *her* room, but merely a temporary billet I had offered when she'd appeared, looking so helpless, at my door. I waited for her face to cloud over, but she only gazed at me, though her smile vanished.

'I think we must talk about what you will do next, as well. You are getting better and better as a writer, which is splendid to see, and you seem to really like French life, so you may wish to stay, at least for a while. But you are also in flight from guilt over your mother's death, and perhaps from other things, perhaps from your own life. Only you cannot escape forever, especially if you wish to be a real writer. Nor can I be your refuge forever. I will help you with your work, as much as I can, but my dear, soon you must move on.'

She lowered herself heavily beside me. Tears were clustered on her lower lashes like little seed pearls, but she spoke clearly. 'Don't send me away, Sebastian. Don't forget how you chose me out of all your students. You chose me because we have an *understanding*. Nobody understands your novels like I do. When I first read them, I felt that you were speaking directly to me. And our life here together is so good, and you paid for my lovely haircut. Don't betray me like the others.'

I resisted an impulse to ask who 'the others' were. Probably her parents and brother, and the Dublin playwright. Sighing inwardly, I regarded her forlorn face. Once more she had managed to fluster me, this girl who could inspire affection, exasperation, revulsion and pity all in a single day. I had thought she would turn into her dragon self tonight, but instead she was looking like one of those sentimental pictures of street urchins with enormous eyes that one sees in the *brocante* sales along the Cours Saleya.

Suddenly she stood, walked over to my small table, and examined Julie's book, which was lying there. 'Poetry,' she murmured. 'I'd never bother to write poetry. It isn't *ample* enough. Though it can be nice to read. Sometimes.' She returned to the bed and asked abruptly, in a low voice, 'The woman who wrote that book, Julie Simon, is she the person you had dinner with tonight?'

I corrected her pronunciation of Julie's surname, then said simply, 'Yes.'

Once again she did not scowl or deride me, as I would have expected. She merely stared, head tilted slightly, in that blackbird way she sometimes had. I suddenly remembered a novelist pal of mine, more an acquaintance really, a saturnine man who had started out in journalism and to whom a certain sardonic journalistic attitude continued to cling. (You could nearly see a ghostly raincoat thrown over his shoulders, and hear the clamour of a phantom newsroom behind him.) One night the year before, during my Trinity term, I'd called on him at his flat in Rathmines, where we had stayed up late, drinking whiskey and smoking his terrible cigars. Discussing a friend we had in common – an accomplished, middle-aged poet – he'd said, 'You know, old Gerard is getting married, finally.' I had laughed incredulously, because 'old Gerard' had been a confirmed bachelor and libertine. But 'Don't laugh, Sebastian', my friend had said, chasteningly. 'The girl is very pleasant. Much younger than Gerard, of course. She began as one of his groupies, then moved on to girlfriend, and now onwards to near-wife. Quite an interesting young woman.'

My friend's description of this shadow-girl had disturbed me.

I had been shocked to hear her described, indeed praised, exclusively in terms of the man who, it seemed, had 'chosen' her from amongst what was presumably a throng of acolytes, aspirants or 'groupies'. And the account of her 'progress' had chilled me: how our poet friend had apparently elevated her from groupie to the exalted state of girlfriend, before deciding to marry her – which meant, as far as my novelist pal was concerned, that she now deserved our respect.

I was recalling that occasion now because I did not wish for Ursula to fall into the category of either 'groupie' or 'stalker'. Her presumption that she and I were involved in a close relationship, that she *understood* me, seemed to place her in the latter category, but her pilgrimage to Nice in order to breathe the air around me made her seem more like a literary groupie. Though what was she, really, in her own right? A promising young (though not all that young) fiction writer, or so I hoped. And I hoped that she considered herself in those terms, as well, and not as something inert or hollow, a marionette that came to life only if animated from the outside.

She continued to stare at me. It struck me that her face had taken on the still, lighted quality I had seen there before, when she had lain beside me the first time, after our failure to make love, and I had noticed a kind of radiance in her eyes, almost as if two candles were burning behind them. And then again at the dining table, when we had discussed my story and she had briefly seemed to glow like a slender, steady flame. She said, 'You're right. My real problem is that I'm practically doubled over with guilt. Because of my mother. I'm a bit like you were with *your* mother: afraid of being *swallowed up*. That's why I didn't go to her funeral. My bossy brother would have eaten me alive, and I thought my mum had let me down and that I hadn't loved her very much, anyway. But now I see her face the whole time, and her voice seems to cry out to me. It's, like, I must expiate this guilt somehow. Only I feel that I have no one. My brother and I do love each other, in a distant way, but I have no one of my *own*. Just you.'

I could not answer for a moment, because I was at once moved by her honesty and unnerved by this revelation of daft devotion. Then something struck me. 'Ursula, it's true. You *are* like me. We are both horribly guilty and grief-stricken, underneath our unflappable demeanours.' She caught the irony and laughed. I went on, 'Which I suppose is normal after one's mother dies, but it's rather more thorny when the mother was . . . difficult, shall we say?' Then I repeated the advice I had given Antoine. 'You do not have only me in the world, Ursula, though I hope to remain your friend. You have yourself, your gift, and that is where your solution lies. If you are a writer, you must write about it. *Write it out*. Everything else will flow from that. This is the only truth for a writer. He – or she – must write. Do you see what I mean?'

'Yes,' she whispered, her face still full of that strange candle-like glow. I wondered why she was all lustrous now, she who was so often without repose, who generally emanated, if anything, a kind of bristling electricity. Why should that light gleam from her at the moment when I was finally releasing myself from her clutches? I had expected shrieks and abuse; I certainly hadn't expected her to shine. Perhaps I felt vaguely disappointed, even affronted. But I was also relieved, of course, and I was marvelling, too, at this light in her, as if she had all of a sudden come close to a source within herself.

She paused, lowering her eyes to examine her feet, in their black ballet slippers. Then she looked up with a proud little smile. 'Well, Sebastian, I shall go to my *own* bed tonight. And don't ask me to come back if you change your mind. I think I'll quite like it there alone.'

*

Next morning, the air smelled curiously empty, until I realised that it was not redolent of coffee. I ventured out of my bedroom to regard an unlaid table – and a fully dressed Ursula sprawled on the sofa, eating a *pain au chocolat* while reading Kundera's *The Art of the Novel*.

'Hi there,' she said brightly. 'I was up early, so I went to the café. I was totally ravenous, so I ate three whole croissants and drank two huge coffees. It was gorgeous. But I was still really *yearning* for chocolate, so I bought this to eat here, only I hadn't thought to get one for you. Sorry.' She buried her teeth in the pastry so that it shattered into buttery shards, the chocolate oozing out on either side.

'That's all right,' I muttered, swallowing. 'I can go down to the breakfast room. Or I suppose I can do without breakfast.'

'Good,' she said, smoothing a pink tongue over chocolate-smeared lips, and returned to her book.

*

Around midday, I was writing a letter to my French publisher when I heard her talking on the phone. First her voice seemed subdued, but then she broke into girlish laughter. I put down my pen, sighing. How could I concentrate with all that adolescent gurgling going on next door? And whom was she speaking to? And furthermore, wasn't it just like Ursula to make a phone call without asking permission? Who did she think paid the bills? I rose, prepared to march out and rebuke her, only suddenly I heard the door close. She had left. Left the suite altogether, without bothering to say goodbye, much less tell me where she was going. I settled back at my desk with another sigh, and reread the first paragraphs of my letter. But I found them wooden, my usually fluent French grown stilted. I crumpled up the page, threw it in the bin, and decided to take myself out to lunch at the café, since it didn't seem likely that Ursula would be preparing one of her pleasant little collations for us today.

*

I had half-hoped that Léon and Max would be there, wound round with their habitual scarves and smoking their habitual cigarettes. But there was only André the barman, and Monsieur Bricoleur, who seemed more cheerful since the weather had improved. I called for the *plat du jour* and a half-litre of wine – considerably more than I would usually drink in the middle of the day. While I ate, I read *Le Monde des Livres*, and also thought of Julie. The image of her, and the sound of her voice in my mind's ear, lifted my spirits, although I did not see why they should have been low in the first place.

*

Blurred with wine, I slept through the afternoon, and dreamt that I was a child, playing on Stephen's Green with my teddy bear – who is remarkably well dressed, as teddy bears go. He wears a red ribbon round his throat, a red waistcoat and red boots. (Even as I slept, my dreaming self was moved by these details of memory, for I'd had just such a teddy bear. His red gear had embarrassed me when I was small; he had seemed ostentatious compared to the more or less naked bears of other children, but I'd loved him anyway.)

My mother appears, and says, 'Come, I will bring you to the secret garden.' Then we are walking along a wooded path. All I can hear in the stillness is the faint rustling of her skirt. I clutch the teddy bear, excited and a bit afraid.

We arrive at a clearing with a pool at the centre. It is unruffled where the sun glints on its surface, but when I look inside I see a green-gold light through which marvellous fish are weaving in a kind of dance. 'Oh,' I breathe, and reach for the teddy bear, only to register that he is gone. I look about wildly and see him waddling away into the trees that encircle the clearing.

I call to him, but 'Let him go, darling' murmurs my mother, putting her arm round my shoulder. 'Let him go. He is happy.' Then my eyes opened and I remembered *ursus*, the Latin for bear, and I began to laugh.

*

We were meant to go out to dinner, but the moment she opened the door – wearing, this time, a white dress – I knew there was no question of leaving the flat that night. I took her in my arms immediately and she raised her face to mine, and then we were making love on the sofa and on the floor, before staggering, still caressing each other, into the next room, since there was, after all, a bed available.

About two hours later, she rummaged in the fridge and produced some of the Corsican cheese from the night before, and a bowl of olives. There was a bottle of red *vin du Var* as well, so we went to the sofa and ate and drank a bit, and I described my talk with Ursula.

She asked me about Ursula's stories, and when I described

the young boy and his cousin, the painter called Isolt, who lives in an enchanted garden, Julie said, 'Ah, this Isolt is her ideal self.'

'How so?' I murmured, staring at her black hair and lovely white throat. (We had put on dressing gowns, since the evening was chilly, but all I wanted was to drag hers off, and kiss her again. She had been so sweet and ardent, and so abandoned in my arms that I was still thrumming.)

She said in her thoughtful way, 'The Isolt character is a flour-ishing artist, and also independent. Ursula wishes to be strong like that, I imagine. Strong and wise, and, of course, successful.'

I embraced her then, and once more we made love on the sofa while children sang and called to each other in the street below – since French children never seem to go to bed. At one point, cradling her body against mine and looking into her green eyes, I whispered that old cliché, 'Where have you been? How could I have lived so long without you?'

And she answered with that other cliché: 'Waiting for you.' But they didn't feel like clichés, not to us.

*

I had not seen Ursula since she had left abruptly after speaking on the phone. When I arrived home next morning, it was clear that she had not slept there either; it was strange to see both her bed and mine undisturbed. And indeed I had noticed an almost amused expression on Hervé's usually sardonic face, when he'd lifted his great head to mutter *bonjour* as I came in. I drowsed for about an hour, then had a bath and drank a coffee. Presently she arrived, wearing, yet again, her pretty black dress, and eating a brioche. She seemed different; there was something dreamy about her smile, and her eyes looked remote.

'Don't get those buttery crumbs on your nice dress,' I said.

'Mmm.' She showed me a bag from the boulangerie. 'I didn't forget you this time. There's a croissant and a kind of fruit thing in there.'

'Thanks, Ursula. I *am* pretty hungry this morning. Would you like a coffee?'

'Mmm,' she repeated, and collapsed onto a chair with a little, satisfied sigh. I stood there until she decided to gaze drowsily up at me, her vast eyes still distant and dreamy. She said, 'I went to visit Noel yesterday.'

'I see. Did you have a nice time?'

She smiled haughtily, and explained in a voice of supreme condescension, 'I stayed over there, Sebastian. I stayed with him last night. And in fact I did have an absolutely *brilliant* time.'

I felt a bit embarrassed, as though I were a father whose daughter had offered him an unseemly confidence. I was also, I had to admit, ever so slightly piqued. I'd had a feeling about that pushy American; I'd known he would try to insinuate himself into Ursula's life and future, after I had worked so hard to encourage her. Now it was my turn to say, 'Mmm.'

'Yes, I'd love a coffee,' she said airily. 'Just let me change.' And she glided past me and into her bedroom, while I stood in the middle of the kitchen, my arms dangling stupidly at my sides.

*

Two things occurred that very day which may explain, at least to some degree, what happened next.

The first was that Julie rang to tell me she would be flying to London the following afternoon on literary business. She had nearly completed a semi-autobiographical novel about her brief early marriage to an older, distinguished though domineering academic, and her agent wished to see her to discuss certain contractual details that had suddenly become urgent. She thought she would return home via Paris, to call on her French publisher as well as some relations who lived there. She would be back home in two weeks' time. 'Or perhaps a week and a half, if I miss you too much,' she said shyly.

The second thing was that I – along with most of my friends – received an invitation in that morning's post which would immediately create a minor scandal throughout the bohemian community of Nice. Léon and Max had decided to establish their own salon to rival the gatherings of Trudy and Alice!

Examining the invitation (which was printed on very fine, heavy paper), I decided that it was cheeky of Léon and Max to encroach on Trudy and Alice's traditional territory. Also, Trudy was a writer, and I thought that her fellow writers, like myself, Babette, Katherine and Antoine, should champion one of our own 'happy few', as opposed to indulging Léon and Max, who were merely psychoanalysts. But their *nouveau salon littéraire* was to take place early next week, as if to throw us all off balance by providing too little time for reflection. Yet I resolved to decline, as tactfully as possible, and I hoped my friends would as well.

Only that afternoon Antoine phoned to say that Léon and Max had told him they intended to combine their salon with a champagne supper, or else a complete buffet dinner involving smoked salmon, caviar, loads of good wine, and *digestifs* like Armagnac and ancient brandies. This was a diabolical lure, since everybody had agreed long ago that Trudy and Alice's shop cake and cups of tea were a drag, and that their whiskey and wine always appeared too late and were of inferior quality.

To everyone's relief, the matter was resolved three days later, when the two couples agreed to 'stagger' their salons. In other words, each would conduct a gathering every second month. That way, we could honour our local tradition and also partake of a good table without offending anybody. I hoped it would be a bit like Dublin in the old days, or Proust's Paris.

In the midst of all this, where was Ursula?

Basically, I did not see her except fleetingly. She was no longer making meals or coffee for us; in the mornings she hurried out, after leaving her wet toothbrush in the basin and strewing crumpled towels all over the bathroom. I had thought to discuss the Max and Léon problem with her, since that new beau of hers, Noel the Great American Deflowerer, had probably been invited to their salon. And of course there was the issue of her accommodation. No doubt she was intending to move in with this Noel. But when? She was never around long enough for me to ask.

Until the following Wednesday. I was listless that morning, slightly hung over after Léon and Max's salon the evening before, and missing Julie acutely. At about ten o'clock Ursula appeared at my bedroom door, approaching so softly that I jumped when she spoke.

'Wasn't it brilliant, the party last night?' She walked in, grinning, although I had not invited her.

I said, 'I saw you in the corner, talking to your novelist friend and some other people. But you didn't bother to come over and greet me, even though we live together.'

She made an actually rather Gallic gesture involving a pout and a certain movement of her shoulders and hands. 'Well, you didn't say hello to me either. Wasn't the food fab?'

'Yes, I'm afraid it was. I think even Trudy and Alice enjoyed themselves. Ursula, we must talk. Take that other chair.'

She complied, settling beside me at the desk, where I had once more been trying to write letters. I said brusquely, 'I think it would be only courteous to let me know what your intentions are, don't you? We talked some time ago about how important it is for you to move on. I suppose you will go and live with the American now?'

She placed her elbow on the desk and sprawled a bit, disturbing my papers. I felt that she was uncomfortably close; I could see the down along her thin forearm, and smell some new scent she was wearing. Tilting her head in her blackbird style, she said, 'I think it would be only courteous to call him by his name. "The American" doesn't sound very nice, Sebastian. In fact, it sounds as if you were a bit jealous.'

'I am most certainly not jealous,' I said stiffly. She gave a loud laugh; I knew that she was amused, once more, by the old-fashioned and pompous quality of my diction. Then suddenly she was serious again, regarding me from those large eyes, and continuing to incline her body too close, so that her breast was nearly touching my arm.

The French have an expression, so-and-so has 'seen the wolf', to describe the change that takes place in people after their first experience of sex. And now it flashed through my mind that Ursula had changed in this way. As she continued to tilt suggestively near my arm, I couldn't help thinking that she had finally come to inhabit her own skin. Her restlessness had at last been channelled, and her body, which had seemed so gawky and boyish that first night in my bed, felt, in its nearness at this moment, quite different. I imagined that, literally overnight, she had realised how to use that body, as well as her intelligence, in a sensual way, and that if I made love to her now, she would be supple, wiry and burning.

Was I tempted? Oh, yes, at that moment I was tempted. How could I not recall her first night in my bed, how she'd thrown her leg like a plank over mine, how clumsy she had felt beneath my hands? And how could I not be curious now, to learn for myself how she had changed? She was obviously signalling those changes to me, as she breathed against my cheek and I tried to keep my own body relaxed so she would not guess that she'd disturbed me.

Then, lowering her lashes like the heroine of a Victorian novel, she said, 'You know, I'm really not all that mad about Noel. He's not nearly as good a writer as you are.'

Now it was my turn to laugh: thank God the spell was broken. She stared at me indignantly while I continued to smile, and to think, *Jesus, what a manipulator she is!* Though I couldn't blame Ursula, for hadn't I been, up until now, her all-too-tractable victim?

I reflected that she was a bit of a sycophant, and that the sycophant is invariably a manipulator, gushing praise – though never in genuine admiration, but only fatuously, for self-promotion. All those toadying courtiers of literature – Iago fawning over Othello, Lear's two daughters buttering up their fool of a father, Brutus flattering Caesar – it's always the same, always the parasite saying to him or herself, 'Time to take that fellow over and then push him out of the way. He's had the limelight long enough. My turn now!' Devious, yes, but successful only if the target is vain enough, or stupid enough, to covet such attentions.

Ursula was ambitious – which was fine, since she clearly had a gift. But she was also conniving, and I had been tempted, even though I was stronger now than I had been when people like Clive had entered my life. I did believe Ursula was perfectly capable of deceiving herself. She would gladly seduce me now to save her new-found sexual pride, or to triumph over Julie, or to convince me that she should stay on in the hotel – or all three of those things, though she would never admit to any one of them. And then she might decide to make Noel jealous by telling him that, in my blundering way, I had come on to her, and she had succumbed, out of pity or gratitude. Ah, yes, she could easily deceive herself, but I was relieved to think – or anyway, to hope – that she could no longer deceive me.

X

Two years on, and the love between Julie and myself continues to ripen, though we do not live together – which seems to puzzle some of our friends. I imagine they have surmised I am still reluctant, after Claudia's death, to make a second home in Old Nice, but that's not the reason – or not any longer. It is simply that I have come to adore hotel life. I love the public part of it: my occasional visits to the breakfast room, where I can observe or sometimes talk with the other, passing guests. And the television room and little bar, and the chambermaids, whose names I know. And I love my private life in the midst of the public bustle, my placid suite overlooking the garden. I even like Hervé, with his glaucous, cynical eye.

Whereas Julie loves her flat in the old quarter, so close to the food and flower markets, to the harbour and the shimmering sea. So we come and go between both places, and we are, I suppose, happy. (I have begun a new novel, in a looser, more contemporary style, while Julie is working on a book-length poem about her parents.)

I say 'happy', but of course my happiness will always be rueful now. Claudia lives on in the deepest part of me, and my mother's death has made my own past a kind of myth or dream, with all of my ancestors gone to the land of the shades.

*

It has occurred to me that all along, I had suspected, indeed hoped, that eventually Ursula would abandon me for another writer on whom she could fasten her ambitions, along with her certainty that she 'understood' him. And after all, it had made sense to choose Noel, since she was writing those intriguing stories about America, which Noel (himself from New York) must have appreciated. They lived together for about six months. Julie and I bumped into Noel soon after she'd left him to live in an arid yet beautiful Italian village with a middle-aged English painter. Noel, looking exhausted, had told us that Ursula had been 'a handful'. Remembering her childlike enthusiasms rent by sudden tantrums, I'd thought it best not to inquire too deeply into what he meant.

Currently she is living in Paris with her new boyfriend, a French accountant. We exchange letters now and again. Hers assure me that she continues to write fiction, 'only I can't seem to finish *anything*'. Although in her most recent letter, she said, 'You and Julie should come up to visit us. I am very happy, and I think every artist should live with an accountant; they are so sensible. I'm trying to write a novel now. It takes place in Nice, and it's about a passionate girl who changes the life of an expatriate Irish writer. He's a sweet man but slow-witted. Maybe when I've finished, I'll send you down a copy.'

*

Perhaps Ursula's fervent admiration of me, her extreme behaviour in pursuing me to Nice, and then her abrupt abandonment of me there – perhaps such things are considered normal nowadays. Perhaps I am old-fashioned to expect 'relationships' (surely an over-earnest Americanism, that word?) to grow and deepen slowly. But I cannot help it; that is the world I am used to, and Ursula's world of ferocious attachments casually broken still shocks me.

Stalkers. I am not at all certain I know what one is. But the whole business seems emblematic of some flaw in human relations these days, a rift in the social web. Of course there is the lurid stalker one sees in films. The kind who tirelessly dogs the poor heroine, showing up at her office or in her kitchen, where he gives an icky smile and says, 'Come, come, my dear, you know that you have always loved me . . . ' before trying to plunge a knife into her boyfriend's heart. And of course there are those famous real-life stalkers, that man who tried to assassinate an American president because he thought it would please the movie star he'd been stalking, or the lunatic who killed John Lennon.

Then there are the others, harder to define. I remember Claudia discussing pity, how dangerous it can be, since it is neither love nor mercy. And how she said that we love those who belong to us, who live within us, and it is to them that we must extend our care. Hadn't I myself spoken to Julie of 'care' in the Irish sense? But of course one also has a duty to one's student, say, or a neighbour. Only what if the student or the neighbour is desperately lonely, or feels empty inside, or is slightly barmy?

Have stalkers always existed? When Edith Wharton lived on the Côte d'Azur, did a version of Clive or Ursula try to break through the carapace of her privileged life and engulf her? My own guess is that yes, there have always been stalkers, though nowadays there are more of them.

I also remember Max and Léon telling me how psychoanalysts have that intriguing concept called transference. The patient falls in love with you, and you foster this for a while, for as long as it bears fruit. And when it ceases to be fruitful, you give your patient his (or her) power back; you say, 'What you love lies not in me but within yourself. Here, have it back.' I've had to do that kind of thing with students who wrote me letter after letter, even though I never corresponded in return. And once to a woman who sent me gushing postcards after I'd danced with her once at a writers' festival, yet whose face I could not even recall. I have had to say to such people, in effect, 'The light you glimpse in me is actually your own promise and your own purpose; it has been inside you all along. Here, take your power back.'

As for Clive, I realise that he regarded himself in a curious way as my son and heir. He expected me to adopt him. In his view, I was meant to take him into the café and introduce him to my colleagues and pals because he was entitled to such privilege; he wished to inherit my life.

Something in me has always felt forlorn. And Clive's father abandoned him, as Ursula's vagabond father forsook her. So perhaps I feel too much for the plight of the marooned, the lost, as Claudia told me that day in Cannes. Yet I was playing with fire. Claudia sensed that Clive regarded her as an impediment. She was the Rival, and if we had continued to employ him, he might indeed have tried to harm her. Trudy and Alice felt it too, that violence in him which was never very far from the surface. Only I did not feel it, or refused to feel it. It was a kind of hubris, indulging him as I did, and in a less dangerous way it was hubris to indulge Ursula, too.

*

One morning a few months ago, I gathered up my post from Hervé's desk and walked to Julie's flat. It was late May, and the city felt festive, although not excessively so: the streets were not yet too crowded, and while the weather was fine, it was not unendurably hot, as it would be in July. Yet even in my more northern quarter, the breezes were seasoned with brine, and everyone had begun to have their drinks and meals outside on the *terrasses* of the restaurants.

I let myself in and put my post on the hall table, on top of Julie's own. She was in the kitchen, heating water for coffee, and I came up noiselessly behind her and kissed her on the nape, which made her give a little jump. She was wearing a beautiful kimono – ivory-coloured with a swirl of black dragons – and her hair was half up and half loose, in the slightly messy way that I love.

We took our coffee to the dining table, and I began to read *Nice-Matin*. It was full of photos from the Cannes Film Festival, which had just ended. I thought that the stars smiling on La Croisette, encircled by the usual frenzy of paparazzi and tourists, looked too perfect and gleaming; I supposed that many of them had had plastic surgery. *How shallow they seem*, I said to myself, *yet they are the new aristocracy*. Or even the new deities, in our godless age: they must have bevies of Ursulas in constant pursuit of them.

'Oh, sorry,' Julie cried suddenly. 'I've just opened one of your letters.'

'Never mind. Anyway, *I'm* sorry, for muddling my post with yours. Who is it from? Is there a cheque?'

Julie, sweeping her eye down the page, was silent. Then she looked up and murmured, 'Extraordinary.'

*

Claudia was a closet writer. She had found it hard going at first, because working as an editor had so sharpened her critical eye, she could barely bring herself to write a sentence without looking at it narrowly, then laying down her pen and rising from the desk. Also, there had been the problem of living with me. 'I can't do it,' she'd said once. 'Even if an editor accepts me, they'll compare my work to yours and find it wanting, or they'll think you used your influence to get me published.'

'Who are "they", Claudia?' I had answered. 'And even if "they" exist, who cares?'

I remember that she had turned away without speaking.

I have not mentioned Claudia's writing until now because she herself was so half-hearted about it, almost ashamed, and to be honest it didn't really seem to matter very much to her; for instance, Alice's cookery book had excited her more than her own efforts. But then illness had made such squeamishness seem juvenile. As she got sicker and sicker, the page became a solace, that empty white space a source of hope. There was this story in her, and now it was urgent to tell it, to save it, even as she struggled to save her life. So she began to rescue it, little by little, preferring pen and paper to the computer, writing in bed when she was weak, her fine head inclined over the page, anchored on a board against her knees, the scratching of her pen the only sound in the room. After she had finished a number of pages, she would transfer them onto the computer and then save them on a diskette. These details are important in the story I am about to tell.

It was a book for children she was writing. The heroine is called Penny. She has mousy-brown hair, gathered into two bunches. Because Penny is shy and dreamy, she often finds herself alone, making up stories inside her head. One day she strolls by a river and sees a willow tree. She walks inside its green curtain, where the air is full of watery green light. When she parts its ragged leaves on the far side, she is in another country.

So this tree is liminal, a border between worlds. On the Other Side, Penny has adventures. Her first adventure starts when she finds an apple tree heavy with fruit. She plucks an apple and eats it hungrily. But when she has finished it and there is just the core left, the apple restores itself by magic and lies whole once again in her hand.

There is a darker side to this Penny story. When she meets and befriends certain characters on the Other Side, she tells them why she is so solitary, why she makes up stories and games instead of playing with the children next door: there is trouble at home. These details emerge slowly, subtly. As does the fact that sometimes Penny dislikes herself. *You are a deceitful, horrible girl,* says a harsh voice in her head, *always spinning lies.* But we come to understand that Penny weaves stories to comfort herself, that they are incantations or prayers, to protect her from the trouble at home.

Claudia had written almost one hundred pages before she grew too ill to continue. After her death, I kept the diskette, along with some of her other effects, in a drawer in the guest bedroom. I wanted to try to publish this delicate novel but it was a long way from being finished, and I couldn't bring myself to complete it. I considered asking Katherine, but it would have felt like a desecration; the prose was absolutely Claudia's, measured and light-hearted yet also serious, with the special seriousness of a lonely child, like the solemnity I had found so endearing in wee Charlie. And Katherine's most brilliant stories were *about* children, whereas Claudia's book was *for* children – a different thing. So I kept it in that desk, along with her scarves and necklaces. There was also a small brown book in which she had written recipes; she'd sometimes talked about this book with Trudy. And recently I had described it to Julie, who had said that she'd love to look at it. As for *Penny*, I was aware Claudia had shown at least parts of it to Trudy, and I would have liked Julie to read it, but somehow I could not bring myself even to touch the disk. Claudia had written that story during her final months, weeks, days, and it was as if it held the embers of her life.

*

With a silent sigh, I recognised Ursula's large handwriting.

Dear Sebastian,
Guess what! I'm finally getting published. Not the Nice novel I told you about, but another one that I was working on at the same time. I finished it last month and sent it off to this English agent and, lo and behold, he sold it for me. It's a really good house, Tate & Wyndham. I bet you're proud of me.

Actually the novel is a children's book. When I was living with you, I found this disk in my room with some chapters on it by Claudia. I guess you must know about it because you were keeping it with some other stuff of hers. Well, the more I thought about it, the more it ignited my imagination. I realised I could turn that raw material into something really great.

Transforming those early clumsy chapters into a truly fine novel was also a way to thank you. The time I spent with you still haunts me. Our days together were so intimate and rich; we really understood each other. You introduced me to France and to great writers like Trudy and Antoine, and I looked after you and fostered your gift. Without me, I fear you would have grown sour and exhausted. I suppose we loved each other, didn't we? Anyway, my period with you was one of the most important times in my life, and I suspect in yours as well.

Only I couldn't finish anything! My Maggie character, a kind of alter ego, I guess, just wasn't inspiring me. So it seemed like destiny when I found the disk, almost as if I was a reincarnation of Claudia. It was actually a mystical feeling, like the way I felt when we were living together, that I could nearly read your mind as if you were a part of me. Now, finally, I could finish a book, and also thank you by realising Claudia's dream, changing her awkward writing into razzle-dazzle prose. I know you'll love the novel. (It is of course absolutely MY novel, though I guess Claudia lies behind it as a kind of muse or inspiration or whatever.)

I've directed my editor to send you a proof copy: it should arrive any day. Loads of love, Ursula

All I could think at first was that she had touched Claudia's things. She had rummaged through my desk, fingering Claudia's red silk scarf, which still exhaled a vague scent of her, trying on her pearl necklace, reading through the small brown book of recipes with, no doubt, a superior smile on that sharp animal face. Directly after Claudia's death, I had tried to offer the scarves and jewels to her sister, but she had said, 'No, Sebastian, keep them with you. You loved her so.'

But then Ursula had arrived, a Grendel shambling through my rooms, opening drawers and cupboards, cackling over private things. I felt violated; I felt soiled, as if she had loosened my clothes and felt about my body with her greedy guttersnipe hands. I knew that I was trembling, and lowered my scalded eyes for fear they would upset Julie.

Presently, 'I want to kill her', I said in a low voice. 'It shocks me, Julie, this ice-cold desire to simply kill her.' It was true; an image of my hands curving round her scrawny throat had jumped into my head, and with it a kind of dark exhilaration. To see that complacent smile turn into a grimace, that face turn purple: this fantasy filled my mouth with bile and my heart with a black joy.

Julie murmured, 'There is only one thing to do.'

I stared at her. She looked very still and thoughtful. It occurred to me that she resembled Claudia slightly. She said, 'We must ring Trudy.'

*

Trudy and Alice received us that very day, at teatime. After reading the letter, Trudy looked especially sombre, hands clasped on the table beside the familiar green cups and plates of yellow cake. She said, 'This kid is sicker than we realised. I mean, I always thought she was kind of ignorant as well as pushy, but I had no idea . . . ' She touched the letter.

Alice said softly, 'Tell them, Trudy.'

Trudy gave a bitter smile. 'Did you know Claudia gave me a copy of the novel? I thought it had real potential. She was too modest to let a publisher see it, but you know me. Modesty is not one of my virtues. So I gave one copy to my London editor, and a second to my *maison d'éditions* in Paris. I thought maybe they would buy it and that this would hearten Claudia so much, she'd finish it.' There was a pause. Trudy reached across the table and squeezed my hand. 'But she got so much sicker, so fast.'

'We knew then that she'd never complete it,' Alice said. She squeezed my other hand. 'But they've read it, those editors. We didn't tell you, Sebastian, when you were so upset and grieving. But they have the novel, Trudy's editors in London and Paris. They have copies of Claudia's manuscript.'

I looked from her to Trudy, who was still smiling. 'I think,' she said, 'that I should throw a party.'

*

Summer arrived precisely on the first of June, with dazzling skies, a din of gulls, and terrific heat every afternoon. And on the second of June came a proof copy of Ursula's novel, sent by her publisher with a 'Compliments of the Author' card inside, and an inscription on the title page: 'For Sebastian, who saw the light in me'.

She had turned Claudia's book into a muddle of fantasy and science fiction. In fact, it recalled me to a visit I had made many years before, to the Freemason's Hall in Molesworth Street in Dublin.

Like many Irish Catholic children, I had received the impression from my mother and teachers that the Freemasons were furtive, devious, powerful and, most dreadful of all, Protestant. Later on, I learnt that Blake had been a Freemason, as had Yeats, but I still believed they were highly arcane, that their Hall in Molesworth Street, with its Mason's sign above the lintel, was a bastion I could never breach.

Only one morning when I was in Dublin on some literary business, I noticed, walking out of Buswell's Hotel, where I'd been having coffee with my agent, that the door of the Freemason's Hall was open. I thought of how little I knew of the Masons beyond a dim idea of secret handshakes, single eyes gazing out from pyramids, and semi-religious initiation rituals. Then I considered how handsome their building was. I walked across the street and simply went in.

I do not know why no one stopped me. I suspect that the Masons were launching a friendlier policy towards the outside world. Anyway, I was alone but for an elderly man behind a desk at the entrance. When I wavered, he smiled and said, 'Welcome.'

So I moved, alone, from one silent chamber to another. They were gloomily opulent, those rooms, full of temple gods and winged sphinxes, thrones and crucifixes, vast painted eyes and golden serpents. It was as though someone had rummaged in the chest of the collective unconscious, uncovering Greek gods, Egyptian glyphs, Jewish stars, Byzantine ikons and Celtic amulets, and had simply thrown them together in an almost frenzy, an incoherent celebration of all the mythologies ever created by humankind.

And Ursula's appalling reworking of Claudia's novel evoked the Freemasons Hall in Molesworth Street because it was a similar iconographic hodgepodge. Penny becomes a kind of warrior queen who searches for a magic chalice *à la* King Arthur, descends into the Underworld like Orpheus, travels to the centre of the earth as in Jules Verne, subdues a giant like a female King David. She even makes a sea voyage in search of a golden fleece. If I'd had any compunction about what we intended to do, it vanished after I read her plagiarised book. In Claudia's delicate narrative, Penny's journeys to the Other Side are tender, and full of sweet details, like a red ribbon from her bunched hair appearing and disappearing on a bough of the willow tree to show that her adventures are not merely a dream. It was an account that would have delighted adults as well as children. Ursula's novel, on the other hand, was a pastiche, and a nearly fascist fantasy, a coarsened version of C. S. Lewis or Tolkien, full of cheap violence, utterly specious, entirely a desecration.

Perhaps Noel, a commercial novelist, had taught her how to write for that market. No doubt he'd dismissed her story fragments as too literary, too inward-looking, too difficult to place. He had probably suggested she read some fat popular novels for inspiration. I imagine all this was innocent enough; he could not have known that she would filch Claudia's book, that she would feel it was her right to do so. As Trudy said, she was sicker than we thought.

Julie was surprised by how cold I was during the next few days. In fact, my coldness surprised even myself. One morning an image entered my head, a memory actually, of Claudia writing in bed when she was sick, the sun turning her short hair into points of light, her face in shadow, and her hand writing that story of the Other Side, where perhaps she herself would soon go. And this image so seared me that I banished it, and everything else, from my mind. I sheathed my heart in ice and thought only of quotidian things, and the letter I must write. And when I came to do the letter, I was still completely cold, feeling nothing.

Dear Ursula,

Thanks for the novel. What terrific news! Of course I've told all the gang, and we are very proud of you. Indeed Trudy wishes to propose a salon in your honour. I suggest you accept, since, as you know, Trudy's influence in the publishing worlds of France, America, England and even little Ireland is considerable. She intends to invite all the literati, and you could glad-hand to your heart's content. And of course it would be splendid to see you again. The summer here is quite as hot as in Paris, only the sea breezes soften the air and we are bathing every day like proper 'Azureens'. So do come and visit us. Trudy has chosen the evening of the 9th, if that would suit.

Her reply arrived two days later, by e-mail.

Dear Sebastian,

It would be a shrewd move for me to hobnob with journalists and editors before my novel is officially launched. That lot will be receiving review copies pretty soon, and meeting me may encourage them to give the book more space. So I'm happy to accept Trudy's invitation. Would she mind if I brought along my publicist, agent and editor? And of course Gaspard, my boyfriend?

Oh no, I thought. She certainly would not mind.

*

Trudy, God bless her, had flown over half the literary establishment of England, or so it seemed. Actually there were not so many London literati there: only Trudy's publisher, along with a man who edited the books pages of a newspaper and who sojourned on the Côte d'Azur in June anyway, and Ursula's editor and publicist from Tate & Wyndham. It was just that their pleasantly fluting English voices nonplussed me somehow; I nearly expected to see mist-shawled street lamps and Regency houses outside Trudy's window, in place of the familiar vivid sky of Nice in summer.

Ursula's editor was a tall fellow with a headful of blondish hair, called Peter Stuart. (He wished for me to know that his name was spelt *Stuart*, like Mary, Queen of Scots, as opposed to *Stewart*, which would have placed him amongst the Ulster Protestants. In fact, he impressed me as being unusually class-conscious even for an Englishman, with a deliberately dry and laconic manner, as if he practised his style before the mirror each morning. Or perhaps I was just biased against him.)

It was good to greet some of the regulars: Max and Léon; Katherine, wearing a crisp white dress, and her husband, a white hat; Antoine; Phebus; Trudy's Paris editor, Sonia Dumas, who often attended her salons; and the others, who knew what we were going to do that evening. We tried to move casually among those who did not know our plan, shaking their hands, exchanging bits of literary gossip, but I could feel a tension in the air, a kind of thrumming, and I wondered when Ursula would deign to honour us with her presence. At one point, Trudy gave me a whiskey and muttered, '*Courage.*'

When she arrived, accompanied by her agent and the accountant boyfriend, I had to admit that she was looking much better. Someone had taught her how to play up those lovely eyes with makeup; she had drawn tapering black lines around them, which gave her an exotically feline look. And she was dressed like a real Parisienne, in a well-cut frock and cunningly arranged scarf. She could never be truly pretty, but she had become chic and confident. The confidence was evident in her insouciant smile and the way she seemed so relaxed in the midst of her entourage: her agent, a middle-aged rotund man, and her slightly ragged-looking publicist, a young woman as thin as Ursula herself. The accountant boyfriend was tall and blond and wore a suit.

She sauntered over to Julie, who was standing beside me, and cried '*Hello*', kissing her exuberantly on both cheeks in the grand French manner. 'You're looking *fabulous.*' I presumed that she intended this style of greeting as practice for the Hollywood parties she was expecting to attend before long. 'And *Sebastian.*' Finally she turned to me, extending a manicured hand. 'It's been *so* long. How *are* you?'

'Grand.' I was finding it hard to look at this new-and-improved Ursula, who seemed as brushed and polished as a new car. 'Why don't you greet your hostess?' I suggested, indicating Trudy across the room.

She laughed her low, flirtatious laugh and said to Julie, 'Just like the old Sebastian. You see, when we lived together he was *always* telling me what to do. I didn't mind, though. It was one of the many little intimacies between us, after all.'

Julie gave her a mint-green look. 'But you must realise, dear girl, that I would naturally know more about you than you do about me.'

Ursula frowned; clearly she was struggling to figure out what Julie meant by that cryptic reply, though probably she suspected she'd been wrong-footed. In any case, after a minute she brightened again with that new brittle shine, and spoke once more to Julie, 'So, how is *your* work going? I suppose quite well, though we all know how exasperating the poetry-writing business can be. I mean, hardly anyone reads the stuff, do they?'

Alice rescued us, appearing at my elbow with a platter of pâté on bits of bread and furls of smoked salmon with fromage frais inside. (Max and Léon's salons had raised Alice and Trudy's culinary standards.) Of course the ever-ravenous Ursula fastened on these hors d'oeuvres, examining them intently and plucking one after the other. I took Julie's elbow and we slipped away.

Julie went over to speak to Noel, who had just arrived and was standing apart, throwing furtive looks in Ursula's direction. He was among those who knew what would take place that evening. I approached Sonia, Trudy's Paris editor, a tall young woman of African descent with a slender Modigliani head and skin the colour of cinnamon. 'I'm rather nervous,' she confided in a soft voice.

'*Bon courage*,' I said, echoing Trudy. I hesitated, then continued, 'You know, I am a bit nervous, too, as well as a bit rueful about what we are up to. I liked her story fragments, even if they clung too closely to my own style. I suppose one is always ambivalent.'

She laughed. 'It will not ruin her, Sebastian. In the climate of these days, such a scandal could even give her a certain cachet. She will be – how do you say in English? – a "comeback kid". No, it will not ruin her.' She tilted closer and murmured in my ear, 'But we hope it will teach her the lesson of her life.'

I settled on the dreadful brown sofa beside William, the English novelist who lived on Cap Ferrat. He had the slightly pouchy, slightly ravaged face of a man somewhat addicted to brandy and cigars. But it was an intelligent face, with large, sunken, burning eyes. He was homosexual, or perhaps bisexual, and his work seemed to reflect this ambiguity, for the critics were always disputing as to whether his books were 'light' or 'serious'. He was also a bit of a dandy and today was clothed in a linen coat of indeterminate colour, with a silk cravat about the throat. He greeted me with his slight stammer, which I found charming because it betrayed his shyness. 'Oh, g-good evening, Sebastian. God, that girl looks full of herself. I don't suppose she realises that most of the p-people in this room either knew Claudia personally, or were familiar with her work as an editor.'

'Honestly, William, I have no idea what she knows or doesn't know. I'm only sorry that I loosed her on myself – and upon all of us. I knew she was mixed up but – '

'But you had no idea she was a m-monster,' William finished for me, taking a gulp of whiskey.

At that moment, Trudy spoke from the centre of the room, her strong voice creating an immediate hush. 'Greetings, dear friends.' Her heavy eyes surveyed the crowd; there must have been twenty or more of us there. 'And what friends! Alice and I are honoured to receive so many distinguished visitors this evening, especially those who have come from Paris, and of course, *most* especially, those of you who travelled all this way from the distant island of Angleterre.' We laughed obligingly. She paused again. Her face wore a smile that I could tell was deeply ironical but which the innocent among us were probably mistaking for mere good humour. I glanced at Ursula, standing next to Peter Stuart. How slight she looked; it was hard to believe that so much ruthlessness was contained within such a fragile sheath. For a moment I felt a tremor of pity: yes, she was a monster, but she was – or had been – *my* monster, and I could still manage to feel sorry for her.

Trudy went on, saying fulsome things about Ursula, how gifted she was and how we – the literary and artistic community of the Côte d'Azur – had always believed in her. And how wonderful it was that editors and journalists, as well as Ursula's fellow writers, had come for this reception. 'It is so important to support the young,' cried Trudy earnestly, 'to foster talent in this increasingly illiterate age, to celebrate the passionate artist at a point in history when so many people regard art merely as merchandise.'

Ursula's thin publicist, who had an absurd flower name like Marigold or Tulip, was busily writing all of this down, probably to use later as publicity or marketing material. Although upon thinking this, I immediately reproved myself, as I had done after Peter Stuart spoke to me. After all, I did not know that he was a prat, or that she was rapacious. They were both probably amusing, intelligent people; I was just prejudiced against them because they intended to publish that novel.

Trudy had swung into full orotund form, gazing solemnly at us while making ample motions with her arms. 'Two years ago, Ursula Dowling arrived at Sebastian Clare's door on a pilgrimage. She wished to blossom into a writer, a real writer. She was concerned not with fame or material success but with the truth, the artist's truth. And now she has indeed fulfilled her dream, and we are here to praise this young and gifted writer, who is bearing the lamp of art into the next generation.'

There was a smattering of uncertain-sounding applause; the ignorant among us must have been a bit puzzled by Trudy's fervour. She resumed, 'Yes, let us raise our glass in praise of Ursula, for in an age when many covet – and some achieve – instant celebrity, she has worked hard and unwaveringly at her art, which has now borne fruit in this, her first publication. To Ursula!'

We all toasted Ursula with our glasses of whiskey or wine, or our cups of tea. She stood there, stiff with pride, between her editor and her accountant boyfriend. Then Trudy said, 'And to further honour this occasion, some of us have decided to read extracts from Ursula's manuscript, so that those of you who are not familiar with the book can begin to appreciate just how fine a work it is.'

The thin publicist threw a baffled look towards Peter Stuart, but he did not catch it, because he himself was frowning perplexedly at Trudy. She began to read the opening paragraph of Claudia's original *Penny*, which Ursula had purloined in full: 'This story is about a girl called Penny. Penny liked her house in the daytime when her mother and father were not there. She liked the dry, quiet face of the grandfather clock, and the sunlight streaming in to touch chairs and tabletops and the leaves of her mother's green plant. She liked the stillness inside and the muffled sounds of motor cars and people calling to one another – the whole busy grownup world – outside. You may wish to know why Penny was often alone in her house. But first I will tell you what she looked like. Her mousy-brown hair was so thick and curly, it had to be tied up into two bunches, one above each ear. She had a round face full of mousy-brown freckles, and big round eyes that were "hazel", which means they were sometimes green and other times brown, depending on the light.'

Peter Stuart interrupted. 'I'm terribly sorry, Trudy, but I don't understand.' He spoke to Ursula. 'Surely you remember our agreement that no one but ourselves would see your text until the launch.' Once more he addressed Trudy. 'For publicity purposes, yes? We had considered trying to serialise it, and so on, but then we decided that releasing bits of the book before its official release would only dilute its impact. We wanted to make a splash, so to speak, by keeping it under wraps until the last moment, if you see what I mean.' He turned to the publicist, 'Isn't that right, Poppy?'

Poppy said to Ursula, 'You asked me to send one proof copy to Sebastian Clare as a special present, but you assured me that no one else had read – or would read – the book until the pub date. Yet Trudy is holding *manuscript pages.*'

Ursula did not reply. She was standing as before, with a glass of wine in her hand, but her lips had turned white. Alice rose from a chair in the corner, and in her firm clear voice read Claudia's second paragraph.

Before, I had imagined that people would begin to move at this point, to rustle and murmur, or even cry out. I had pictured them throwing bemused or outraged glances at Ursula, the whole room drawing itself away from her as if even the curtains and furniture were recoiling. But instead, everyone remained curiously still, caught in some thrall. Even Ursula did not move. Beside me I could hear William breathing heavily. Julie, across the room, looked at me and mouthed the catchword of that evening: *Courage.*

Katherine produced a sheaf of pages from her handbag, and quietly read the third paragraph.

At this point, the woman called Poppy demanded, 'What's

going on?' She rounded on Katherine, who was looking nearly translucent, in her white dress. 'How *did* all of you get your hands on Ursula's novel?'

Still in that quiet voice, Katherine answered, 'It is not Ursula's novel.'

'Christ,' said Peter Stuart.

The editor from Paris spoke. 'Most of this book was written by Claudia Byrne. Trudy posted it to me some years ago and I was greatly taken with it, as were certain of my colleagues in Paris and London. We would have made an offer but then, alas, Miss Byrne died. So it remained, unfinished, in the hands of her partner Sebastian Clare. Until Ursula Dowling appropriated it, completed it in her peculiar fashion and submitted it as her own work.'

Poppy mumbled, 'I always thought the first half was better. Too much pseudo-science-fiction-fantasy crap in the second half, if you ask me. But that stuff sells these days.'

'I knew Claudia Byrne quite well,' said Peter Stuart in a marvelling voice. 'A fine editor, she was. And a lovely woman.' Staring at Ursula, he repeated, 'I knew her quite well.'

Suddenly Ursula cried in a rather horrible, nasal wail, '*Sebastian*, how can you let them *do* this to me? You're supposed to be my *mentor. Tell them to leave me alone.*'

I looked at her. Always, as a writer, I had cherished words for their nearly mystical power. I had always believed that if an idea or a feeling were wrought into powerful language, it could change people. Only finally I'd been forced by circumstance to realise that some people cannot be changed. No words of mine would have convinced Ursula that *she*, not ourselves, was the villain of this particular piece, that it was she who had done the betraying, that she was not entitled to my protection. It was terrible to realise this hard truth that Claudia had discussed with me so long ago over lunch in Cannes: some people cannot be changed; they are simply too damaged. But now I knew, so I just looked at Ursula and said nothing.

After a moment she wailed again, though this time to the room at large, 'You *can't* withdraw my novel. You *can't*. I *rescued* that book. It would never have been published only for me.' Her voice rose to a shriek. '*You can't take it away from me now.*'

Antoine, forever troubled by bad manners, murmured 'Dear God', but no one else spoke.

Suddenly she turned furious, as I knew she would. Good old Ursula, predictable in her unpredictable temper, that swift change from pixie to harpy. She narrowed her eyes at Peter Stuart and said in a kind of hiss, 'You'd better not let me down. I wrote the only sellable bits of that novel, and you know it. The early parts were just twee bullshit.' She repeated more loudly, 'I rescued that book.'

She indicated the lot of us with a contemptuous sweep of her arm. 'What do *these* people know, with their old-fashioned literary pretensions? Who cares about Katherine's stupid stories or Antoine's dreamy plays, in this day and age? You're all just dodos.' She glared at me. '*All* of you. Your books are dead, and you are dead. You're all just names in a school book. The rubbish you write says nothing to me or my generation. *Nothing.*'

Next, she fastened on Poppy. '*You're* a publicist. *You* know the real world. You know I'm the only person in this whole fucking room who has managed to write a contemporary book that people will actually *read.*'

Suddenly Gaspard, the accountant boyfriend, spoke. 'But you *didn't* write it,' he said, almost too softly for us to hear.

She whirled round and screamed at him, 'Who cares? Who cares that some dead woman gave me a leg up? Don't you see? This book was going to make me *famous*. It'd be a film and everything. And then after I'm famous, I can write the kind of novel I've always longed to write, the kind of novel that I'm *destined* to write.' She stopped then, her mouth half open, and I realised that the admission couched in her last sentence had surprised even herself. Despite her ostensible disdain for fuddy-duddies like Antoine, Katherine and me, she actually did want to write a serious novel, had always dreamt of doing so. That had been the purest of her reasons for descending on me here in Nice, only it had got drowned in the brackish waters of her ambition and her terrible pride.

She said in a much fainter voice, 'It was just that I could never *finish* anything. Everything always dried up on me. Until I found that disk . . . '

Her burly agent, who had kindly eyes above a dark beard, asked all of us, 'What in heaven's name are we to do now?'

Finally we became animated, rising from our chairs and sofas, gazing questioningly at each other. Julie appeared at my side, while Trudy and Alice moved about, replenishing people's glasses. Only Ursula remained stiff and alone in her corner, for even her abashed-looking boyfriend had glided away to accept a large whiskey from Alice.

'Poor wretched girl,' murmured Julie. 'She looks like a sacrificial lamb.' She laughed dryly. 'Even though she's only a humiliated plagiarist.'

I recalled my desire to actually kill Ursula. Considering her miserable face, I did not feel like that now. Antoine came up beside us and asked, 'Well?'

I realised that everyone was looking at me. 'It was a subtle book,' I said. 'I mean, Claudia's was a subtle book. Even the name Penny was chosen quite deliberately. Claudia meant it to evoke Homer's Penelope, since little Penny weaves stories as Penelope wove her tapestry. It was all quite serious, and genuinely imaginative, I think, without being whimsical.' I paused. 'It should be finished. I kept that diskette in a desk drawer because I just didn't know what to do with it. But at least Ursula has achieved that much. She has made me see that the novel deserves to be completed and to appear in the world.' I glanced over at Ursula, whose eyes looked stricken, but whose jaw was set in a stubborn way that I found all too familiar.

'Ursula's bowdlerised version cannot possibly be released,' I said firmly.

'Hear, hear,' muttered Peter Stuart, throwing her a baleful look.

I continued hastily, 'But I do not wish to blacken her name forever. She is young. She has a gift. Perhaps she will realise it one day. I wish her luck. But not on these terms.'

Once again I glanced at Ursula. I was feeling puzzled by myself, by that pattern in my life which had dismayed the only two women I had ever truly loved. Why, Claudia and Julie had wondered, did I let them in – the stalkers, the predators, the silly vain women and arrogant men, those who feel entitled to invade the deepest precincts of one's life but who understand so little? There had been a girl before Claudia whom I had liked for her slightly daft character; she had amused me but I could not love her. Only after I'd rebuffed her, she continued to write to me in her curious round hand like a child's, postcard after postcard, year after year. In fact, just a month before, I'd had to throw yet another into the bin. Stalkers, I was at long last realising, were not like other people. They don't take no for an answer. But why was I so susceptible?

Ursula was staring back at me with a look I could not read. I said bluntly, 'Ursula, you're a good stylist, but what you wrote is rubbish. We're living in an age when loads of people are perverting any spiritual or psychological text they can lay their hands on.

All that New Age lot, with their very imperfect understanding of Jungian archetypes and Buddhism and *The White Goddess*. As well as the fundamentalists, who see nothing of the mystery and oblique beauty of the Bible, but who read it as concrete truth and who brandish God about like a gun, using Scripture to threaten and judge and moralise. That was the kind of mystical muddle you indulged in, Ursula. Probably you were thinking it would make a good movie, with lots of lovely violence and special effects. But it was not Claudia's truth.'

She raised her chin even higher. I wondered if we were getting through to her at all, or if she was merely full of scorn for us. Suddenly I remembered myself at the age of nine or ten, lying sprawled on my stomach in what my mother liked to call the drawing room. I was reading *She* by H. Ryder Haggard, with panels of thick sunlight falling across the pages, and a certain smell in the air which was the smell of our house – a mixture of tea, polished floors, upholstery and my mother's scent. And I was recalling this now because it was striking me with the force of revelation that I had always felt the particular loneliness of the fatherless child. And all my adult life, I had been trying to offer others the comfort that had been denied to myself. I had been forever searching for the perfect candidate, who would allow me to utter the words that I, as a lonely boy, as a kind of male Penny, had longed to hear: *I will look after you; I will be a father to you. Don't be afraid.*

And I had always been drawn to what we still call bohemia, to those who tilt towards the margins of life. I had thought this was because I myself was a nonconformist, like most artists. Only it was occurring to me now that I had also been afflicted with a Good Samaritan complex. As a student, I'd made my Dublin flat into a kind of doss-house, inviting down-and-out types to come up for a glass of whiskey or a cup of tea, sometimes letting them stay the night. I'd never told my mother about the pasty-faced little prostitute from somewhere in the midlands for whom I would occasionally cook breakfast in exchange for her relatively innocent services. Nor had I mentioned the fifty-year-old drunk whose wife had thrown him out and who slept chastely beside me for a couple of nights, a foreshadowing of Ursula. No, I had not spoken of these things to my mother, but when she arrived at the end of term to help me clean the place up, she'd taken one look at the unchanged bed linen and thrown it into the dustbin.

So Ursula was right. I was in fact a bit of an *homme sec*, stiff and old-fashioned, but there was also that renegade part of me which had loved wildness ever since I was a young man at university. Perhaps throughout my life I had confused bohemian behaviour with mere craziness. Perhaps I had failed to realise that sinister men like Clive, or those schizophrenics and dipso-maniacs I'd harboured in my student flat, may not be grateful for my ministrations, or really interested in work. Whereas even the wildest, the most bohemian, of true artists will rise from bed with a parched throat and a killer hangover and drag himself to the easel or the piano or the desk, for work, the discipline of work, must always come first.

Yet I myself had been undisciplined, and self-indulgent, over the matter of Clive and Ursula. Ursula! I had let that crazy girl into my life and into my bed, although I hadn't even got any sexual pleasure from it. And I hadn't even really been so alarmed by my foolish behaviour. As with Clive, others had been alarmed for me, while I had felt virtuous, and therefore invulnerable.

Katherine came over and touched my arm. 'We shall figure out something,' she said. 'We shall do something to finish the book. You know, when they discovered that posthumous unfin-ished novel by Edith Wharton, somebody, a Wharton scholar I suppose, completed it. We could do something like that. A collaboration, perhaps? I could work on it with you, or Trudy or William. Or even David, although he doesn't like me any more.' She paused. 'It's because of the illness, I think. He sees it burning away at me and it makes him afraid, since, of course, he has it too.'

The sunlight was flushing her cheek, and indeed I saw the illness there. It reminded me of that moment in our old flat when I had looked at Claudia's face, also touched by sunlight, and had felt a frisson of fear. Katherine didn't know how much time remained for her; it made sense that she would wish to redeem the work of a woman she had loved.

'Obviously we couldn't get it absolutely right,' she went on. 'The style, the *texture* of Claudia's writing will always be her own and no one else's. But we could do our best, and publish it *honestly.*'

At that mention of honesty, I looked round for Ursula. Phebus was speaking in his fervent way to Sonia Dumas; Antoine, Julie and some others were clustered in a corner; Peter Stuart, his face drawn, was talking into Poppy's ear. But Ursula, her boyfriend and the kindly-looking agent had gone: they had probably slipped away when we were too preoccupied with the challenge of Claudia's novel to notice.

Poor Ursula; how could I blame her entirely? Just the week before, I had read in *Nice-Matin* of a young woman, the heiress to a yachting or hotel fortune (I forgot which), who was famous for being famous. Various photos had accompanied this article, of the heiress in party gear, in jodphurs, in a bikini. I had regarded her cunning shop girl's face and pampered body, and had marvelled, as I never cease to marvel, at the mindless vulgarity of our age.

Despite everything, as a writer and a man I have chosen my two pillars: work and love. I believe that every real writer must try, through an effort of imagination and of love, to enter into his or her mystery, to write with passion, to transform the water into wine. To hell with sarcastic distances, with snide references, with abstraction! There is only the fact of love, ordinary love, through which we may even be brushed by the wing of the divine, for it is love that makes us human, since we are not born human; we are made so by choice, through love.

But what would such convictions mean to someone like Ursula? I still believed that she had it in her to become a serious writer. Only she had got lost along the way.

I wondered if I would ever see her again.

EPILOGUE

Periodically, I continue to wonder why I live here in Nice, instead of Ireland or England, where my books appear in their original form and I could enjoy literary exchanges in my native tongue. Or if I must make France my home, why not Paris, why not the thrumming *soigné* capital as opposed to a beach town in the remote south?

The answer I come up with is invariably the same. Of course there is the beauty of the place: the Mediterranean basin – that deep source – the light, the mountains. But beyond this has always lain my aversion to the literary life back home, to the rivalries, the hype, the endless aspirants pouring out of workshops. (These days most workshop graduates do not read their elders, or even each other, very much. That's one of the reasons I liked Ursula: at least she read novels with real hunger.)

So I love Nice for its obscurity, and for the company of old-fashioned writers like Antoine and Katherine, types that barely exist any more outside of our little community, as if they – and I – were relics of a bygone age, quiet ships in an old harbour.

*

October arrived, with the sea still warm enough for late-season bathers. I continued to work on my new book while Trudy and Katherine cobbled away at Claudia's manuscript. That project would have been too close to the bone for me, whereas I was pleased to leave it in the hands of two such good writers, one so shrewd and tough and the other so delicate. And they both loved her.

One morning, early in the month, I was up very early, writing on my terrace before the day grew too bright. I have always liked to work in a kind of gloaming, dawn or dusk, that half-light when the membrane between the day and the world of dreams is still slightly porous, like the willow tree in *Penny*. Only at about half past nine, I realised that I was tired and feeling like a *chocolat chaud*, so I descended to the breakfast room, where ancient, kindly Delphine, who had been making the morning meals for ages, would look after me.

Ever since coming to live in the hotel, I had visited the breakfast room only sporadically, and of course during Ursula's stay I had descended not at all. Delphine made the coffee very early and let it stew, so that if one arrived after, say, eight o'clock, it was often thick and acrid; also, Hervé was not opposed to recycling the previous day's dry bread. Whereas I had enjoyed taking Ursula's delicious collations at my own table overlooking the garden. Before and after her, if I did have the hotel breakfast, I would try to choose a time when the place was fairly full, so that the coffee and bread would be replenished all morning.

Or if I simply felt lonely and inclined to savour a bit of hotel life, or felt the novelist's need to observe people obliquely, I would come down to take a pot of Delphine's hot chocolate without food. And I would look round at the tourists or at the occasional business traveller eating a hurried, solitary breakfast. (Over the years I have found that the Germans eat the most

abundantly, followed by the Americans, whereas the native
French and nearby Italians are the messiest, munching exuberantly and leaving empty butter packets, sticky knives and crumpled napkins scattered over tables furred with crumbs.)

Today Delphine and I had our usual exchange. ('*Pas de croissant? Pas de pain? Monsieur Clare, vous êtes maigre. Vous devez manger
quelque chose, alors?* 'Non, Delphine. Non, merci. Votre chocolat est
suffisant.*')

A middle-aged American woman and her adolescent daughter occupied the table on my left. They were both fat, with sullen
faces. Or at least their expression struck me that way. Many
Europeans of my acquaintance complain that Americans are ill-
mannered, that they look at one suspiciously and do not smile,
that they are without *joie de vivre*. But I have come to think that
Americans abroad are often merely shy, that the plunge from
their immense country, where nearly everyone speaks the same
language, into the splendid bazaar of Europe simply nonplusses
them, and that, as a result, they can seem guarded or cold. Yet I
did have to conclude that the two beside me were without
charm. The lumpy daughter, called, I gathered, Marisa, seemed
unhappy with everything. The coffee was too strong, the butter
too cold; she reminded me of Ursula demanding cream for her
apple tart not so long ago. The mother kept trying to placate her,
imploring in a wheedling voice, 'Marisa, don't you like your
croissant? Marisa, why aren't you drinking your orange juice?'

They were dressed in shorts and T-shirts, and the sunlight of
southern France had not been kind to their skin. In other words,
they looked and sounded awful, though in a curious way my
heart went out to them, as it had gone out now and again to
Andrew and Lucy. They were plucky enough, venturing off to a
foreign country, and I thought that the mother was probably trying her best, since it seems that adolescent children are never

easy, with their hormones forever on a rampage.

I turned my attention to the table on my other side. Two young women, perhaps twenty-five or twenty-six, were taking breakfast there. Three things struck me more or less simultaneously. First, both were wearing dark glasses even though the morning light was still soft, and also muffled by the hotel's curtains. Second, in contrast to the pair on my left, both were very thin and sharp-featured, and in fact resembled Ursula. And third, unlike Ursula, they were barely eating. One girl plucked at a croissant as if bored by it, while her companion kept breaking rolls onto her plate without ever raising a morsel to her mouth. Now and again they took a listless swallow of coffee.

Suddenly the fair-haired girl diagonally across from me lowered her sunglasses and said, 'Mougins? I mean, *really*.'

I couldn't place her accent. It seemed English but contained an American flatness; it could even have been Irish, that new Irish accent with peculiar vowels.

The other girl, whose hair was dark, flapped her hands and cried, 'Yeah. So B-list. I mean, totally B-list. We *can't* go there.'

The blonde girl murmured, 'But there's that Monte Carlo thing tonight.'

Once more the dark girl waved her hands about. 'Yeah, only how will we ever get in? They'll never let us in.' She paused. 'Will they?'

The blonde gave a soft laugh. 'Sweetie, I know the doorman. The doorman, remember? That cute bloke from the Irish pub in Cannes.'

Now it was the dark girl's turn to lower her sunglasses. 'This is *so* fantastic. The cute Irish doorman! Who'll be there?'

'Oh, everyone,' the blonde said airily. 'Doug and Melly, and the director of that cool new film about Jesus, and Teddy from International Gigolos, and what's-his-name the techno star, and

Adam and Jojo, and about a hundred models.'

'Fantastic,' repeated the brunette. 'This will totally change our lives.'

They talked a while longer, in excited voices, while the milky coffee turned grey in their cups. Just before they rose, the blonde gathered up three magazines from the floor beside her chair. I glanced at their covers: *Vogue*, the *Riviera Times* and something called *Heat*. I wondered did they ever read a book.

Delphine, scowling first at the girls' retreating backs, then down at their uneaten breakfasts, muttered, '*Les jeunes femmes sont trop gâtées, aujourd'hui.*'

*

So perhaps stalkers are indeed a sign of some modern malaise, a kind of short-circuit in society. Perhaps in the past people felt more *whole*, more certain of their true and separate selves. And through this separateness, this *intactness*, they could receive and fathom some other self, with all its own colours and textures, its past, its dreams. And by this balance of self and other, human relations become possible. Intimacy becomes possible, and love. Or so I believe. Only what of the stalker, the 'classic' kind, who sees the 'stalkee' as an object to be wooed and then pushed aside, or else consumed?

I believe the man who killed John Lennon declared that he loved his 'stalkee' so much, he could not bear that they should be separate, sheathed in their separate bodies and separate consciousnesses. He *had* to kill Lennon in order to overcome this schism. Through the act of murder, he could absorb his love object into himself, swallow him and become him. And thereby assuage his terrible loneliness.

Perhaps in the past, people trembled with religious fervour as they now seem to tremble with awe before film stars and the like. In the past, they could retreat to a monastery or take the veil and devote their lives to the worship of the beloved. (I am thinking of Bernini's St Theresa, head thrown back, draperies swirling, as Christ thrusts His presence into her soul. And also that nun for whom Jesus bared His bosom, revealing His Sacred Heart to her alone.) In other words, in the past certain people stalked God, who understood their hunger with an infinite understanding, and fulfilled it. Whereas these days there are so many of us lost and unfinished, searching for completion, hoping to touch the mantle of a star, to be smiled upon by a star, to become a star.

Of course, my own first stalker was my mother. She never separated from me in the traditional Freudian sense. She was 'symbiotic', I suppose, and as a child I did feel that I was almost a part of her. For instance. I would panic when she was displeased with me, as if I were falling down a well. So for a while I was indeed her creature and she had what she wanted from me: docility, dependence. But perhaps the price of that early thraldom was higher for her than for myself, because when I finally managed to separate, I recoiled too violently.

Immediately after she died, I dreamt now and again of her voice, ashen with sickness and fear, calling to me. But I could not rescue her from death, and while I did love her, she had also filled me with annoyance and even rage. At times I am still guilt-stricken, and wonder, as Ursula (who did not go to her mother's funeral) must wonder: how does one atone? How can I make reparation to my dead?

Lately, my dreams of Claudia are peaceful. She appears to me smiling, and when I open my eyes, my heart is calm, although sometimes my face is wet with tears. And recently my mother was also smiling when she visited me in a dream. 'Don't worry,' she soothed, extending a hand that was her true, remembered hand. 'Don't worry, Sebastian. I am all right now. Just get on with it. Get on with the business of living.'

*

Three weeks ago, Julie drove us across the border into the terraced mountains of Italy. We ate a delicious though stupefyingly heavy lunch in Pigna, and then explored the squares, where old people were benignly arrayed upon benches in the formation that the French call *la brochette*. On the way home, we stopped in Villefranche and walked along the *voie obscure*, with its timbered ceiling, like moving inside a cavern. And I thought how in medieval times people had met one another in this labyrinth, where pirates in the harbour could not see them. Their robes had swirled along these very stones as they had hurried to keep an assignation, something innocent like buying salt or bread, or else clandestine – a clasping of hands, a kiss – before vanishing through a door in the wall.

Back in Old Nice, we walked down the rue de la poissonnerie to the chapel of Saint Rita in the Church of Notre Dame. Rita is a patron saint of this place and there is something, a glow, in her chapel, as if the lucent sea just outside had offered her some of its light, or as if she were in fact a numinous presence. Anyway, I find it a comfort to pray to her, and I did so on that day with Julie beside me, while the bells clanged overhead.

I prayed, actually, for Ursula, that she would learn how to temper her overweaning ambition and would realise success honestly, for I do believe she has a gift. Yet thinking of her rapacious expression, her brass neck, her unslakeable appetite for both food and fame, I also found myself praying that she would leave us alone.

But she did not.

*

At about that time, I began to experience one of my intermittent periods of insomnia. All my life, even as a little boy, I had been afflicted with sleeplessness from time to time, had occasionally kept a kind of all-night vigil in my bed while the sky changed, and changed again, and the greyish shapes in my bedroom slowly took on colour and grew solid. Often, during those periods, I would finally fall asleep just as dawn broke, as if something in me believed I would at last be safe.

But this time I wasn't sleeping at all, except for a brief, ragged slumber in the afternoons. And one very early morning I was so exhausted, and so exasperated with myself, that I rose from my hotel bed, threw on some clothes, and went out for a walk.

I will never, ever be able to convey to anyone the beauty of this light, I said to myself as I walked southwards along avenue Jean Médecin. *How could I possibly describe the way it is so bright without being at all hard? And how the sky is the blue of certain ceramic plates, rich and deep and with a faint patina like pearls, or else a film of very thin milk?* I trudged on, thinking these things in an almost-stupor of fatigue; I was nearly alone except for the early-morning *boulangers,* and delivery vans, and one or two mendicants.

As I had passed through the Place Massena and was nearly in Old Nice, I decided to go to Julie's. In fact, I had probably, unconsciously, intended to do so from the moment I started out: my insomniac loneliness had grown stronger than the reluctance to disturb her sleep. So I turned into her street, let myself into her flat and fell into her bed, and she took me in her arms and mumbled something, and we slept, but not before I wondered why I had waited so long for this solace.

She let me sleep until midday, when she came into the bedroom with a bowl of coffee (and a boiled egg!) for me. I showered while she went down to collect her post; she returned as I was buttoning up my shirt. Coming out to greet her at the dining table, I was thinking how refreshed and happy I felt, when I saw her face.

'What is it, darling?' I took the chair next to hers. 'Another letter from Ursula?'

'Don't joke.'

She passed the envelope over to me, and there it was, Ursula's large print, spelling out my name above Julie's address. Immediately I felt the same revulsion – coupled with a strange light-headedness, a darkly euphoric tingling – that her tirades had produced in me before.

I said, 'We could just *not open it*, this time.'

We both surveyed the innocent-looking envelope. Julie sighed. 'I wonder why she sent it here, instead of the hotel? I suppose she must have wanted to be sure I would see it – no, that I would read it, along with you.'

'Oh, *merde*, anyway,' I muttered, and tore open the envelope with my finger. Inside was just one page – Ursula's familiar foolscap – but typewritten:

Sebastian,

I believe the time has come to settle our account. For quite a long while I was repressing the memory of your odious behaviour towards me because I could not stand to recall it. But now I am strong enough. (Pain and betrayal have made me strong.) So at last I am going to confront you, and confront the world, with the true story of your abuse of me, of how you took me into your rooms and into your bed, of how you lived and worked with me, intimately, over a long period, thereby convincing me that we were a couple, of how you accepted my valuable editorial help without ever once offering me payment or written acknowledgement. And of how you betrayed and humiliated me sexually, emotionally and, most important, publicly.

I have a new boyfriend now, a much stronger and kinder man than you could ever hope to be. And he is a shrewd Parisian lawyer. I was reluctant to pursue this course because I feel a lingering affection for you despite your perfidy, but my boyfriend convinced me of my moral obligation to myself and my work. Therefore, I intend to contact *everyone* connected with your professional and personal life: your English, Irish, American and French publishers; your agents; the literary pages of every major Irish, English and American newspaper; the broadcast media; and others among your friends and colleagues. Do you think any of them would believe you if you tried to convince them that we lived together, and slept together, for an extended period without ever having a sexual relationship? Or that you did not encourage me to improve Claudia Byrne's manuscript and publish it under my own name, as a form of thanks for the editorial advice I was generous enough to bestow on you? You exercised your charm and your guile in order to convince Julie and other members of Nice's literary milieu that you had had no intimate relations with me (despite sleeping in the same bed!)

and that you were 'shocked' by my revision of *Penny*, but I do not believe you will be as lucky with the literary establishments abroad once they have read my exposé.

*

We went to see my lawyer, who had on office close to the Rialto cinema and whom I had been consulting on property and literary matters since coming with Claudia to live in Nice.

Her name was Maître Véronique Millo. She was extremely competent; she was also pleasant to look at: about forty, with short rough blondish hair, a golden complexion and intensely blue eyes. I had only ever found one fault in her: she smoked incessantly and inelegantly. In fact, she was a filthy smoker, crumbling ash all over her desk, grinding fag ends into the already excessive rubble of her *cendrier*, and enveloping herself and her office in a perpetual, tobacco-smelling miasma.

After reading Ursula's letter, she looked at us with raised eyebrows. I said, 'Well? What do you think I should do? Retaliate in some way? Perhaps just let the matter drop?'

She was silent for a moment. Then, lighting another of her infernal cigarettes, she asked, 'You never had sex with this girl?'

'No. Never.'

Once more she was silent. I continued irritably, 'I know it seems bizarre. But she did make my life easier in some ways. She cooked good meals for us; she discussed books fairly intelligently; she *did* help me with my own work, once or twice. Also, she came to me soon after my mother died, and a helplessness about her made me think of my mother. I don't know what else to say except that I found her unattractive, which at the time seemed a blessing. We could live together and work companiably without any emotional entanglement – or so I thought. I didn't see the danger. I should have, but I didn't.'

Julie burst out, 'Surely she couldn't harm Sebastian now? She was exposed as a plagiarist, right here in Nice, before a gathering of eminent literary people.'

Maître Millo removed a fragment of tobacco from her tongue. 'We are living,' she said, 'in a time without ambiguity.' She raised her eyebrows again. 'People are moralistic these days. They do not honour the nuances, the *ambiguities*, of human relations, you know? The newspapers are full of scandal: presidents and film directors and football stars who have had affairs or dalliances with prostitutes, et cetera. And always the people cry out, "How disgraceful! How shocking! Off with his head!" They do not consider that human beings and their relationships are complicated, ambiguous. They oversimplify; they have little mercy. And this is dangerous.'

I watched as she blew a tendril of smoke towards the ceiling. 'You are saying that Ursula could, in fact, blacken my name quite easily, in the current climate?'

She touched the letter on her desk. 'She hasn't threatened legal action so far, thank God. But to an outsider, your arrangement would seem . . . odd. She was not your cousin or Claudia's cousin. She was not a friend. Yet you brought her in to live with you, to *sleep* with you. Under those conditions, even her filching of the manuscript could seem reasonable. You had opened your rooms and your life to her. You were encouraging her in her writing. Why shouldn't she complete an unfinished book she had found in what was, essentially, *her home?*'

Julie was playing nervously with the tassels of her green scarf. I thought about all those literati: Julie, Trudy, Alice, William, Katherine (along with Sonia in Paris, Peter Stuart and Poppy from Tate & Wyndham, and Ursula's agent), all those valorous people who had denounced her attempt to desecrate Claudia's truth. And yet again I reflected that we were, it seemed, different from many of those outside our little world: different from those who ogle tabloid newspapers and glossy magazines; different from the publishers of lurid best-sellers; different from the gossipmongers, the hardened, the cynical and the snide; different from Ursula? Perhaps we were just pathetically old-fashioned.

Maître Millo continued, 'I suppose she may maintain that you exploited her sexually and then reviled her among your friends when you had fallen in love with Julie and wanted her out of your life. Or something like that.'

'She was already out of my life! She was living in Paris with an accountant!'

'If she really is a stalker,' the lawyer observed quietly, 'she might have been presuming an ongoing relationship nonetheless. She may even believe the two of you have always remained central to each other, despite other people. Clearly her letter is an attempt keep up the connection with you.'

'But such a venomous, hostile connection . . . '

'She may not mind that it is a hostile connection, as long as it exists.'

'What would you advise us to do?' asked Julie.

She fished around for another cigarette. 'Wait. It is all you *can* do.' She looked up with a tight smile. 'You do realise this is probably just a hollow threat? Most likely, she only wanted to scare you. Try not to be scared. And certainly you mustn't write or phone her. Be patient. Wait.'

*

And so we wait. Another three weeks have passed, without a murmur from Ursula. She has contacted neither me, nor any of my colleagues in Ireland or elsewhere – at least as far as I know. Nor has her litigious new boyfriend advanced any kind of court action (if he even exists).

But while I am afraid, I do manage to work. I will not let Ursula triumph there, in the house of my craft. So I write every day, and I think the work is good.

But how porous we are, in this world! How vulnerable, our separate selves! A woman files a paternity suit on the internet; an 'escort girl' appears on television to accuse a pop star of rape; a Dublin thief steals the 'identity' of an elderly lady, plundering her bank account. At times the whole world seems charged with menace. Look at me! I should have protected myself and those I loved from Clive, from the importunate Andrew and Lucy, from Ursula. But I did not.

For now, I try to praise. I praise my life on the Côte d'Azur; I praise my love for Julie and for my friends and for my work; I praise Heaven.

But I also wait.

POSTFACE

This novel is about stalkers. It is also about Nice. In it, I have conflated time, so that while the major action takes place during more or less our own day, characters from Nice's literary and artistic past make appearances as if they were contemporaries of the main character and of one another.

I do not try to be biographically accurate in my portrayal of these illustrious figures who lived, at one period or other, on the Côte d'Azur. I present variations or interpretations of them, sometimes changing their names. Colette, for instance, becomes Babette.

Some characters are disguised more thinly than others. I think most readers would recognise Katherine from New Zealand as Katherine Mansfield. The Russian playwright Antoine is of course Chekhov. Livia is modelled on Lydia, the hapless young woman for whom he wrote *The Seagull*. Trudy and Alice are versions of Gertrude Stein and Alice B. Toklas. Phebus and Loulou are meant to be Apollinaire and his beloved Lou. The American dancer glimpsed by Sebastian on the Promenade des Anglais is Isadora Duncan. James the American novelist is James Baldwin. Mention is made of characters resembling D. H. Lawrence, Somerset Maugham and Friedrich Nietzsche. Sebastian admires a painting by an artist called Pierre, who is meant to suggest Bonnard, while Henry M. and April are intended to evoke Henry Miller and his wife June.

In this way I have tried to work spatially rather than temporally, fashioning a kind of mosaic or frieze in which my subjects are some of the fascinating characters who remain part of this marvellous place.

Elizabeth Wassell
Nice